Bug Out! Texas
Book 4

Texas Battle Cry

Robert Boren

South Bay Press

Book Layout ©2017 BookDesignTemplates.com
Cover design: SelfPubBookCovers.com/Fantasyart
Bug Out! Texas Book 4– Texas Battle Cry/ Robert Boren. – 3rd ed.
ISBN 9781973197225

For Gwen

We view ourselves on the eve of battle. We are nerved for the contest, and must conquer or perish. It is vain to look for present aid: none is at hand. We must now act or abandon all hope! Rally to the standard, and be no longer the scoff of mercenary tongues! Be men, be free men, that your children may bless their father's name.

—Sam Houston

Contents

Previously, in Bug Out! Texas Book 3:

The Texas Patriots living at the Fort Stockton RV Park saw Islamist fighters try to hijack a convoy of four M-1 Battle tanks on I-10, being moved on massive flatbed trucks. They swept in and took the tanks away from the enemy, using Curt's heavily armed Barracuda Off-Roader. The tanks became part of the group's armament and were used to guard the RV Park. The group figured out later that the hijacking was an inside job, aided by Islamists who had infiltrated Fort Bliss.

Falcon Lake was attacked with a device which created a giant wave. The wave took out the dam, draining the lake in minutes. Brendan, Juan Carlos, and Richardson barely got their patrol boat to the beach before the wave hit.

All the characters saw news reports of nuclear attacks in the US and elsewhere. Panic spread quickly to every corner of the globe. Austin locked down during the attack, with leadership heading to the bunkers under the State Capital building.

Kip Hendrix helped Maria with her disturbed younger sister after a suicide attempt. This and the rapidly approaching war pulled them closer together. Maria realized that Kip had fallen in love with her, but she wasn't sure what to do about it.

Curt fabricated a weapon mount for Kyle's truck, using his 3D Printer and machine shop set up in the back of his toy hauler. He installed a remote-controlled .50 cal machine gun on the truck's roll bar, with a sight unit inside the cab.

Brendan, Juan Carlos, and Richardson were relocated to the Gulf Coast, near South Padre Island. Richardson's girlfriend Lita was there, working in her father's bar. She introduced her friends Madison and Hannah to Juan Carlos and Brendan. Sparks flew from the start.

Eric, Kim, and the people from Deadwood finally made it to central Texas. They had to fight their way through a terror attack on the freeway in Austin, eventually taking refuge at the Finley family homestead outside of Fredericksburg.

Austin was attacked by thousands of Islamist fighters with tank support, turning the south side of the city into rubble. Kip Hendrix and Maria barely escaped with their lives. They took refuge in a bunker under the President Pro Tempore's residence. Love blossomed between them while they were there.

Curt used his cellphone tracking program to find the enemy supply depot supporting the Austin attack. He gathered up Jason, Kyle, Kelly, Junior, and others. They headed for the small town of Mountain View to carry out an assault, leaving their women behind to worry.

South Padre Island and nearby Port Isabel were rocked with a massive air strike by the enemy, causing Richardson, Brendan, and Juan Carlos to flee with their women. They got out just in time…

Road to Laredo

Madison was in bed, propped up on her elbow, looking at Juan Carlos as the sun came up. The explosions and flashes of light went on until after 2:00 in the morning, but Juan Carlos fell asleep anyway. She looked at his peaceful face, strong and yet gentle. *Is he the one?*

Juan Carlos stirred, eyes opening to see her staring at him. He smiled. "Good morning."

She smiled at him. "You look proud of yourself."

"Yeah, I am," he said, pulling her naked body back against him. "What time is it?"

"It's not even six yet," she said. "Uh oh, what's that I feel?"

"Guess."

"Oh, God, again?" she asked. "Last night won't hold you for a while?"

"I'll never get enough," he said, bringing her in for a kiss. Madison gave in to him, moaning as his body came over hers. They built each other into a fever pitch, laying back afterwards, breath coming down slowly.

"Listen, you hear that?" Juan Carlos whispered. The muffled sound of a woman moaning and crying out floated into their room.

Madison giggled. "Hannah is getting it good."

"You sure that's Hannah?"

"I'm sure," she said. "We're roommates, remember? I don't remember her sounding quite this passionate before, though."

"It's having an effect on me," Juan Carlos said, moving closer to her.

"No!" she said. "I'm sore. I need some recovery time."

"Okay," Juan Carlos said, covering her forehead and cheeks with kisses, ending up at her mouth, where they kissed each other deeply. Then he stopped and pulled back, looking into her eyes with an intensity that made her uncomfortable.

"What?" she asked, trembling. "You look scared."

"Son of a bitch," he said. "This is what it's like."

She watched as his expression changed from fear to reverence. He reached out and petted her cheek. "Oh, *shit,*" she whispered.

"Something wrong?" Juan Carlos said, looking in her eyes again.

"You're looking at me the way Richardson looks at Lita, *and I like it.*"

"You do?" Juan Carlos asked.

"Tell me you don't feel it," Madison said.

Juan Carlos sighed. "Okay, I feel it. What now?"

"We wait and see if it sticks around."

Suddenly Juan Carlos felt calm and warm, becoming joyful. "This hasn't happened to me before. Not like this."

"It's scary," Madison whispered. "How can this happen so quickly? I feel out of control."

"What do you mean?"

Madison opened her mouth to speak, but then stopped.

"Out with it," he said.

"No, it's embarrassing," she whispered.

"C'mon," he said.

"Let's get up now," she said.

"No," Juan Carlos said. "What did you mean?"

"Dammit. Don't hold me to this. I don't understand it, and don't feel like you have to do anything about it."

"Out with it, all ready," he said softly.

"Okay, okay," she said. "I keep having images of us together, and I want it so bad."

"We're together right now."

"No, you don't get it. I want to be your woman. I want to follow you everywhere, and have your babies."

"Oh," Juan Carlos said.

"You look scared," she said. "I should have kept my mouth shut."

Juan Carlos laughed. "You don't know why I'm scared."

"This is too much pressure on you," she said. "I'm sorry. It's probably just me being scared."

He pulled her against him and kissed her again. "Now it's you that doesn't get it," he said softly. "I'm having the same thoughts."

She looked at him, tears flowing down her cheeks. "You aren't going to run away?"

"Only if you're with me," he said. "You can consider me yours."

She studied his eyes, looking for that hint of doubt.

"What are you thinking?" he asked her.

"I'm looking for doubt in your eyes," she said.

"Well?"

She took a deep breath. "There isn't any."

"So what does that mean?"

"It means you can consider me to be yours, I guess," she said. "I can't believe I'm saying this."

He kissed her again, passionate and hard, then pulled back, eyes intense again. "I lo…"

"No! Don't say that yet. Let's give this a little time, all right?"

There was silence for a moment as they studied each other.

"Okay, let's see how it goes, but can we act on what we feel?" Juan Carlos asked.

"Meaning what?"

"Meaning we act as if we're together. Give it a chance to grow."

"Or die," Madison said.

"Yeah, or die, but it's not going to."

"What makes you so sure?" she asked.

"I just know," he said. "Let's get up. We need to be going pretty soon."

"Okay." Madison threw back the sheet and stood up, turning to him, showing him her soft white curves.

"My God you're beautiful," he said.

"Stop it or we'll never get up," she said. "Sounds like Hannah and Brendan finally finished."

"You think they feel the same as we do?"

"Oh, I'm sure I'll get a detailed report." Madison giggled as she reached down for her clothes. "Get dressed."

They were startled by a knock on the door. "You guys up?"

"Yeah, boss," Juan Carlos said. "We're getting dressed now."

"Good," Richardson said. "We need to be out of here sooner rather than later."

"It's just past six," Juan Carlos said.

"I know, but the enemy is on their way. We need to be on the road in ten minutes, so chop chop."

"Oh, geez," Madison said. She watched as Juan Carlos jumped out of bed and dressed.

"Don't be scared, sweetie," Juan Carlos said. "We'll be okay."

"Sweetie?"

"You're mine, remember?"

"Yes," she said softly.

They went down the stairs into the entryway. Lita and Richardson were there, putting food and water into a box.

"Juan Carlos, put this into the suburban, all right? I parked it in front of the door."

"Will do," he said.

"Need help from me?" Madison asked.

"Yeah, I have more food we can bring," Lita said. "C'mon." Madison followed her into the kitchen.

"Hurry up, Brendan," Richardson called up the stairs.

"The parental units left lots of food here," Lita said. "We're lucky they flew out."

"We all going to fit in a Suburban?" Madison asked.

"It seats seven," Lita said, "with room in the back for supplies and guns."

"Hey," Hannah said, walking into the kitchen. Lita and Madison looked at her and snickered. "Was I too loud? I'm so embarrassed."

"You really like him, don't you?" Lita asked.

"I could get used to him," Hannah said. "How about you, Madison?"

She had her back to them, loading dry goods into a box.

"Are you crying?" Lita asked, rushing to her.

Madison turned around, wiping the tears out of her eyes.

"He didn't hurt you, did he?" Hannah asked.

Madison smiled and shook her head no.

"Oh, *hell no*," Lita said. "Already?"

Madison shook her head yes.

"Him?" Lita said.

Madison shook her head yes again.

"Get out of here," Hannah said. "You just met the guy."

"You aren't feeling anything?" Madison asked. "I know what you usually sound like. You sounded different. Last night, and especially this morning."

Hannah's face turned red. "Shut up."

Lita giggled. "Struck a nerve there, I see."

"Okay, so he knows how to push my buttons," Hannah said. "All of them."

"C'mon, girls," Richardson said. "We have to leave right now."

"Coming," Lita said. "This will be enough. Let's go."

They rushed out through the front door with the boxes of food. Juan Carlos and Brendan loaded them into the back. Lita locked the house as the others got in, Richardson behind the wheel. Lita got into the front passenger seat. "I know a short cut out of town."

"As long as it's heading north," Richardson said. "Juan Carlos and Brendan, keep your eyes open, and keep the SMAW close by, but don't fire that thing from inside the car."

"Got it," Brendan said.

"My shortcut will take us to the road your boss said to get on," Lita said. "I-69E. If we try to use route 100 to get there, we'll sit for a while. That road clogs up too much."

"Okay, which way?"

"Turn right at the first stop light. The road will get smaller as we get out of town. Part of it is dirt. Just trust me, okay?"

"Got it," Richardson said. He got to the stop light and made the turn. Before they went two blocks there were explosions behind them.

"Damn, dude, that sounds like artillery," Juan Carlos said.

"Sure does," Richardson said, speeding up. "What next, honey?"

"The road goes into a low-rent residential area. Keep going past all the houses and take the dirt road it turns into."

"How long is the dirt part?" Richardson asked.

"Six or seven miles. If any of it's wet, just pop this sucker into four-wheel drive."

Richardson nodded, keeping his speed up as the road thinned. Then there was a huge explosion behind them.

"My God, look at all that fire," Hannah said. Lita looked back and cried.

"Port Isabel," she said between sobs. "Oh no."

"Good thing we got out when we did," Brendan said. He pulled Hannah close as she began to cry. Madison leaned against Juan Carlos in the third row of seats, taking his hand and holding it tight.

"There's the dirt road up ahead," Richardson said. He glanced into the rearview mirror when he caught a flash of movement. "Dammit, we're being followed. Got that SMAW handy?"

Juan Carlos passed it up to Brendan, then grabbed a couple more rounds from the box behind the seat.

"I got it," Brendan said.

"I'll pull behind that tree. You jump out and fire at the vehicle. Juan Carlos, hand up the rifles and get ready to fire."

"You got it, boss," Juan Carlos said.

Richardson swerved off the road behind a huge oak and Brendan got out, diving into the road, getting a bead on the vehicle. He pulled the trigger and the rocket flashed out, hitting the vehicle and exploding.

"Holy shit!" Juan Carlos said, looking out the back with a rifle in his hand. "Look at it burn. Nobody survived that."

"Yeah, and it blocked up the road real good," Richardson said. "Get in, Brendan."

Brendan climbed in and Richardson took off before he got the door closed.

"Nice shot, bro," Juan Carlos said. "You're getting good with that thing."

"It's handy," he said, handing it back to him. "Don't touch the barrel. It's hot."

"How did they know to follow us?" Madison asked.

"Yeah, I'm wondering the same thing," Lita said.

"Maybe it's our cellphones," Brendan said. "Remember what we heard in that briefing?"

"We haven't talked to anybody who's infected," Juan Carlos said.

"Correction. We haven't talked to anybody who we *know* is infected," Richardson said. He fished his phone out of his pocket and handed it to Lita. "Call Captain Jefferson. Put it on speaker. His contact name is Cappy. Should be pretty high up in the recents."

"What's your passcode."

"Your birthday," Richardson said. "Month and day."

Lita gave him a sweet look. "I guess you *do* like me."

"Stop it," he said, looking at her and smiling.

Lita hit the contact and pushed the speaker button. It rang twice.

"Lieutenant Richardson, thank God," Captain Jefferson said. "We feared the worst, since I told you to stay later."

"What the hell was that?" Richardson asked.

"Field artillery. Hit some LNG tanks. Blew up most of the town. Glad we got so many people out over the last couple of weeks. Still lost a lot."

"I know where those tanks were," Lita said. "Probably would have killed us all."

"Who's that?" Jefferson asked.

"Lita, my girlfriend," Richardson said.

"Where are you guys?"

"On a dirt-road shortcut that Lita knew about," Richardson said. "It leads to I-69E. That route still safe?"

"No route is safe, but that's better than most," Jefferson said. "We underestimated the strength of the enemy."

"Shit," Richardson said. "Figures. I called for a reason. Got a question."

"Shoot," Jefferson said.

"Remember that business about the cell phone tracking?"

"Yeah," Jefferson said. "You think your phones might be compromised?"

"We got followed on the dirt road by an enemy vehicle," Richardson said. "They had no other way to know where we were."

"Dammit," Jefferson said. "We were told there was no problem. My suggestion is to dump the phones. Buy burners when you get to the first town. Call the headquarters land line as soon as you get the new phones. Don't call any DPS cellphones."

"Got it," Richardson said.

"You talk to Lita with your cellphone?"

"Of course," Richardson said.

"Then her phone has to go too. And the other women if they've talked to her."

"Roger that. Thanks, Captain. Talk to you soon."

"Take care of yourselves."

"You too," Richardson said.

Lita ended the call. "Dammit, I love my phone."

"I love being alive more," Juan Carlos said. "Where can we dump them?"

"There's a stream by the road up about half a mile," Lita said. "I'll show you where to stop."

"Okay," Richardson said. "Guys, make note of any numbers you need to keep track of."

"Got it," Brendan said.

"I got a small pad and a pen in my purse," Madison said. She pulled it out, then took out her phone and got a few numbers off of it. Then she handed the pen and pad to Juan Carlos. He finished and passed it up to Brendan and Madison as Richardson pulled over.

"You guys ready?" Lita asked.

"Yeah," Madison said. "I'm not happy about throwing away this new iPhone."

"Me neither, but you can always get a new phone," Juan Carlos said.

"I got that insurance on mine," Hannah said. "As far as they know, I just lost it while I was hiking."

Brendan snickered.

"When you replace it, don't clone from a backup," Richardson said. "Chances are the virus is on there. You'll be right back in danger."

"Yeah, we'll use burners for a while," Juan Carlos said. "No muss, no fuss."

They got out of the SUV, taking their guns with them. The stream was about thirty yards from the car.

"Bye bye," Juan Carlos said, tossing his phone into the rapids. The others did the same.

"Let's go," Richardson said. "We need to put some distance between ourselves and this place. If they're watching, they know exactly where the signals disappeared."

"Yeah," Lita said. They headed back in a hurry.

Madison watched Juan Carlos take a long look down the road. His strong form standing there made her flutter, with his hawk-like eyes staring. "Think there's still somebody after us?" she asked.

"Could be," he said. "We'll keep our eyes open for a while."

"Hey, while we're young," Brendan said. "We can't get in until you do."

"You could sit in the way back," Juan Carlos said.

"No," Richardson said. "Brendan may need to get out quick with that SMAW. C'mon, you two."

"Okay," Juan Carlos said, holding the seat down for Madison to get in, then climbing in behind her. The others got in and Richardson took off.

"Hey," Madison whispered, getting close to Juan Carlos, her hand on his thigh.

"What?" he asked her.

"I'm breaking my rule," she whispered. "I love you."

"I love you too," Juan Carlos said. He kissed her hard. Brendan and Hannah snickered in front of them, causing them to break the kiss.

"Be nice," Madison said.

"Watch out the back window," Richardson said. "Might be somebody else. You can make out later."

Madison smiled at Juan Carlos and mouthed the words to him again. Then they both got sideways so they could watch out the back window.

{ 2 }

Mountain City

Jason drove the Jeep down the highway in the early morning darkness.

"Long ass drive," Jason said to Curt.

"You want me to spell you yet? Slept a little."

"I slept some too," Junior said from the back seat. "I can take over if you need me too."

"Okay, next stop," Jason said. "We should be hearing from the bikers pretty soon."

"I know," Curt said. "Hope they didn't get caught."

Curt's phone rang. He put it on speaker.

"Curt?"

"Hey, Kelly, what's up?"

"We're gonna trade off in a minute, so we'll be pulling over," he said.

"We were just talking about the same thing," Junior said.

"Hear from Gray's bikers yet?" Kyle asked.

"No," Curt said. "They ought to be pretty close now, though."

"All right, I'll pull over," Jason said.

Both vehicles parked and the men got out. Curt rushed behind the Jeep to check the Barracuda. Kelly and Kyle walked over from the truck, the .50 cal looking monstrous on the roll bar behind the cab.

"How far is 290?" Kelly asked.

"Another half hour," Junior said. "I should drive, guys. I slept the longest."

"Fine by me," Jason said, brow furrowed. "Haven't heard from Gray's bikers yet. Should have."

"Yeah, I was thinking the same thing," Curt said.

Jason still looked concerned.

"What?" Kyle asked him.

"Eric. He's at the homestead in Fredericksburg. Maybe I ought to call him."

"Let's not take the time to drive there," Kyle said. "That dirt road would cost us too much time."

"I was thinking more about him meeting us. He's really good in a fight, and he's got that Bronco."

"Call him," Curt said.

Jason nodded and hit Eric's contact. It rang four times, then clicked.

"Jason?" Eric asked in a groggy voice.

"Yeah, it's me," Jason said. "We're about half an hour away from 290. Headed for Mountain City."

"Really?" He sounded more awake. "You get attacked in Fort Stockton?"

"Not yet," Jason said. "You heard about what happened in Austin, right?"

"Yeah," Eric said.

"Curt figured out where they have their supplies and fuel hidden. Fuel for the tanks."

"It's in Mountain City?" Eric asked.

"Yeah," Jason said. "We're gonna blow it up."

Eric snickered. "I got that case of grenades. Maybe I should join you."

"Oh, yeah, forgot about that. Where'd you get those again?"

"Took them from the enemy when they were attacking Deadwood," Eric said. "Where should we meet?"

"You know where that big BBQ is? On 1826?"

"The Salt Lick," Eric said. "Yeah, I can be there in about half an hour."

"It'll take us a little longer. We're in my Jeep towing Curt's Barracuda, and in Kyle's truck."

"Okay, I'll get going now. I've got some friends from the Deadwood battle with me. I'm sure they'd be interested."

"Okay, brother. Be careful."

"You too," Eric said.

Jason ended the call.

"He's gonna join us, ain't he?" Junior asked.

"Yep, and he's got a case of grenades," Jason said.

Curt snickered. "Good. Let's haul ass."

"Junior, you know where the Salt Lick is, right?"

"Hell yeah," Junior said. "No problema. We go south from Dripping Springs. Maybe they'll be open on the way back."

Kelly chuckled. "Think they'll let us back in?"

"Uh oh, you guys caused some problems there, I take it?" Kyle asked.

"Yeah, but it was a long time ago," Junior said. "I doubt if they remember."

"Let's saddle up," Curt said.

The men got back into their vehicles and took off into the darkness.

{ 3 }

Dark Road

Eric got out of bed after Jason's call, trying not to wake Kim. She was already awake.

"Who was that?" Kim asked.

"Jason," Eric said. He pulled on his clothes. "He needs my help."

"Oh crap, what's going on?"

"Curt figured out where the enemy has their supplies for the Austin attack. They're on the way to blow it up."

Kim got out of bed and dressed. "I'm going with you."

"I'm okay with that," Eric said. "You know how to handle yourself. I'll go wake Dirk and the others."

"Okay, sweetie. I'll load the guns and ammo in the Bronco."

"Leave some room for that crate of grenades, and Paco."

Eric left the trailer and rushed to the house. "Dirk! Chance!"

"What, we under attack?" Dirk asked, getting off the couch. Chance stirred and sat up. Don woke up on the recliner.

"Jason called me. They figured out where the supplies for the enemy attack on Austin are. They're on the way to blow them up. I'm gonna go help. Interested?"

"Hell yeah," Dirk said. "I'll go wake up Francis. He and Sherry are in the trailer."

"We might want to leave a couple men here," Eric said. "To protect the girls, for instance."

"Yeah, you're right," Don said. "I'll stick around. Francis should too."

Kim came into the house, Paco trotting behind her. "Everything is loaded except for the grenades. That box is still too heavy for me."

"I'll get it, sweetie," Eric said, rushing to her side. Eric lifted the grenade crate into the back end of the Jeep. "I didn't think we had so many left. We're gonna mess the enemy up good."

"Sure you want to take Paco?" Kim asked.

"Yeah," Eric said. "Good early warning."

Dirk and Chance ran out, guns in their hands. "Where we meeting them?"

"At a BBQ in Driftwood called Salt Lick," Eric said. "Ready?"

"Hell yeah," Chance said. "Let's haul ass."

Eric got into the driver's seat of the Bronco, Kim in the passenger side. She pulled one of the AK's on her lap. "How far is it?"

"Just over half an hour," Eric said. "Mountain City is a little further."

"Careful on those switchbacks," Kim said. "They scare me when it's *light*."

Eric chuckled. "Don't worry, sweetie, the Bronco handles it a lot better than our motor home."

"Yeah, well no hot-rodding." She held onto the sides of her seat as Eric turned onto the first switchback, the road getting more and more narrow. "How's Dirk handling it?"

"He's got a four-wheel-drive truck," Eric said. "He'll have no more trouble than we will."

It took only ten minutes to get to 290. Eric sped up to sixty-five.

"I'm worried about Alyssa and Chloe," Kim said. "They were crying last night. I heard it before we went to the trailer."

"Maybe the news bothered them," Eric said. "That video of the Islamists chasing down civilians in south Austin was enough to scare anybody."

"Maybe they lost people in Deadwood," Kim said.

"Wonder what happened to Alyssa's mother? Don's not wearing a wedding ring."

"Sherry told me that Don's wife became an addict. Overdosed about five years ago."

"Oh, geez," Eric said. "What?"

"Meth," Kim said. "I had a friend get into that. It ruined her."

"What about Chloe?"

"Parents both dead."

"How did that happen?" Eric asked.

"Mom died of cancer," Kim said. "Pancreatic. Dad killed himself about six months later. Don took her in, since she was Alyssa's best friend."

"Oh my God," Eric said. "That's tough. Don's a good guy for taking her in."

"Small towns have their problems, but people take care of each other in them," Kim said. "That says a lot."

"True," Eric said. "I've lived in the city and in small towns. They both have their strong and weak points, but I'd have to give the advantage to the small towns. You have to be careful in them, though."

"Careful how?"

Eric chuckled. "Everybody knows everybody, and gossip gets out of control sometimes. If you get on the outs with the wrong circle of people, you might have to move away."

"That's true," Kim said. "Cities are much more anonymous. You can re-invent yourself and nobody bats an eye."

"What's the biggest city you've lived in?" Eric asked.

"Atlanta," she said. "You?"

"San Antonio," Eric said. "It was a little too big. I like Austin better."

"Atlanta was fun when I was younger," Kim said. "Bar hopping with my girlfriends."

"Yeah, I'll bet," Eric said. "You probably got a lot of attention."

"Oh, I suppose so," Kim said. "I was pretty lucky, now that I think about it."

Eric laughed. "Yeah, when you're young you feel invincible. I used to bar hop on my motorcycle. Not so bright. And of course that was before helmet laws."

"Geez," Kim said. "Oh well, I might have gotten on the back with you."

Eric laughed. "Yeah, maybe so. I could've done a lot worse."

"Hey look!" Kim said, pointing ahead. "Is that more flatbeds with tanks on them?"

"Looks like it. Maybe we ought to pull off into the woods there. Call Dirk."

Kim hit Dirk's contact on her phone as Eric slowed the Bronco and turned it onto the dirt road to the right.

"Dirk, get off the road. Tanks on flatbeds coming."

"Roger that," Dirk said. "I'll follow you."

Eric made it into the trees and shut off the engine. Dirk pulled up behind them. They got out and listened as the flatbeds approached. Paco stood at attention, staring at the road, growling softly.

"Quiet, boy," Eric whispered.

"He's a good judge of character," Chance whispered.

"Think they saw us?" Dirk asked.

"We had our headlights on, so yes," Eric said. "Get your rifles out in case they send a scouting party back here."

"Yeah, and grab a couple grenades," Chance said.

"Can they see us from the road?" Kim asked.

"No, but they saw where we turned, if they were paying any attention."

"Here they come," Dirk said, checking his rifle. The big flatbeds flew by on the highway, one after the other.

"How many is that?" Kim asked.

"I counted twelve," Eric said. "Wonder if they're going to attack Fredericksburg?"

"Think they'll hit our place?" Chance asked.

"It's way off the beaten path," Eric said, "so I doubt it."

"Something turned onto the dirt road," Kim whispered, eyes filled with fear.

"I see it," Eric said. "C'mon, let's get them before they get in range of our vehicles."

"Yeah," Dirk said, his AK-47 at the ready. They rushed forward and dropped, all of them firing at the military vehicle, bullets crashing through the windshield. It rolled to a stop, and three men piled out of the back, racing for cover. Dirk hit one, Chance another. The third ran. Eric got up, running towards him.

"Damn that guy can run fast," Dirk said, watching as Eric lifted his gun and fired, taking the man down.

"Thank God," Kim said to herself as she saw him trot back over with a new AK-47 in his hands.

Dirk hurried to the vehicle in a crouch, checking the inside. "They're all dead."

"Get their weapons," Eric said. "Check for grenades."

"What the hell is this thing?" Chance asked as he checked it out. "Looks like a Humvee but it's not."

"That's a GAZ Tigr," Dirk said. "Russian-made Humvee-style vehicle. They had guns – usually a 7.62 machine gun and a grenade launcher. Let's take them."

"Maybe we should just drive the vehicle," Chance said.

"No," Eric said. "There might be other good guys around."

"I got a better idea," Kim said. "Let's hide it back in the brush there, and get it later."

"Good idea," Eric said

"I'll help," Dirk said. They rushed over, cleaned out the driver and passenger seat and hopped in, driving it back into the brush. Then they checked the back with their phone flashlights.

"Lots of 7.62 ammo we can use for the AKs," Eric said. "Might as well take that."

"See those long, thin covers in the floor?"

"Yeah," Eric said.

"Open them."

Eric opened the one closest to him. "Bingo. Machine gun. Probably mounts on the bar up there."

"The other one is probably an auto-grenade launcher," Dirk said.

Eric opened it. "Looks like it. Maybe we can mount this stuff on one of our vehicles."

"Maybe," Dirk said. "You want to bring the ammo? I'll get Chance to help me drag the bodies out of sight."

"Okay," Eric said. He picked up two big metal boxes of ammo and walked towards their vehicles, putting one in the back of Dirk's truck and one in the back of the Bronco. Then he helped Dirk and Chance with the bodies, stripping them of ammo and their handguns.

"Ready to go?" Kim asked. Paco was next to them, watching the road like a hawk.

"Yeah, let's go," Eric said. Dirk gave them a thumbs up, and then they all got into their vehicles and took off for 290.

"Hope none of those guys called us in," Kim said.

"Seriously," Eric said. "We'll have to be careful if we come back here. It's obvious that we hid that vehicle and the bodies. They'll expect us to come back. Might be the death of us."

"Shit, you're right," Kim said. "Maybe we ought to forget it."

"We should play it by ear," Eric said. "We'll have Jason, Curt, and Kyle with us after the mission, assuming we live through it."

"Mission?" Kim chuckled. "Wow, we're really in this, aren't we?"

"Damn straight. Glad it's still dark for a while."

{ 4 }

Secrets

Kip Hendrix sat next to Maria, looking at the video feed on the monitor.

"That's the last of the cameras," Hendrix said. "Looks like the coast is clear."

"This scares me," Maria said, clutching him closely. "I should go with you."

"No, somebody has to be here to manage communications," Hendrix said. "You're gonna do your job, and I'm gonna do mine, okay?"

"Okay," she said.

"I'll bring down a bunch of those long t-shirts and other things you can wear, also stuff for myself, and some of the perishables I have in the fridge up there."

"You want me to lock this behind you, right?"

"Yes," Hendrix said. "I'll Facetime you when I'm back down here. That way you'll be able to see my face. If I try to call instead, don't open the vault door, okay?"

"Okay," she said.

Hendrix pushed the button to open the vault. The bolts receded and the door slowly opened. Hendrix slipped through with his rifle, and turned to look at Maria. She blew him a kiss and hit the button to close the vault.

Hendrix walked out to the door, cracking it open and peering outside. Nobody there. He could see the early-morning sunshine flowing down the hall from the kitchen. He crept towards it, listening for anybody who might be sneaking around. The kitchen was clear, so he checked the other ground-floor rooms, and then headed up the stairs into the master bedroom. He opened the walk-in closet and walked all the way to the end, then pushed a button. The wall opened, revealing a dark spiral staircase. After a last look back, he climbed up, pushing the trap door open as quietly as he could. The roof was deserted, the walls around the perimeter hiding him from view. He walked over to a small shack against one side and sat in the observation chair, pulling the periscope in front of him. "Love this thing," he said as he scanned the area.

"Dammit," he said under his breath. There was still a line-up of tanks bottled up on South Congress Ave. There was smoke and flames to the south, near the area where Maria lived. Enemy troops were moving around on rooftops along South Congress, firing shots into buildings nearby, then getting down as fire erupted from surrounding windows. He pushed the periscope eyepieces away and slipped out of the shed, running in a crouch to the trap door and slipping down onto the spiral staircase, his heart pounding.

Back in his bedroom, he took pillow cases off of both his pillows and rushed them to the dresser, stuffing them full of clothes. Then he went down to the kitchen, grabbed several re-useable grocery bags and filled them with food from the fridge. Fresh vegetables and fruits and milk and other things. Rushing down to the hallway leading to the vault, he set the food bags inside the door, then went back to fetch the two pillowcases. He moved everything in front of the vault door and got on Facetime, hitting Maria's contact. Her smiling face showed up, and he heard the bolts opening behind the vault door. It swung open slowly and he slipped inside with the grocery bags, then reached back and grabbed the pillow cases.

"Should I shut it?" Maria asked.

"Yeah, go ahead," Hendrix said.

She pushed the button and the vault door closed, the bolts extending.

"I hope you can wear some of what I brought," he said.

"Looks like you got a lot of groceries," she said, looking inside the bags. "I'll take them to the walk-in."

"I'll help," Hendrix said. They picked them up and walked through the kitchen to the pantry and walk-in area.

"See much out there?" she asked.

Hendrix pulled open the door of the walk-in. "Yeah, tanks bottled up on South Congress Ave. Enemy fighters on the rooftops, shooting at buildings. Citizens returning fire. Looks like a stalemate to me."

"Why aren't the tanks moving?"

"I don't think they can," Hendrix said. "I think the first few are disabled, and the others can't get around them. Hard to tell from where I was, though."

"Nobody was close by here?" Maria asked as she unloaded the grocery bags.

"Not that I could see," Hendrix said. "I hope whatever citizens are left were well stocked up with food. This is liable to be a long siege."

"Good, you brought some milk," Maria said. "I saw some boxes of cereal. You getting hungry?"

"Yeah," Hendrix said. "Let's eat."

They got bowls down and made cereal, then sat at one of the three tables in the kitchen.

"No way could thirty people all eat in here at the same time," Maria said.

Hendrix finished chewing his first spoonful. "Yeah, it would be a little cramped. The protocol was based on submarine practices. Hot bunking, rotation of meal times, and so on."

They finished eating. Hendrix looked Maria in the eyes. "Regrets?"

"Regrets?"

"About last night," he said.

"Not even a little bit," she said. "It was what I needed. What we both needed."

"Good, I was hoping," he said, still looking at her face. "If you change your mind, I'll understand."

"Will you stop that?" Maria asked. "I gave myself to you because I wanted to, and I'm not one for one-night stands or casual relationships. You can tell that, I hope."

"Yes, I can," Hendrix said. "Sorry to be so nervous about this. I don't want to become a disappointment. I don't want you to feel trapped."

She giggled. "I don't see that being a problem."

"What's funny?"

"Oh, I was just thinking about you, saddled with a wife and several kids. You're in more danger than I am."

"You'd have babies with me?"

"Yes," she said softly.

The buzzer went off.

"Duty calls," Hendrix said, standing. He and Maria hurried to the console. Maria got onto the keyboard and input the codes. Holly's face came on the screen.

"Good morning, you two," he said.

"Morning, Holly," Hendrix said. "What's up?"

"It's been quiet," Holly said. "Too quiet. You been up to the roof yet?"

"Yes, a few minutes ago. Tanks are bottled up on South Congress Ave, and there's skirmishes going on between enemy fighters on the rooftops and citizens in buildings. Looks like a stalemate."

"The tanks are low on fuel," Holly said. "We're waiting to see where they go to replenish. Gallagher thinks they know we're watching for that. He's afraid they're waiting to make a move until more troops show up to hold their positions."

"More troops are coming in?" Maria asked. She moved closer to Hendrix, hand going over his on the desk.

"We saw another eighty thousand last night, but they never showed up. We don't know where they are. They might be trying to enter the city a different way."

"So you think they'll try to keep us busy with a new front while they start rushing tanks to their service area?" Hendrix asked.

"That's what Gallagher is afraid of," Holly said. "Since Dallas is in so much danger, we're really low on men and materiel around Austin."

"Why did you call me?" Holly asked. "You're getting ready to ask me something that you don't want to ask me. I know you too well. Spill."

Holly sighed. "Nelson wants you to work your Fed connections. We need access to the satellites so we can have a better chance at seeing their troop movements and supply depots."

"Oh," Hendrix said, glancing at Maria. "I'm certainly willing to try that. I'll need something to trade."

"Nelson has authorized you to provide them info, but we'll need to tiptoe around some things."

"Like what?" Hendrix asked.

"Our relationship with the Air Force, for starters," Holly said. "The administration knows that we're getting some help from the Air Force, but they think it's just a few renegades. We need them to continue to think that, so they don't know they've lost control of the entire Air Force."

"I take it the Air Force has been playing them, then," Hendrix said.

"Exactly," Holly said. "There's a close association with certain high-ranking Air Force officers and some agency folks in the Administration. FBI mostly, but also Homeland Security and the CIA."

"You aren't going to tell me they suspect the Administration is behind this invasion, I hope."

Holly was silent for a moment.

"Shit, what do you know?" Hendrix asked.

"Not much more than you do," he said. "Nelson knows something, though. So does Gallagher and Landry. Also General Hogan and General Walker. I have a feeling they've got the administration dead to rights on this, but they can't act on it...yet."

"This will kill the progressive movement in this country for years if it's true," Hendrix said.

"I know," Holly said. "We're lucky we got onto the right side."

"Seriously," Hendrix said. "The Feds might apply a lot of pressure on me, you know."

"I know," Holly said. "So does Nelson and Ramsey, so you need to be careful. You'll have to walk the razor's edge. Understand?"

"Yeah, I understand," Hendrix said.

"Good. That's all I've got."

"You safe?" Hendrix asked.

"For now, yeah, but I'm stuck in the city."

"Know where Jerry Sutton ended up?"

Holly was silent again, his brow furrowed.

"Oh, dammit, he didn't get killed, did he?" Hendrix asked, feeling the tears around his eyes.

"He disappeared," Holly said. "Last night, as he was trying to get to the checkpoint. He was in a bad place when this started."

"How bad a place?" Hendrix asked.

"Not far from where you and Maria were," Holly said. "Nelson has people looking for him."

"He knows a lot," Hendrix said.

"If there *is* a connection between the enemy and the Administration, this could be bad for us," Holly said.

"It could also backfire on the Administration," Hendrix said, leaning back in his chair. "I'll be able to tell if they've talked to him."

Holly was quiet for moment.

"What's the matter?" Hendrix asked.

"We need to have a classified conversation. Would you mind sending Maria away for a moment?"

"We don't have to do that," Hendrix said.

"It's okay," Maria said, getting up. "I'll go in the other room and shut the door."

"Thank you, Maria," Holly said. "It'll just take a minute."

She nodded and went into the next room, shutting the door behind her.

Hendrix looked at Holly's image on the screen. "Okay, what?"

"I'm worried about her," Holly said. "She could be an opportunity for the enemy."

"What are you talking about?"

"You're in love with her," Holly said. "The Feds know things about you that she might not. They may threaten you with that."

"You think they'll blackmail me," Hendrix said.

"Yeah," Holly said. "Have you told her everything?"

"I've told her some, but not the worst stuff. I've put that behind me, now. You know that. I've paid the victims."

"It'll look like you've hushed them up," Holly said, "so be careful. If I were you, I'd come completely clean with her before you talk to the Feds, just in case. Better than getting yourself caught while trying to walk the tightrope."

"Okay, I understand," Hendrix said. "Good advice."

"All right, then see if you can get that satellite access turned back on. It's important. Might save thousands of lives."

"I understand," Hendrix said. "Talk to you later."

Hendrix shut down the call and went into the next room.

"Sorry about that," he said to Maria.

"Don't worry about it," she said. "Was it some of the stuff you told me that I'm not supposed to know?"

"Yeah," Hendrix said. "Time to call my contact in DC. Wish me luck." He walked into the bedroom and picked up the land line phone receiver.

{ 5 }

Rendezvous

Eric slowed the Bronco as they approached the dark Salt Lick barbecue. Dirk's truck pulled up next to it. They got out.

"How long till your brother gets here?" Dirk asked.

"Oh, I'd guess twenty minutes to an hour," Eric said.

"That's a pretty big range," Chance said.

"I know," Eric said. "They're towing, so they may be going slower. You know they might run into those flatbeds too, right? They might have to fight."

"Shit," Kim said. "Maybe you should call them."

"Yeah," Eric said, pulling his phone out of his pocket. He hit Jason's contact. It rang twice.

"Eric," Jason said. "What's up?"

"We just got to the Salt Lick," Eric said. "Saw an enemy convoy on the way. You run into them?"

"Yeah, but we ducked into the woods before they saw us," Jason said.

"They didn't see your headlights?" Eric asked.

"No, we've been running without them since we made it to the area," Jason said.

"That's tough to do," Eric said. "Dark out here."

"I live around here, remember," Jason said. "I know these roads like the back of my hand."

"Glad you didn't have to stop and fight them, anyway," Eric said. "How far out are you?"

"Half hour, give or take," Jason said.

"Good, we'll be waiting," Eric said. "Be careful."

"You too," Jason said.

Eric ended the call.

"They see the convoy?" Dirk asked.

"Yeah," Eric said. "They've been running without lights, so they were able to get into the woods without being seen."

"Wow, really?" Chance asked. "I wouldn't want to try that."

"Those guys all live around here," Eric said. "I haven't for years and years."

"Makes a difference," Dirk said.

"How long till they get here?" Kim asked.

"Half an hour or so," Eric said. "We've got a little while to relax."

"Yeah, like that's going to happen," Kim said.

"I'm going to double check the guns," Chance said.

"Good idea," Dirk said. "We should load up those AKs we got from the Tigr crew also."

"Wish we would've grabbed the machine gun and the grenade launcher before we left," Chance said.

"Too heavy," Eric said. "We're going to be flying through rough terrain during this attack. Better not to have them if we can't use them."

"Good point," Dirk said. He went to the back of his pickup truck and started checking out the new AKs.

"Let's check ours, too, sweetie," Eric said. Kim nodded and followed him to the back of the Bronco. Eric opened the tail gate and they got to work.

"You think we'll survive this?" Kim asked. "I'm more scared than normal."

Eric chuckled. "Maybe you're just nervous about meeting my family."

She shot him a glance. "Oh, please. It's just your brother."

"He's all the family I have left," Eric said.

"You think I'm worried that Jason won't like me?"

"No, I'm just trying to take your mind off the battle," Eric said. "Don't think it's working. Being scared doesn't mean you'll do poorly. Most of the time it's exactly the opposite."

"Hope you're right," Kim said.

"We're all checked out," Dirk said, walking over with Chance. "Those weapons look newer."

"Yeah, I don't see a lot of evidence of hard use on any of them," Chance said. "Maybe the people coming in are green."

"Or maybe they aren't and they just got new weapons," Kim said.

"We'll be more than a match for them," Dirk said. "If they wouldn't have had a huge advantage in numbers at Deadwood, we would've killed them all. We lost less people than they did in the battle. There was just too many of them."

"We have the home-field advantage," Eric said. "It helps."

"I suppose," Kim said. "How long has it been?"

"Fifteen minutes," Eric said. "They'll be here."

They gathered next to the Bronco, leaning on it, thoughts inward as the minutes crept by. Then they heard the sound of vehicles approaching.

"Should we get out of sight?" Chance asked.

Eric thought about it for a second. "Yeah, just in case."

They scurried into the bushes and waited as the vehicles approached, coming into view after a few seconds. A Jeep towing a Barracuda with a big gun mounted on top, and a pickup truck with a machine gun mounted on the roll bar.

"It's Jason!" Eric said, rushing out to greet them. The vehicles stopped, Jason getting out and rushing to Eric. They embraced.

"Boy am I glad to see you," Jason said, looking at Eric. Kim walked over. "This your woman?"

"Yes, I am," Kim said. "Nice to meet you."

"Kim," Eric said. "This is Jason."

Kelly, Junior, Curt, and Kyle came over.

"Eric," Kyle said, taking his hand and shaking it. "Long time no see."

"Yeah, too long," Eric said. "This is Kim."

"Nice to meet you," Kyle said.

"Wow, not bad," Curt said. "How you been, Eric?"

"Good," Eric said, shaking hands.

"This is Kelly and Junior," Curt said. "Comrades in arms."

"Heard about you guys," Eric said. "Good to meet you."

"Likewise," Kelly said.

"Yeah," Junior said. "Me too."

"Dirk and Chance have been with us since the battle for Deadwood," Eric said.

"Good to meet you guys," Curt said. The others nodded in agreement.

"This all we got?" Eric asked.

"We have a group of bikers on the way," Kelly said. "Gray's men. Haven't heard from them yet. I don't want to call them now – might interrupt them in a bad place."

"Hopefully they've made it there safe and sound," Kyle said, "someplace where we can link up. Those guys are good in a fight."

"We probably better get going," Jason said. "We've still got some miles to go."

"Anybody else around?" Jason asked. "Enemy, that is?"

Curt pulled out his phone and looked at his tracking app.

"No," Curt said. "They're all bunched up in one place, but I have seen a few hits coming towards their position from Austin. They might be re-supplying some of their folks already."

"Then let's get our butts in gear," Kelly said.

"How we getting there?" Eric asked. "Just in case we get separated."

"Take 967 until you get to 1626, then go south," Curt said. "Easy peasy."

They got into their vehicles and got back on the road.

"Jason looks a lot like you," Kim said.

"That's what everybody tells me, but I don't see it that much," Eric said. "He looks more like mom's side of the family than I do."

Kim chuckled. "There is a resemblance. I would have guessed you were related if I didn't know."

Eric chuckled as he struggled to keep up with the others on the dark road.

"Did you know Kelly and Junior before?" Kim asked.

"No, but I heard about them, mostly from Curt," Eric said.

"Kelly's kind of scary looking."

"I've heard he's good in a fight, and has a heart of gold," Eric said.

"These guys drive fast back here," Kim said, clutching the sides of her seat.

"Don't worry, I'm following them fine. Easier when I can see somebody in front of me."

They drove silently for a while, getting to route 1626 and making the right turn, heading south.

"How big is Mountain City?" Kim asked.

"Not very," Eric said. "Remember going there a few times when I was younger. It's a bedroom community for Austin, mainly."

"Hope they didn't kill off most of the population," Kim said.

"There are some remote parts of that area," Eric said. "Good for ATV riding. Hopefully everybody got out the back way when the enemy came in."

Eric's phone rang. He put it to his ear. "Yeah, Jason?"

"Their supply depot is next to Onion Creek," Jason said.

"Is there a good way to approach?"

"Probably not with vehicles," he said. "How many grenades do you have?"

"About thirty," Eric said. "Think we ought to go in on foot first? I've got my bow in the back of the Bronco."

"Yeah, we might want to soften them up with the grenades, and then drive in the big guns to finish them off."

"The fuel is gonna be the most important part, right?" Eric asked.

"Yeah, that'll insure that they can't operate their tanks in Austin for long. There might be a lot of men at their depot, though, so we've got to be careful. I heard there was another eighty thousand troops that were on their way into Austin but then disappeared. They might be around here."

"Dammit," Eric said. "Maybe they're trying to make it to Dallas."

"Maybe," Jason said. "We've only got a couple more miles. They might have sentries posted pretty far out, so stay sharp. Keep your eyes open."

"Roger that," Eric said. He ended the call.

"Getting close?" Kim asked.

"Really close. We'll probably go in on foot to check things out, maybe blow up their fuel before we hit them with our mobile assets."

Kim snickered. "Mobile assets? You mean that jury-rigged off roader and the pickup truck with the machine gun on it?"

"Yeah," Eric said. "I recognized the gun on that off-roader. Don't know where the hell Curt got it."

"What is it?"

"Mark 19 automatic grenade launcher," Eric said. "Those things will fire grenades as fast as you can pull the trigger."

"Geez," Kim said. "So why are we going in on foot?"

"To make sure that they can't protect the fuel," Eric said. "They might hear us coming in the vehicles in time to block us from it, especially if there are any tanks around. Remember, the fuel is job one."

"They're slowing down," Kim said. "Look."

"See it."

"Glad we brought Paco," Kim said.

"I'm worried about the homestead," Eric said. "Almost decided to leave him. He's a good early warning system. The Islamists would love to get their paws on Alyssa and Chloe."

"Oh, God, I don't even want to think about that," Kim said.

"Here we go," Eric said, following Jason and the others onto the bumpy dirt road. "Hope they don't hear us coming."

"How much faith do you have in Curt's tracking ability?"

Eric glanced at her. "Total. The guy's a genius."

"Hope you're right. They're pulling over ahead."

Eric slowed and parked next to Jason's Jeep.

"Keep quiet!" Jason whispered as the others gathered around. "If they've got sentries placed, they might be pretty close."

"I'll get my bow," Eric whispered. "Let's distribute some grenades. Meet me in back of the Bronco."

He walked to the tailgate with Kim and opened it as quietly as he could, then carefully removed the top of the wooden crate.

"Let's see, two a piece?" Eric whispered.

"Wait a minute," Curt said. "Got an idea. Instead of all of us sneaking in on foot, how about if Kyle and I wait here with the Barracuda and the pickup? When we hear you guys blowing things up, we'll come on over and give them a real bad day."

"I'm game," Kyle said. "I'll help you unhitch the Barracuda while they take off."

"Not a bad idea," Jason whispered. "Just keep an eye out so you don't get jumped."

Eric handed out the grenades. They all checked their guns, and then started into the trees along Onion Creek. The eastern sky was just starting to show a glow as the sun rose.

"Hear that?" Jason whispered.

"Yeah, sounds like an electric pump," Eric whispered.

"They might be filling some tanks," Junior whispered. "Be a good time to surprise them."

"Yeah," Kelly whispered. "We know they aren't asleep, so be quiet."

Eric stopped, staring. "Sentry, see? In that tree. Dozing."

"Think you can hit him with the bow?" Kim whispered.

"Yeah, if I get a tad closer. You guys stay here."

Eric nocked an arrow and walked quietly forward, eyes darting around. The sentry woke for a moment, shaking his head, but not looking in Eric's direction.

"Get ready," Junior whispered. They watched Eric creep closer, then aim is bow. He let an arrow fly, hitting the sentry in the chest, dropping him silently.

"Nice," Kelly said. "Look, he sees somebody else. He just nocked another arrow."

Eric crept forward to a ring of rocks overlooking a bend in the creek, and poked his head up. The fuel tanks were about fifty yards ahead of him. Two M-1 tanks were parked next to them, hoses running into each. He could smell kerosene. Another sentry stood thirty yards in that direction, with his back to Eric, watching the tanks. Eric got a little closer and aimed his bow. The arrow flew, hitting the sentry in the back. He gasped as he fell. One of the men fueling the nearest tank whirled around, but saw nothing and turned back to his job. Eric turned back towards Jason and gave him a thumbs up. They all crept up behind as Eric continued.

"You no move!" shouted a man with a heavy Arabic accent, standing to the right of Eric. He froze, bringing up his hands, one of them hiding a grenade. "Turn towards me now!"

Eric looked at the man, heart pounding, hand sweating around the grenade. *Don't see it.*

Jason aimed his BAR at the Islamist, not sure what to do. Then there was a double shotgun blast from behind the Islamist, nearly cutting him in half. Jason squinted through the dust. Gray's men were there with sawed-off shotguns.

There was yelling in Arabic in the camp. Eric threw his grenade, landing it right next to the fuel tanks. It blew up, starting a fire along the hoses into the tanks, engulfing the closest one in flames as the Islamists opened fire in their direction, shooting wildly in a panic.

Eric tossed his second grenade, hitting the side of the fuel tank and rupturing it, spreading a sea of flame around the area. The far tank was trying to drive away. Dirk, Chance, Kelly, Kim, and Junior ran up, all of them throwing their grenades, blowing up the tank servicing area, sending the Islamists fleeing for their lives. Jason opened up with the BAR, hitting as many as he could.

"Look, they're running towards those transport trucks!" Junior yelled.

Suddenly there was a roar behind them, as Curt flew onto the scene with his Barracuda, firing grenades into the camp, blowing up both of the trucks before the Islamists could escape. Grays men ran in, blasting their shotguns at anybody who moved as Kyle pulled up on the perimeter. He opened up with the .50 cal, making a mess of everything, killing the remaining Islamists in minutes. Then there was silence. Kim rushed over to Eric.

"You okay?" she asked

"Yeah, you?"

"I'm good," she said. "I don't think any of our people got hit."

Gray rushed over with his men. "We ruined their party, didn't we?"

"You must be the bikers," Eric said, shaking hands. "I'm Eric, Jason's brother. Thanks for saving my ass."

"Don't mention it," Gray said. "Good to meet you."

The group rushed into the camp as Kyle and Curt kept watch above in their vehicles.

"Look, there's a tank that didn't get blown up," Gray said. "Wonder if there's anybody in it?"

He rushed down with his people. There were several men next to the tank, dead among the rubble. Gray cautiously opened the hatch.

"Toss a grenade in there," Jason shouted.

"No way," Gray said. "There's nobody in here, and we know how to run these things now, remember?"

"It's probably out of fuel," Curt shouted. "It was next in line. We ruined the gas station."

Kelly and Junior laughed.

There was sound approaching. Engine noise and the squeaking of tank treads.

"Hear that?" Jason asked. "There's more tanks coming in. They have to know something happened. Look at all the smoke."

"And the flames," Dirk said. "Hey, maybe we ought to aim the cannon in that last tank at them. Part their hair."

"I heard that," Gray said. He rushed over to his men, and several of them climbed into the tank. There was a whir of motors as the tank's turret turned towards the incoming road.

"This is gonna be a mess," Kim said. "Maybe we ought to get back."

"Hey, there's two troop transports and a mobile artillery unit behind that M-1," Curt said in a loud whisper. "I can take on everything but that tank. We got to disable it with the first shot."

"That's the plan," Gray said, half his body sticking out of the turret.

"Here it comes," Kim said, fear in her eyes as she glanced at Eric. Suddenly there was a loud boom, the approaching tank blew up, pieces of the turret flying off.

"Let's get 'em," Curt yelled, driving the Barracuda closer and firing grenades at the trucks and the mobile artillery unit. Kyle joined in, sweeping the area with .50 cal fire as the enemy fighters ran in a panic. Then Gray's men fired the tank again, blowing up the enemy tank, flames and shrapnel flying in every direction.

"Get down!" Jason yelled. Everybody hit the dirt as debris fell around them.

Gray popped his head out of the tank. "There's several more tanks coming down the road. I can't get them all before they return fire. We'd better split."

"I'm gonna hit those three buildings over there before we go," Curt yelled. "Probably ammo."

He drove the Barracuda closer to them and opened fire, the buildings shuddering and then blowing sky high as the ammo inside exploded.

"Yes!" Junior yelled, laughing and jumping up and down.

"Contain yourself," Kelly said, shaking his head.

"Let's get the hell out of here," Jason yelled. "Before those tanks start lobbing shells at us."

"Yeah, let's go," Curt yelled. He drove the Barracuda back to the other vehicles. Kyle pulled up next to the others on foot.

"Hop in," he said. Jason, Eric, Kim, Dirk, and Chance all piled into the bed. Gray's men ran to their bikes, which were a couple hundred yards away, getting on them and roaring away as the enemy approached.

"They're really screwed," Eric said. "They're gonna run out of gas in a hurry. They won't be able to chase us."

"They couldn't catch us anyway," Jason said. "Let's go to dad's spread."

"Yeah," Eric said. "Should be pretty safe there."

"I need to call Chief Ramsey," Jason said. "Let him know that we took out their fuel and ammo supply. They need to make it rough on those tanks, force them to move."

Everybody got back to the vehicles. Curt already was halfway done hitching the Barracuda to Jason's Jeep.

"Damn, buddy, that Barracuda is awesome," Dirk said. "Wish we would've had that at the Deadwood battle."

"Yeah, it's a nice little toy," Curt said. "I got several more of those M-19s at my place in San Antonio. It's not that far from here. Once we're settled I'm gonna go get them. We have several more vehicles we could put them on."

"Hell yeah!" Chance said.

Junior laughed. "We're back on the enemy's shit list again. We'll need all the firepower we can get."

"By the way, we damaged a GAZ Tigr back on the road," Eric said. "It was with that convoy that I told you about. There was a grenade launcher and a machine gun in the storage compartments in back.

Curt froze and looked over at him, a grin washing over his face. "Oh, really now? You hide it?"

"As best we could," Eric said. "We have to be careful. It's obvious that we tried to hide it. If the enemy found it, they know we'll probably be back. We could walk right into a trap."

"Sounds risky," Kelly said, "but it might be worth it."

"C'mon, let's get the hell out of here," Jason said. "Before something arrives that can catch us."

"I'm ready," Curt said. "Let's go."

Everybody got into their vehicles and took off towards Fredericksburg.

6

Change of Route

The DPS team was still on the road, Richardson behind the wheel.

"Finally," he said. "I-69E."

"Looks okay," Lita said.

"Yeah, everything looks okay," Juan Carlos said. "Until it's not."

Brendan laughed. Madison and Hannah shot each other a worried glance, then looked at Lita.

"Look, there's a gas station," Richardson said. "Let's go pick up a burner phone."

"Only one?" Madison asked.

"For now, yeah," Richardson said as he pulled into a parking stall in front of the store. He rushed inside, leaving the others in the car.

"We're sticking out like a sore thumb," Juan Carlos said. "Maybe we should've parked in the back."

"Don't worry about it," Lita said. "He's already coming out."

"Got it," Richardson said as he got back in. "What a piece of crap. I'm gonna send a text to Jefferson so he knows the number." He focused on the phone for a moment, put it in his pocket, then drove back onto I-69E.

"I wouldn't worry about this road. You sure they really want us on Route 2? That runs right along the border, you know. Right by Falcon Lake, or what's left of it."

"Jefferson told us to go to Laredo," Richardson said. "That's the fastest way to get there."

"There's a safer way," Lita said. "Take route 77 north. This road turns into it eventually. Then use route 285 to go west."

"That's way out of the way," Richardson said.

"We got plenty of drivers," Lita said. "We can drive straight through."

"I'll have to check with Jefferson," he said.

"Why do they want us in Laredo, anyway?" Brendan asked. "The lake is gone. Patrolling the river is easier to do with ground assets. You know that, right?"

"Might just be a good place to meet with Gallagher and Landry," Richardson said. "They'll probably call pretty soon. I'll go along with the northern route for now. Lita has a good point. Don't want our women in danger."

"Our women?" Hannah asked.

"Yeah," Brendan said, pulling her close. She rolled her eyes, but he stared, causing her to take in a breath.

"Don't look at me that way," she whispered.

"Why not?" Brendan whispered back.

"It makes me feel uncomfortable," she said. "Out of control."

Madison giggled. "Now it's our turn to tease you guys."

"Shut up," Hannah said. "At least I'm not telling Brendan that I love him already."

"You guys watching our back?" Richardson asked. He glanced over at Lita and grinned.

"Yes, sir," Juan Carlos said.

Richardson's burner phone rang. He took it out of his pocket and handed it to Lita. "Put it on speaker, okay?"

"Sure," Lita said. She held the phone to her ear. "Putting you on speaker." Then she set the phone on the center console.

"You hear us okay?" Richardson asked.

"Yeah," Jefferson said. "Change of plans. We want you guys up at Riviera Beach. You didn't get to route two yet, did you?"

"No, we decided it wasn't safe. We're gonna go up route 77 and then go west to Laredo."

"Perfect," Jefferson said. "We're getting ready to mount an assault on South Padre Island from the north. There's other boats already operating there, and the new ones were delivered last night. One of them has your name on it. It's more capable than your last one."

"How much time do we have?" Richardson asked.

Lita was looking at her phone. "It's just over an hour from here, honey."

"Good," Jefferson said. "Check in at the base. You can't miss it. Take route 771 from route 77. Then take route 1155 to the end. We're using the docks that used to belong to a seafood outfit."

"Okay, we'll be there soon. You going to be there?"

"Yeah, along with Gallagher and Landry."

"Where's General Walker?"

"That's classified," Jefferson said.

"Roger that," Richardson said. "Talk to you later."

Lita ended the call. "Want to leave the phone on the console?"

"Sure," Richardson said. "Well, you guys heard that. Looks like we're getting back into it."

"Where are we gonna stay?" Madison asked.

"Oh, I'm sure they'll have someplace set up for us," Richardson said. "Let's turn on the radio for a while, okay? I'd like to hear what's been happening."

"Me too," Lita said. She reached over and turned on the radio, then searched for a news channel.

"I'm scared," Madison whispered to Juan Carlos. "What if you guys get killed?"

"Shhhh," Hannah said. "Don't even talk about it."

"Oh, so you *do* care," Brendan said.

Hannah looked at his face, tears forming in her eyes. "Shut up."

"Quiet, here's a report about Austin," Lita said.

"We finally have good news at this hour. The enemy fighters are beginning to leave the Austin area. Their supply depot in Mountain City was discovered early this morning. Their fuel and ammunition stocks were destroyed, and all of their technical support staff were killed."

"Yes!" Juan Carlos said.

"Sshhh." Lita put her finger to her lips, looking at him.

"The enemy fighters are leaving on foot, trying to regroup south of the city. Citizen militias are following them, picking off as many as they can."

"They aren't saying who found the depot," Brendan said. "Wonder if it was the military or some citizens?"

"Good question," Richardson said. "I heard that the military in the Austin area was being moved to protect Dallas."

"Oops," Lita said.

"I thought we were gonna get sent to Dallas," Richardson said.

"Why?" Juan Carlos asked.

"Those big lakes up there," he said. "The brass was afraid of a device like the one that destroyed Falcon Lake."

"Don't blame them," Brendan said. "Lot of people would be killed if the dams got blown up there."

"Yep," Richardson said. "Maybe they figured out another way to protect against them."

"Did they ever tell you what they used?" Juan Carlos asked.

"Nope," Richardson said. "It's classified. I did some research, though. The Russians have an anti-submarine weapon which could cause what happened in Falcon Lake."

"I thought Russia was on our side," Madison said.

"They are, but they haven't always had good control over their military assets," Richardson said. "If one of those devices got used, it's because somebody stole it."

"This just in. Houston is under attack, similar to the attack in Austin. A large number of M-1 tanks and at least fifty thousand men have arrived. Houston still has numerous military personnel, so a large battle is expected. Citizens are fleeing to the east as the enemy enters the western side of the city."

"Dammit, where are all these men and tanks coming from?" Brendan asked.

"They must have another source," Richardson said. "We locked down Fort Bliss tight."

They rode silently for a half hour, listening to the radio. There was news of more nukes going off in small harbors, and of the beginning of martial law in California. Hannah was getting more and more agitated. Brendan tried to comfort her, but she stiffened when he touched her.

"What's wrong?" Brendan asked.

She looked at him, tears in her eyes. "You're going to get killed. I don't want to get too close. It'll be hard enough as it is."

"Don't count me out yet," Brendan said.

"Yeah, quit talking about that," Madison said. "It scares me."

"It ought to," Hannah said. "You went and fell in love already."

"So did you," Madison said. "You just aren't admitting it to yourself yet."

"Shut up," she said quietly. Brendan brushed her hair out of her eyes, looking at her face.

"Is it true?"

"I'm not talking about that now," she said. "Survive this and we'll talk."

Brendan smiled. "You don't have to tell me. Just don't leave me."

Lita turned off the radio.

"Had enough?" Richardson asked.

"The world is going nuts," she said. "I don't want to wait so long."

"For what?" Richardson asked.

She rolled her eyes. "Marriage, dummy."

Richardson shot her a glance and smiled. "You're the one who wouldn't go for it, remember?"

"Yes," she whispered. "I'm sorry."

"Nothing to be sorry about," he said. "I'd pull over to a Justice of the Peace right now if I saw one."

She laughed. "They still have those?"

"Probably," he said. "Maybe there's a courthouse in Riviera Beach. Unless you want to wait for a big wedding."

"Oh, please," she said. "None of our families are close by, and it's not exactly a good time to travel."

"So why rush it, then?" Richardson asked. "We *can* wait until things settle down and do it proper, you know."

"I'd rather have kids *after* we get married," she said. "I've got the urge bad. *Right now.*"

Richardson chuckled. "Oh, *really* now?"

"You don't want to?"

"I didn't say that," Richardson said. "Doesn't it scare you with the war going on?"

"It scares the hell out of me, but the fear isn't as strong as the desire," Lita said.

"You know we can hear you back here, right?" Hannah asked.

Lita put her hand over her mouth. "Oops."

Hannah laughed and looked at Madison, who had a serious, thoughtful expression on her face. "Oh, *shit.* No way."

Madison glanced at her, a soft smile coming onto her face.

"You too?" Hannah asked.

"No comment," Madison said. Juan Carlos smiled and pulled her closer.

"You two better be careful," Hannah said.

"So should you," Madison said. "I know you want it. I could hear it this morning."

"What? No way," Hannah said.

"I don't know," Brendan said. "Sounds kinda nice to me."

Hannah rolled her eyes and turned to look out the side window. Madison started to say something but Brendan shook his head no at her.

They settled in for the ride.

7

Sydney

Jason lead the way to the homestead in Fredericksburg, Kyle's truck following with Kelly and Junior in the cab, Eric behind him, and Gray's motorcycles at the rear.

"You gonna call your boss?" Curt asked.

"Yeah," Jason said. "As soon as we get on a straighter piece of road."

"You're almost on that," Curt said.

"Pretty country," Dirk said.

"Yeah," Chance said. "Miss East Texas, though."

"Been to Deadwood a couple times on hunting trips," Jason said. "Eric too. He probably found his way around okay back there."

"He did," Chance said. "Took dirt roads into Texas. We met up with him on one of them. Ran into a group of Islamists as they were murdering citizens."

"Yeah, Eric told me about that," Jason said. "You guys had quite an adventure. Hope you didn't lose too many people."

"We *did* lose too many," Dirk said. "Good people. Some of our women are still missing. Scares me to think about that. Wish there was something we could do."

"There is," Curt said, "and you guys just took part in the opening battle."

Chance smiled. "Yeah, I guess we did. We have the makings of a kick-ass team here."

"You got that right," Curt said. "Wait till we get the other grenade launchers set up."

"The road is straight enough now," Justin said, pulling out his phone. He hit the contact for the Austin PD land line.

"Austin PD. How may I direct your call?" the operator said.

"This is Jason Finley, for Chief Ramsey."

"One moment please," she said. "I'll see if he's available. Is he expecting your call?"

"Yes," Jason said. He held the line for a moment. Then there was a click.

"Jason," Ramsey said. "Everything okay?"

"Better than okay," Jason said. "We just blew up the enemy ammo and fuel depot in Mountain City. Killed all their technical folks. Blew up a few of their tanks and several other vehicles, too."

"That was you guys?" he asked. "I just got a report on that a few minutes ago from one of our scouts."

"Yeah, it was us."

"How'd you find that location? We've been looking for the last twenty-four hours."

"Curt figured out how to track their cell phones. He found them."

"Curt. Figures. What now? You still in the area?"

"Yeah, but I won't say where we're going over the phone. You guys should give those tanks a hard time, now that their fuel and ammo are destroyed."

"Some of them are already stranded south of town," Ramsey said. "You hear what's going on in Houston?"

"No," Jason said.

"Twenty tanks and about fifty-thousand men are hitting the west side of the city now. At least Houston is better prepared for them than Austin was."

"Holy shit," Jason said. "Think that's where that missing eighty-thousand men ended up?"

"Part of them," Ramsey said. "I take it you didn't see a large group of men at the depot?"

"Nope, there were fifty men there at most."

"Okay, thanks for the info," Ramsey said, "and nice job on that depot. With folks like you out there, we might just win this war."

"You can bet on that," Jason said. "Talk to you later, Chief." He ended the call.

"Well, sounds like he was happy about that," Curt said.

"Of course," Jason said. "He told me that Houston is under attack."

"Dammit," Curt said. "Anything about San Antonio?"

"Not that he mentioned," Jason said. "How close to town is your stockpile?"

"It's a little west of Lackland Air Force Base," Curt said. "Just off of route 90. It's kinda in the boonies."

"That's not that far from Fredericksburg," Jason said.

"A little under two hours," Curt said. "Depending on traffic and *other problems.*"

Dick snorted. "*Other problems as* in enemy fighters?"

"Yeah," Curt said. "After we get settled, I'd like to crank on down there."

"Well, you're welcome to take my Jeep," Jason said. "It's a little lower profile than Kyle's truck."

"If you need more cargo space, we have a pickup at the house," Dirk said. "It doesn't have any *modifications.* Looks like every other well-used redneck truck in Texas."

"We probably should avoid 290 now that it's light," Jason said. "We might get some questions otherwise, with these weapons showing."

"Yeah," Curt said. "Take Ranch-to-Market 32. That way we'll avoid the big towns."

"Way ahead of you," Jason said. "Gonna take about an hour and a half."

Jason's phone rang. He answered it.

"What's up, Kyle?" Jason asked.

"We aren't taking 290, I hope."

Jason laughed. "We were just talking about it. We're taking Ranch-to-Market 32."

"Good, that'll work," Kyle said. "You call the girls yet?"

"Figured I'd wait until we got back to dad's place," Jason said. "As far as I'm concerned, we're still in this. We could run into another fight on the way to the homestead."

"Maybe I ought to get in the lead. My truck has the machine gun."

"Sounds good," Jason said. "I'll pull over the next time I see a wide spot."

"Roger that," Kyle said. "If you hear me start firing, stop and let Curt get into his Barracuda."

"You sound a little worried," Jason said.

"We got off too easy earlier. I'm waiting for the other shoe to drop."

"Well don't get all jittery. Especially near the trigger of that .50 cal."

"Understand," Kyle said. "Talk to you later."

Jason ended the call.

"Kyle got the jitters?" Curt asked. "Pencil neck."

"He's right," Jason said. "We aren't out of this yet. He's gonna pass me as soon as I can move over a little bit. That way if we run into anybody, he can fire on them."

"Good idea," Curt said. "If anything starts up, I'll get into the Barracuda."

Jason laughed. "Yeah, he brought that up too."

"How long will it take to get back?" Dirk asked.

"A little over an hour," Jason said. "Not so bad. All backroads."

Chance snickered. "These aren't backroads to us. Where we come from, the backroads are dirt or gravel."

Kyle passed them after a couple miles. They rode silently for most of the way, holding their breaths as they rolled through the small towns. Nobody was out and around until they got to Luckenbach. Kyle slowed to a stop just inside town.

"Dammit," Curt said. "That a cop walking up to Kyle's window?"

"Doesn't look like a cop to me," Jason said.

"Get your guns ready," Dirk said.

"Wait, he's walking away. Kyle's driving off."

"What the hell?" Dirk asked. Then Jason's phone rang.

"Hey, Kyle, who was that guy?"

Kyle snickered. "Some old coot who hangs around the saloon in Luckenbach. I've met him before, believe it or not."

"What'd he want?" Jason asked.

"He offered me fifty bucks if I'd let him fire off a few rounds with the .50 cal. I told him I needed to save the ammo for the Islamists. He gave me a thumbs up and walked away."

Jason cracked up. "All right. Talk to you later."

"What's so funny?" Chance asked.

"That old man offered Kyle money to fire the .50 cal."

Curt laughed hard. "Man after my own heart."

"Seriously," Jason said.

"There any more towns to go through?" Chance asked.

"No, that was it. It's all back country roads now," Jason said, "and by the way, there's a real scary stretch of dirt switchbacks right before we get there. Don't piss yourself in my car, okay?"

Dirk laughed. "You should see some of the roads where we come from."

They made it to the homestead turnoff without incident, and took the dirt road back, handling the switchbacks with no problem. Right after they got back onto the valley floor somebody fired a weapon.

"Dammit!" Curt said as Kyle slammed on the brakes in front of them.

Jason laughed when he saw a raven-haired woman walking up, gun pointing at Kyle's truck, long hair blowing a little in the breeze.

"You know her?" Curt asked. "She's hot."

"Sydney Merchant," Jason said. "One of the three Merchant sisters. They're *all* hot." He rolled down his window and stuck his head out. "Hey, Sydney!"

She whirled around, gun pointing at him for a second, and then a smile washed over her face. "Jason Finley, is that you?"

"Yeah," he said. "These are my friends."

She lowered her gun and trotted over to Jason's Jeep.

"Sorry about that," she said, her steel-blue eyes piercing everybody in the vehicle. "Can't be too careful, especially after what happened." She paused, brow furrowed. "So sorry about your dad."

"Thanks," Jason said. "We have some others at the house. Eric brought them."

"Eric?" she asked, face lighting up. "Is he here? Really?"

"Yeah, he's behind us. He's got a girlfriend, though."

"He does?" she asked, her face disappointed.

"Hey, I don't have a girlfriend," Curt said.

Jason cracked up.

"Who's he?" Sydney asked.

"Our resident genius," Jason said. "Oh, and in the back are Dirk and Chance. From Deadwood."

"Deadwood?" she asked, eyes getting big. "There was a bloodbath there."

"Yeah, Eric helped us in one of the battles," Dirk said. "We followed him here after the town got overrun."

"Well, I'll let you go," she said. "Maybe I'll come over for a visit later, if that's okay."

"It's more than okay," Curt said. Sydney looked at him and rolled her eyes.

"He always like this?" she asked, shy smile on her face.

"Pretty much," Jason said. "How about your family?"

"Dad and Haley got caught outside of Texas when this mess started. They're staying put with my cousins in Montana for now. Amanda is here, though. I'll bring her over."

"You two are here all alone?" Curt asked.

"Somebody has to keep the family business running."

Jason laughed as Curt gave her a quizzical look.

"What?" Curt asked.

"Never mind," Jason said. "They can tell you when they visit, if they want to. I'll catch you later, Sydney. Nice to see you again."

"Likewise," she said. "See you later."

Jason tooted the horn. Kyle got the message and drove forward, down the long dirt road, then into the gate of the homestead. Jason pulled in next to him, then Eric's Bronco and the motorcycles.

Paco ran ahead of Eric and Kim as they walked towards the house. Don and his daughters rushed out, then Francis and Sherry. Eric introduced them to Jason, Kyle, Kelly, Junior, Curt, Gray, and the other bikers.

"Saw what you guys did on the news," Don said. "Nice work."

"Think we need to keep watch at the narrow part of the road for a few hours?" Francis asked.

"Might not be a bad idea," Eric said, "but we used back roads to get here, so I think we kept a pretty low profile. We weren't followed."

"We hung back pretty far every so often," Gray said. "Never saw anybody back there."

"Yeah," Kim said. "I spent some time looking out the back of the Bronco too. Never saw anybody. There weren't many cars on the road."

"What was that gunshot?" Alyssa asked. "Was that you?"

"No, that was just our neighbor," Eric said. "Actually an old girlfriend of mine."

"Really?" Kim asked.

"Yeah, from when I was about seventeen," he said. "Ancient history. She's a nice person. So were her sisters."

"Amanda is the only one here with her," Jason said. "Haley and the father got caught in Montana."

"Probably a good place to sit this mess out," Curt said. "Think I have any chance with Sydney?"

Eric laughed. "She likes he-men types, but you can't be too crude around her. Amanda is more up your alley, as I remember. She could always get as raunchy as Jason and I. She's also the oldest, so she's a little closer to your age than Sydney is."

"Wish I was younger," Dirk said. "I could stare into those blue eyes all day long."

"There are a couple women in my group who are about your age, and un-attached," Gray said. "They tend to gravitate towards bikers, though."

Dirk laughed. "Hell, I *am* a biker, but I couldn't take my bike with me when we left Deadwood."

"Well there you go, then," Gray said, grinning.

"How old *is* this Sydney, anyway?" Kim asked, her brow furrowed.

Eric laughed. "Seriously, sweetie, you have nothing to worry about."

"Just curious," she said. "I know you're mine."

"She's about thirty-five," Jason said. "That would put Amanda in her early 40s, and Haley in her late thirties."

"I'm gonna unhitch the Barracuda and point it towards that twisty stretch of road," Curt said.

"Go for it," Jason said.

"Think we ought to call home?" Junior asked.

"I'm gonna call Brenda now," Kelly said, walking away with his phone to his ear.

"Okay," Junior said. "I'll call Rachel in a few minutes."

Jason walked into the house with Eric and Kim.

"You clean the place up?" Jason asked, glancing at the hallway to the master bedroom.

"No, it was cleaned up when we got here," Jason said.

"There was police tape across the door," Kim said.

"They got rid of mom and dad's bed and pulled up the carpet," Eric said. Tears were forming around his eyes. Kim put her arm around him.

"He's had a hard time with this," Kim whispered.

"Not as hard as Jason did," Eric said. "He found them."

"That was bad," Jason said, tears running down his cheeks now. "Really bad. At least I didn't see their faces."

"So what now?" Eric asked. "We all go to Fort Stockton, or work out of this location?"

They stood in the kitchen. Jason leaned against the counter. "This will take some thought. There *are* safety problems with the Fort Stockton location."

"Yeah, you told me about it being too close to I-10."

"It's way too exposed," Jason said. "It's also far from where we're needed."

"To continue the battle?" Eric asked.

"Yeah," Jason said. "I don't know if the whole group will fit here, though. Plus, there's the hook-up problem. We'd have to do some serious work to provide power to all the rigs."

"We probably could do it," Eric said. "The infrastructure is here, from what I can tell. This place was a commercial dairy farm before dad bought it. It's got enough amps to power quite a few coaches if we can get the hardware to connect them. We'd have to share a dump station. What worries me the most is the road in. If something happens to it, we'll need four-wheel drive to get out of here."

"Yeah, that is a problem," Kim said.

"The switchbacks are doable with RV's," Eric said. "You got in here with dad's rig, right?"

"Yeah, and it's huge," Jason said. "I don't think anybody in the group has a bigger rig than that. There's a lot of flat ground in that pasture behind the house, so we'd have enough space."

"If it rains, we'll be stuck," Kim said. "The road to that back pasture doesn't have any gravel on it."

"We could fix that too, I suppose," Jason said.

"Probably," Eric said. "You won't want to be away from your family for long, I'm sure. We have to decide in a hurry."

"I'm chomping at the bit to go now," Jason said. "I'm sure Kyle is too. He's got a serious girlfriend. Real serious."

"So I've heard," Eric said. "Nice feeling."

Jason chuckled. "You two look pretty close."

Kim's face turned red. Eric pulled her close. "She's the one, brother. I can feel it."

"Good," Jason said. "I think I'd better call Carrie."

Jason walked outside just in time to see Kelly rush over to Junior and Kyle. He started talking, getting more and more agitated. Junior glanced around, made eye contact with Jason, and waved him over.

"Something wrong?" Jason asked as he approached.

"We need to go home now," Kelly said.

"Oh, shit," Jason said. "Somebody attack the park?"

Kyle shook his head no. "Brenda told Kelly that some character named Simon Orr will be there tomorrow morning, with Chris, Jasper, and Earl."

"Chris - the co-owner of Texas Mary's?" Jason asked.

"Yeah," Kelly said. "He got held up because he went to pick up his sister in Comanche. She's with them too."

"I take it this Simon Orr character is dangerous?" Jason asked.

"Yeah," Kelly said. "He was trying to recruit us into a secessionist militia right before we fled Dripping Springs. I don't want him to recruit our people. He's a spellbinder."

"I'm ready to go any time," Junior said.

"Because of Simon Orr or because of Rachel?" Kelly asked, a smile escaping his face.

"Both," Junior said.

"Okay, let's have a meeting," Jason said. "By the barn, five minutes."

"I'll let people know," Kelly said.

"Me too," Jason said.

Everybody gathered around the barn after a few minutes.

"What's up?" Gray asked.

"Problems at home," Kelly said. "I just talked to Brenda. The last part of our group will be there tomorrow. They picked up a person who is very bad news on the way. A guy named Simon Orr."

"Who is he? One of the enemy?" Dirk asked.

"Potentially, yes," Kelly said. "We met him right before we fled Dripping Springs. He was trying to recruit our people for a secessionist militia. He's an anti-government nutcase, and a dangerous one at that."

"You don't have to talk me into going home," Kyle said. "My woman is there, and I want to get to her as soon as possible."

"I hear you there," Jason said. "I want to get back in a hurry too. Was going to suggest we overnight here, but maybe we ought to take off now. Divide up the drive, go through the night."

"What about the side-trip to San Antonio?" Curt asked. "We need those M-19s."

"Not everybody has to go to Fort Stockton right this minute," Jason said.

"That's right," Eric said. "Some of us can stay here for now. Curt, I'm sure we can get you to San Antonio and back with no problem."

"I'll keep some of my guys here," Gray said.

"You can still use my truck," Dirk said. "I'll go with you, in fact."

"Me too," Chance said.

"Okay, who wants to go to Fort Stockton with us?" asked Jason. "I know you're going, Kyle."

"Damn straight," Kyle said.

"I'm going," Junior said.

"Me too," Kelly said.

"I'll go, to round up my guys," Gray said. "I think it's safer here. Is it okay if we pitch tents back behind the barn?"

"Sure," Eric said.

"What about the tanks?" Curt asked.

"Moe and Clancy were gonna help us get the tires and brake lines fixed on the flatbeds," Gray said. "Maybe they got that done. If not, we can help them when we get back."

"Can somebody drive my rig back here?" Curt asked.

"Sure, we'll find somebody to do that," Jason said.

"Okay, then let's go," Junior said.

Kelly cracked up. "You're awful anxious. Thought you weren't gonna take Rachel up on her offer."

Junior shrugged as Kelly and Jason cracked up.

"I'm missing something here, I guess," Eric said.

"Yeah," Kelly said. "Let's get going."

The group said their goodbyes. Jason got behind the wheel of his Jeep, Kyle behind the wheel of his truck, Kelly and Junior riding with him. Four of Gray's bikes followed. Eric watched them leave, feeling a hole in the pit of his stomach. Kim saw it.

"You okay, honey?" she asked.

"I just got back together with my brother, and now he's taking off again," Eric said.

"He'll be back, sweetie," Kim said.

"It's a dangerous road," Eric said, watching as the vehicles snaked their way around the first of the switchbacks.

{ 8 }

Austin Retreat

Hendrix waited for Maria to open the vault door. The bolts slid over with a clunk and it opened. She was there before him, wearing one of his oversized t-shirts with bare feet.

"How was it out there?" she asked as he walked in.

"The tanks are gone," Hendrix said. "No sign of Islamist troops, either. Something happened. Guess we ought to watch the news for a little while."

"We'll get called if it's all clear, I hope."

"We should," Hendrix said. "I'll report in after a few minutes."

"You can do it now if you want," she said as she bent over the console to close the vault door. Her t-shirt rode up, giving him a show of her lovely rear end.

Hendrix moaned. "You did that on purpose," he said, walking closer to her.

"So what if I did?" she asked, turning to him. She put her arms around his neck and kissed him tenderly. "You can report in later, can't you?"

"I suppose so," he said, in a daze from the kiss. She smirked and grabbed his hand.

"C'mon." She led him into the bedroom. They spent close to an hour together, passion rising and falling and rising again, finally drifting off to sleep. They were awakened by the phone buzzer.

"Dammit," Hendrix said. "I want the world to leave us alone."

"I know, sweetie," she said, "but you've got a job to do."

He nodded and answered the phone. "Hendrix."

"Hi Kip, it's Ramsey."

"Hi Chief," Hendrix said. "What's up?"

"We're just about ready to blow the all-clear sirens," he said. "The tanks fled. Most of them ran out of gas between here and Houston. The fighters are gone too, for the most part. We're rounding up stragglers now."

"Good," Hendrix said. "I was expecting a call. The tanks were gone from South Congress last time I was on the roof."

"You been watching the news?"

"Not for a while. Something going on?"

"Houston is under attack," Ramsey said. "About the same strength as we got hit with, but that's a bigger town. They're running into a lot of resistance. Houston was better prepared than we were."

"Glad to hear that, at least," Hendrix said. "So what now? Back to work?"

"Yep, basically," Ramsey said. "Nelson already took the city off of martial law."

"Okay, I'll get ready to head for the office," Hendrix said. "I've got some business to take care of anyway."

"Yeah, I've got all kinds of stuff to catch up on," Ramsey said. "Thanks for manning the outpost so well. Say thanks to Maria too, okay?"

"Will do," Hendrix said. "Is South Austin safe now? Maria's apartment is there."

"The enemy's gone, but the place is a mess," Ramsey said. "If this was anywhere but Austin, I'd expect looting."

"Understand," Hendrix said. "Talk to you later."

"Take care," Ramsey said. Hendrix hung up the phone and turned to Maria.

"I think I got the gist," she said. "We're getting the all clear."

"You look sad."

"This was our love nest," she said. "Geez, I can't believe I just said that."

"Well, we should be able to get to your apartment now."

"If it's still standing," she said. "What are we going to do now?"

"Head to the office and get back to work, I guess," Hendrix said.

"No, what are *we* going to do now?"

"Oh," Hendrix said, looking into her eyes. "What do you want to do?"

"I asked you first," she said, brow furrowed.

Hendrix chuckled. "Oh, I get it," he said. "Here's what I want. I want to go to your place, get your clothes and your things, and move them here."

"Are you sure?" she asked.

"That's a good start," he said.

Her eyes teared up as she searched his face. "That really is what you want. I can see it."

"I'm an old-fashioned guy," Hendrix said. "Won't live in sin for too long."

"You want to marry me," she said softly.

"Would you?" he asked.

"Yes," she whispered. "In a heartbeat. Can't you tell?"

"I can tell," he said. "I want the other part, too."

"Other part?" she asked, eyes questioning. Then her face turned red. "Oh."

"You still thinking about that?" he asked.

She nodded yes. "I'll go off birth control. Right away. The rest is up to you."

"It's a tough job, but somebody has to do it." He kissed her. It was going to be a peck, but she slipped her arms around his neck and returned it deeply. They trembled as he moved over her.

"You want me again already?" she asked. He didn't answer. He just took her, with more animal passion than before.

They laid next to each other afterwards, trying to catch their breath, covered in sweat. She looked over at him. "Wow."

"I could say the same thing," Hendrix said, moving over to kiss her forehead. "Let's go get your stuff. I want you living with me. *Really* living with me."

She nodded, and they got up to dress. "We moving down here?"

"We can live upstairs, but I suggest we bring some of our stuff down here just in case. You never know what's going to happen."

"I'm fine with that," she said. "Wonder what we're going to find out there?"

"A mess," Hendrix said. "I hope your building is still standing."

"If not I'm going to need clothes and stuff," she said.

"I kinda like you in my t-shirts." Hendrix grinned.

"Yes, I noticed," she said. "Let's go before we start up again. I washed my dress and my underwear. I'll put those on. Only you get to see me in the t-shirt."

"Good." Hendrix checked in at the console as she finished getting dressed, sending a message that they were going outside. The go-ahead came back in a few seconds, along with an invite to a meeting with Nelson and the other Texas leadership in the evening.

"I'm ready," Maria said, walking out in the outfit she wore on their date.

"Good," Hendrix said. "Got to be at a meeting tonight, so we need to hurry."

"Let's go," she said.

Awakening

Brenda came out of the trailer. It was late afternoon, the wind kicking up, dust blowing across the Fort Stockton RV Park. Her bleach-blonde hair fluttered.

"Hey," Carrie said, coming out of her motor home. "You get a call? I did."

"Yeah, just talked to Kelly," Brenda said. "I think I got him scared. They're driving through the night to get here."

"He's that worried about this Simon Orr character," Carrie said. "Jason mentioned it. I'll bet he's also real anxious to see you."

"Mommy, when is daddy getting home?" Chelsea asked. "I heard you talking to him."

"Very early in the morning, sweet pea," Carrie said.

"Will you wake me up?" she asked. "I miss him so much."

"We'll see," Carrie said.

"Okay, I'm going to go color."

"I'll be inside in a little while," Carrie said.

"You're showing more," Brenda said, looking at her belly.

"Yeah, things are moving along," Carrie said. "I should have been to another pre-natal appointment by now. Need to find a doctor around here."

"*If we stay here,*" Brenda said. "Kelly thinks we're going to your in-law's spread."

"Really?" Carrie asked. "Jason didn't say that. Hope it's true, though. I could see my own doctor if we go back there. He's got a second office in Fredericksburg."

"I wouldn't count on everything being back to normal there yet," Brenda said.

"Oh, I know," Carrie said.

The door to Kate's trailer opened and she came out.

"You look like the cat that just swallowed the canary," Carrie said.

"Shoot, she does, doesn't she?" Brenda said, eyeing her.

Kate shrugged, trying not to look excited.

"Shit, he knocked you up, didn't he?" Carrie asked. Brenda giggled.

"Quiet," Kate whispered, "and no telling anybody else, except Rachel."

"Where is she, anyway?" Kate asked.

"She was crying inside Junior's rig earlier," Brenda said. "I asked her what was the matter through the door. She said she didn't want to talk about it."

"You think she was serious about all that stuff she was saying last night?" Kate asked.

"What stuff?" Carrie asked. "That joking around we were doing about her and Junior? She wasn't serious."

"Oh, yeah, you were already inside during the last part of the conversation," Brenda said.

"She was," Kate said.

"So what'd she say?" Carrie asked.

"She said she was going to screw Junior until he got her pregnant," Brenda said.

"It was after we were talking about biology," Kate said. "After I admitted that Kyle and I were trying."

The door to the Brave opened and Rachel came out, walking towards them. Her eyes were red from crying, but her smile was punching through it.

"You okay, honey?" Brenda asked.

"Junior called. They're coming back. Driving right through."

"Yeah, we were just talking about that," Carrie said.

"Why were you crying so much?" Brenda asked. "Sorry, maybe that was too personal."

"It's okay," she said. "I can't answer the question, though. Don't understand it. I was just afraid I wouldn't see him again, I guess."

"Junior?" Carrie asked.

"Yeah." Rachel sighed. "I think my feelings about him are changing."

Carrie snickered. "Yeah, apparently I missed the best part of the conversation last night."

"Oh, they told you?" Rachel asked.

"You don't look embarrassed," Brenda said. "You were just yanking our chains, weren't you?"

Rachel looked serious. "No. Maybe *that's* why I was crying so much."

"I don't get it," Kate said.

"I do," Brenda said. "You weren't thinking about him that way until you started thinking about having his babies. Now your mind is preparing itself."

"Preparing itself for what?" Rachel asked.

Kate laughed. "Oh, shit, that *is* what's going on. It happened to me, too. With Kyle. I resisted him at first. Thought he was one of these wannabe womanizers. That didn't last long. It's like one moment he was a convenient protector and man toy to me, and then a minute later I was just on fire for him."

Brenda and Carrie looked at each other and laughed.

"You said a mouthful there," Carrie said. "You gonna tell Rachel?"

"Tell me what?" Rachel asked.

"I'm pregnant," Kate said.

"You're pregnant? Oh my God, congratulations!" she said.

"Shhhh, not so loud," Kate said. "Only us four know about it, and I want it to stay that way until I can tell Kyle."

"Sorry," Rachel whispered. "Mum's the word."

"Mommy, I'm hungry," Chelsea said from the doorway of the coach.

"I'll be there in a few minutes, sweetie," Carrie said.

"Hurry," Chelsea said.

"You sure you want one of those?" Carrie asked, looking at Kate.

"I'm more than sure," Kate said. "I've got some things to do. See you all later."

"Wait a minute," Rachel said. "You guys said my mind was preparing itself. Preparing itself for what?"

Brenda snickered. "It's preparing *you* to be Junior's woman."

"No it's not," she said.

"Oh yes it is," Kate said. "If you're having *babies* with this man, what do you think that makes *you?*"

Rachel stood quietly for a moment, thinking, then smiling. "Dammit. You're right. Shit. That *is* why I'm thinking differently about him."

"Look at that," Carrie whispered, looking at Rachel's face. "Never seen anything like that before."

"Mommy!"

"In a minute, honey," Carrie said. "How are you thinking differently about him?"

"I was going to give myself to him as a thank you. Figured I could make it work okay for myself. I *did* have a lot of affection for him. Don't feel the same way about it now."

"You're not going through with it?" Brenda asked.

Rachel smiled. "You aren't getting me. I want him all over me. I want to kiss every inch of him. My God, I want him to take me so bad. I want him to possess me."

Kate stood there trembling, watching her. "That's what happened to me. Once it starts, there's no denying it."

Suddenly there was a loud boom.

"Dammit, that was one of the tanks!" shouted Carrie. "Let's get the guns!"

"Oh no!" Kate said.

{ 10 }

Reacquired

The group was getting road-weary.

"How you holding up?" Jason asked over the phone to Kyle. "Kelly or Junior been sleeping?"

"Yeah, both of them have on and off," Kyle said. "Time to switch drivers?"

"Yeah, next stop. Ozona. That's about half-way."

"We'll get there before midnight," Kyle said. "Good thing. Allows us to use I-10."

"Notice we've seen nobody on the road?" Jason asked.

"Yeah, I noticed. Eerie as hell, even for this time of night."

"I'll talk to you in a few minutes," Jason said. He ended the call and hung up the phone, then concentrated on the road, trying to keep awake. Ozona was only a couple miles away. He felt himself drifting, the rumble strips on the road snapping him awake. *Dammit. Hold it together.* His phone rang, startling him. He answered it.

"Jason?" Carrie asked.

"Hi, Sweetie," Jason said. "Everything okay?"

"Yes and no," she said. "I'll fill you in when you get here. You'll have to get off of I-10 at University Road. There's a big mess on I-10. Take the service road instead, and turn off your lights. If you don't, you'll likely get stopped."

"What happened?" Jason asked, breaking into a cold sweat.

"Can't talk more now," she said. "Like before." The call ended.

Cellphones. Shit.

Adrenalin kicked in. Jason gripped the wheel, mind moving a mile a minute. *The homestead. Could the enemy see us there?* He got off I-10, driving into Ozona and pulling over. Kyle parked behind them and they all got out.

"We got a problem," Jason said to the others as they walked up.

"Where?" Kyle asked, fear in his eyes.

"RV Park. Carrie called me. Said to get off I-10 at University Road and run without lights on the service road."

"They're okay, though, right?" Junior asked.

"I think so," Jason said. "She wouldn't tell me anything. Sounds like the cell phones might be bad again."

"No," Kelly said. "Son of a bitch. What about the people at your folk's place?"

"I'll call the land line at the house as soon as we get moving again."

"Let's go," Junior said. "Who's driving what?"

"I'll drive Jason's Jeep," Kelly said.

"Suits me," Jason said. "Let's get out of here."

"Yeah," Kyle said. Kelly and Jason trotted back to the Jeep, Kyle and Junior back to the truck. They took off.

"This is bad," Kelly said. "I hope they don't get attacked again before we can get there."

"You and me both," Jason said as he hit the contact for the house land line. It rang over and over. "C'mon, pick up."

"It's late, and most of the folks there have had a rough day," Kelly said.

There was a click. A girl's mousy voice came on. "Hello?"

"Is this Alyssa?" Jason asked.

"No, it's Chloe," she said. "Who's this?"

"Jason. Could you find Eric for me?"

"Okay. I think he's in his motor home. Be right back."

Jason could hear the phone receiver set on the kitchen counter.

"Everybody's asleep, eh?" Kelly asked.

"Yeah," Jason said. "Chloe is going to get Eric."

"What are you gonna tell them?"

"Pull the batteries out of their cell phones, or destroy them."

"Shit, what about Curt's away team?" Kelly asked. "We can't reach them via a land line, can we?"

"No," Jason said. "I'll get Eric to call him from the land line."

"Jason?" Eric yawned. "Something go wrong?"

"I just got a call from Carrie. She thinks the cell phones have been compromised again. Better round them up. Yank batteries where you can, destroy the rest."

"Dammit," Eric said. "If they're compromised, the enemy probably knows where we are already."

"I know," Jason said. "Also, call Curt on the land line. Warn him."

"His phone might not be hackable," Eric said. "He might even be able to tell us where the enemy is."

"Oh, yeah," Jason said. "You know what to do. I'm getting off."

"Okay," Eric said. "Be careful."

"You too," Jason said. He ended the call. "Here goes another iPhone. Pull over."

"Will do. Need to yank the battery out of my Android too."

Kelly parked. Junior stopped Kyle's truck behind them. Jason set his iPhone in front of the rear tire of the Jeep and rushed over to the truck.

"Just heard from Carrie. She thinks the cell phones have been compromised again. Yank your batteries or destroy your phones."

"Shit," Kyle said.

"Everything okay in Fort Stockton?" Junior asked.

"Sounds like it, but Carrie wouldn't stay on the line. I called the land line at the homestead."

"What about Curt?" Kyle asked, brow furrowed.

"Eric's calling him from the land line, but you know Curt. He'll probably be able to tell us where they are."

"Except he can't call us because our phones will be off or gone," Junior said.

"Glad I bought an Android this time," Kyle said, pulling the back off the phone and removing the battery.

"Me too," Junior said, doing the same.

"Thanks for rubbing it in," Jason said. "At least I bought the Apple insurance this time. Let's get moving."

They got back into their vehicles, the Jeep crunching Jason's iPhone as they drove away.

"You'd better try to get some sleep," Kelly said. "I have a feeling we're in for a busy day."

"I'll try," Jason said. "Not going to be easy."

They rode silently down the deserted I-10. Jason nodded off, but woke every so often. Kelly gripped the wheel, images of Brenda filling his head, pushing the Jeep up to eighty-five. The turnoff to University Drive came faster than he expected.

"Damn, almost missed it," he muttered to himself.

"There already?" Jason asked, stretching in his seat.

"Yeah," Kelly said as he took the off-ramp. "You sleep any?"

"Some," Jason said. "Better than I expected."

"Good," Kelly said.

"Lights," Jason said.

"Oh, yeah," Kelly said. He switched off the lights. Junior did the same behind him. They raced down the service road, going too fast, buzzing past stop signs.

"It's close," Jason said. "Look up ahead. Roadblock on I-10."

"See it," Kelly said. "Army trucks broken on the road. See?"

"Yeah," Jason said. "Wonder if we blasted them with the tanks?"

"That'd be my guess," Kelly said. "Hope we didn't lose anybody."

"Me too," Jason said.

"You think the authorities will confiscate our tanks over this?"

Jason chuckled. "If they try, they ain't the authorities. Chief Ramsey knows where we are and what we have. He told me to keep the tanks, and he's very close to Governor Nelson. If there are authorities throwing their weight around, I'll call Ramsey on the Austin PD land line."

"With somebody else's phone." Kelly chuckled.

"You're gonna rub it in too, huh," Jason said, smiling at him.

"Sorry," Kelly said.

"Should be almost there," Jason said.

"Look, there's the park ahead! Think it's this visible from I-10?"

"Close," Jason said. "That's why we have to leave. Hope Clancy and Moe got those flatbeds fixed."

"Yeah, we want to keep those tanks," Kelly said.

"Here comes Warnock Road," Jason said.

Kelly nodded and turned right. "Not many lights on."

"Good," Jason said. "There's the dirt road."

"This is gonna be fun with no lights," Kelly said. "There's some serious potholes on this road."

Jason chuckled. "You're being generous. I wouldn't call this a road."

"Here goes nothing," Kelly said, turning onto it and slowing down. The Jeep bounced around too much, so he slowed down more.

"This sucks," Jason said.

"Want me to turn the lights back on?" Kelly asked.

"No," Jason said.

"Good, me neither. This vehicle can take it."

"Hope it doesn't screw up Kyle's truck. It's got a lot of extra weight on the roll bar."

"Junior's driving. I wouldn't worry about it. He's got a sixth sense for driving around in the back country. It's like he can feel the road."

"Maybe we should have let him lead the way in," Jason said.

"Yeah, should've thought about it," Kelly said. "There's the gate."

The two vehicles drove through the gate and headed straight for their spaces, Junior parking next to Kate's trailer and Kelly parking next to Jason's motor home.

"Jason!" Carrie cried, rushing over as he got out of the passenger side. She fell into his arms, kissing him deeply.

Kelly got out and saw Brenda running towards him. He threw his arms around her, letting out a loud sigh, then kissing her hard.

Junior and Kyle got out of the truck. Kate rushed out of the trailer and leapt into Kyle's arms. They embraced and kissed, but Kate broke it quickly and whispered something in his ear. He pulled back and looked at her face. "Really?" he whispered. She nodded yes and they kissed again, longer this time.

Junior saw Rachel running towards him, but then she stopped, staring at his face, tears running down her cheeks. She approached him slowly, sobbing now as she went into his arms.

"Thank God," she whispered as she rested her head on his shoulder, Junior caressing her hair.

"We need to talk," Carrie said. "We can finish this afterwards."

"Where? Your rig?" Kyle asked.

"No, we'll wake up Chelsea," Carrie said. "Curt's rig. It's big enough. Let's use his garage."

They followed her to the rear of Curt's toy hauler. Jason and Kyle undid the latches and lowered the ramp. They went inside and gathered towards the front end. Kyle switched on a small light on the wall.

"So what happened?" Kyle asked.

"It was late afternoon," Brenda said. "We were gathered outside talking when we heard one of the tank cannons go off."

"Scared the crap out of us," Carrie said. "We got our guns out right away."

"You didn't have to fight, did you?" Junior asked.

"No," Kate said. "The tank blew up one of the trucks. Apparently it hit something explosive inside, because the whole thing exploded into flames. Killed everybody inside."

"How many trucks were there?" Kelly asked.

"Three," Rachel said. "They hit the second one, but about half the men in the back survived. There was a small firefight by the flatbeds, but we won."

"Clancy is crazy," Brenda said. "He got on his Harley and chased the last truck, tossing a grenade into the back as the Islamists tried to shoot him. His handlebars have a nice nick in them from a bullet, but he didn't get hit. Then he rode up to the cab and tossed another grenade. Killed all three men sitting up there."

"Damn," Junior said. "Good for him."

"The tanks hit them from here?" Jason asked.

"No, they took one tank down to I-10, where they were working on the flatbeds," Brenda said. "We were lucky. We would've had to fight them here if the tank wouldn't have been down there."

"Anybody get killed?" Kyle asked.

"No, but Moe got wounded in the upper arm," Rachel said.

"Oh no," Jason said.

"Don't worry, he'll be okay," Carrie said. "A doctor from Fort Stockton stitched him up. Old friend of Moe's."

"Thank God," Jason said.

"So what now?" Kyle asked.

"The flatbeds are almost finished," Carrie said. "We had authorities here making noise like they were going to confiscate everything and arrest all of us, but then somebody from Governor Nelson's office called and told them to leave us alone, and concentrate on road clearance."

"Somebody call him?" Jason asked.

"No," Carrie said. "The officers called it into Austin. Ramsey let Nelson know about it."

"They're taking their sweet time clearing the road, if this happened at dusk," Kyle said.

"They had investigators down there looking at everything," Carrie said. "They're the ones who warned us about the phones."

"Really?" Jason asked. "What'd they say?"

"They said that Austin PD's new phones already got infected, and they haven't been able to figure out why."

"We need Curt on it," Kyle said.

"Where is he?" Kate asked.

"He took a few guys and went to San Antonio to pick up the rest of his M-19 grenade launchers," Kyle said.

"Hope he knows about this," Brenda said.

"His phone has some special capability, remember?" Kelly said. "He's probably tracking them already."

"How would he know if you guys couldn't call him?" Carrie asked.

"I called the land line at the homestead before I trashed my phone and warned Eric. He said he'd call Curt from the land line."

"This sucks," Junior said. "Maybe we need to get walkie-talkies."

"Not a bad idea to communicate between ourselves," Jason said. "We have a set. Not sure if we can buy a bunch more in this two-bit town, though."

"You know we can't stay here, right?" Carrie asked.

"Yeah, we know," Jason said. "Not sure the homestead is safe anymore, though, now that the cell phones have been infected again."

"Like I said, we need Curt on it," Kyle said. "He should be getting back there pretty soon. Not that far to his stash."

"We need to leave as soon as those flatbeds are ready," Brenda said. "Clancy thought he'd have them done by about noon tomorrow. We should get some sleep. Tomorrow's going to be a long day."

"Did Simon Orr show up yet?" Kelly asked.

"No, and now we can't raise Chris, Earl, or Jasper," Brenda said. "I'm worried sick."

"Mommy, is daddy home?" Chelsea asked, standing in the doorway of the motor home.

Carrie chuckled. "Knew she'd figure it out."

"I'll go see her," Jason said.

"I'm going too," Carrie said. "We need to sleep."

"Okay," Jason said, taking her hand and walking towards their rig.

"Let's all hit the sack," Brenda said. "Big day tomorrow."

Fear and Bliss

Rachel took Junior's hand and led him quickly to the Brave. "I thought they'd never get done talking."

"You okay?" he asked, trying to keep up.

She turned to face him when they got to the door. "We need to talk. You able to do that tonight, or are you too tired?"

Junior watched as she pulled the door open and climbed the steps, his heartbeat quickening. He followed her up and sat next to her on the couch.

"Well?" she asked.

Junior looked into her eyes, in the light of the led shining from above them. "Your eyes are red. Have you been crying?"

She nodded yes, looking down.

"We don't have to do anything," Junior said. "I told you that before we left, remember?"

"Stop," she said, looking at him with an expression he hadn't seen on her face before. "Let me finish. Don't stop me, okay?" She moved towards him and kissed him lightly on the lips.

"Okay, sorry," he said, eyes focused on her, waiting for her to deliver the news he expected but dreaded. A smile crept onto her face.

"You have the wrong idea about this." She moved in and kissed him again, with more passion this time. Then she hugged him tight. "You're trembling."

He started to say something, but she put her finger on his lips. He nodded, moving his eyes from hers, looking down at his lap, hunkering down.

"I *have* been crying," she said. "I didn't stop until you called me from the road."

"Why?"

"Because I can't imagine life without you," she said. He looked at her, not knowing what to say.

"We can..."

"Hush," she said. "I was afraid you were going to get yourself killed. Don't think I could've taken that."

"I worried about you the whole time I was gone too," Junior told her.

"Hush up," she said.

"Sorry," he said, looking down again. She put her hand below his bearded chin and tilted his head back up at her face. "You think I'm about to give you a *Dear John* talk. That's not what this is about."

"You don't have..."

"Stop," she said softly, almost in a whisper.

He nodded, and she smiled at him.

"The way I feel about you has changed since you've been gone," Rachel said. "I was gonna give myself to you when you got back, out of respect and a *kind of* love. I wasn't planning on that before I said it. It just popped into my head as you were leaving, and I blurted it out before I had a chance to think about it."

"That's what I thought," Junior said. "That's why I told you I wouldn't."

"You're interrupting me again," she said, half a grin on her face. "This is like pulling teeth."

"Sorry," he said. "Go ahead."

I began to have different feelings about you when you were gone," she said. "I didn't understand them until talking to the girls. They saw it all over my face; they realized it before I did."

"Realized what?"

"Realized that I was falling for you," she said. "Not love like a brother or an uncle, either."

A tear rolled down Junior's check. Rachel reached up and wiped it off with her fingers.

"I don't know what to say," he said.

"Your eyes are telling me," she said, looking into them. She snaked her arms around his neck and pulled him in for a deep kiss, Junior's arms going around her quickly. They kissed for more than a minute, then broke it and stared at each other.

"So what do you want?" Junior asked.

"In a minute," she said. "How do you feel about me?"

"I'm in love with you," he said. "Have been since we rode together and talked in the motor home. I never imagined that I'd have any chance with you."

"That's what I thought," she said. "Even before I realized how I felt. That's part of the reason I wanted to give myself to you. I knew you wanted it more than anything. I just couldn't lose you."

"Okay, so I put my cards on the table," Junior said. "What do you want?"

She took a deep breath, looking at him nervously. "I want to be your woman. I want to live with you that way. I want you to take me whenever you want." She paused.

"What else? Is there a *but* coming?"

She smiled, looking embarrassed, face red. She got closer, like she was ready to kiss him again, and then whispered. "I want to have your babies. I want to start working on that now. This minute."

They kissed again, their passion rising quickly. Junior's heart was pounding in his chest as his hands roamed over her back. Rachel broke the kiss and stood up, unbuttoning her blouse. Junior watched in awe, trembling with excitement. She pulled off her shirt and then reached behind her back to undo her bra, taking it off, revealing herself to him.

"Oh, God," Junior said, standing next to her, his hands on her. "You're so beautiful."

"C'mon." She took his hand and dragged him into the bedroom, then undressed him frantically. She pushed him back on the bed, then removed her shorts and climbed on top of him, reveling in the feeling of their bare skin touching.

"Is this really happening?" Junior asked as he looked at her face. She stopped him with another kiss, then rose upright and positioned herself.

"I can't wait anymore," she said as she lowered herself onto him. They both moaned, moving against each other slowly, then faster, crying out with each other. It was over in a couple minutes. She collapsed on top of him, caressing his face as he sought her mouth to kiss her again.

"That was unbelievable," Junior said between breaths.

"We aren't done yet," she said, rolling off of him and pulling him over her. They were back into passion quickly, longer and more urgently than before.

They finally fell asleep, spent and exhausted.

The sun woke Junior with a start. He was on his side, spooned against Rachel, her soft warmth stirring him. The night came rushing back at him. She woke and turned towards him.

"Is it time to get up already?" she asked.

"No, it's early," Junior said. "You sleep okay?"

"Best I have in weeks," she said, her hands roaming over his body. "I want you again. Can we?"

Junior moved over her, taking her forcefully, making her lose control time and again. They fell back to sleep afterwards, not waking up until Kelly banged on the door.

"Hey, Junior, you up yet?"

Rachel giggled. "Wonder if they heard us? That last time was pretty intense."

Junior smiled and kissed her forehead.

"We'll be up in a few minutes," he shouted.

{ 12 }

Hardware Run

It was pitch black on the small dirt road. Dirk was driving the truck, Curt was next to him, Chance against the passenger side door.

"How much further?" Dirk asked.

"Another couple miles," Curt said. His phone rang. He looked at the number before he put the phone to his ear. "This is the land line at the Finley place."

"Curt?" Eric asked.

"Yeah, Eric, what's up?"

"Just got a call from Jason. The cell phones might be hacked again. The Austin PD cell phones got infected again, and Chief Ramsey hasn't figured out how that happened yet."

Curt smiled. "I'm on it. They can't hack this phone. I made a couple of modifications."

"Can you still use it to find the enemy?"

"Yeah," Curt said. "I'll check for cretins around the homestead and around the Fort Stockton RV Park."

"There was an attempted hit at the RV Park already," Eric said.

"Oh, shit," Curt said.

"Don't worry, our folks won," Eric said. "They had one of the tanks over by the flatbeds, protecting the team that was working on them."

"Good," Curt said. "I'll do some checking and get back to you. Don't disable your cellphones yet. We don't want them to know we're onto them."

"Fair enough, thanks," Eric said. Curt ended the call.

"Something wrong?" Chance asked.

"The cell phones might be hacked again," Curt said. "I'll check it out."

"Uh oh," Dirk said. "They hurt any of our people?"

"Not yet," Curt said, looking at his phone as he moved his finger around on its screen. "They're right. Numerous attempts to get onto this phone. My modifications blocked them."

"Should we yank our batteries?" Chance asked.

"Not yet," Curt said. "Let me see if they're following us. If they are, we'll surprise them."

He worked silently for a few minutes, then looked out the windshield. "Take that road to the left. My cabin is about a mile down. You can't miss it. Only place around."

"Got it," Dirk said. Curt went back to work on his phone.

Dirk made the turn as Chance looked out the window nervously.

"We don't have much in the way of firepower," Chance said.

"Wanna bet?" Curt said, not looking up from his phone. "Wait till you see what I've got at the cabin."

Dirk snickered. "Hell, I almost hope they *are* following us."

"They are," Curt said. "We've got time. They're about four miles behind us."

"What about the homestead?" Dirk asked.

"Checking now," he said.

"Is that the cabin up ahead?" Chance asked.

Curt looked up. "Yeah, that's it. Pull around back, out of sight of the road."

Dirk made the turn, pulling up on the dirt behind the house. The garage door was in back. Curt pulled his keys out of his pocket and handed them to Dirk. "The round key opens the padlock on the garage door. Go ahead and open it while I finish here."

Dirk took the keys and got out. Chance joined him in front of the garage door. They got it open.

"Holy crap," Chance said as he looked at the hardware. There was a row of six M-19 Grenade launchers, several RPGs and AR-15s, and three mortars. Lots of ammo for all of the devices sat in crates against the wall.

"The mother lode," Dirk said. "Let's start putting this stuff in the truck."

"Keep the RPGs and AR-15s out," Curt said. "We'll need them in about five minutes."

"Roger that," Dirk said.

Curt hit Eric's contact and put the phone to his ear.

"Curt, what's up?" Eric asked.

"You're gonna have company in about half an hour. Better be ready. Keep your phones on. You'll get the drop on them. Use my Barracuda."

"Will do," Eric said. "Thanks."

Curt ended the call and got out to help Dirk and Chance.

"The homestead in danger?" Chance asked.

"Yeah, but they'll handle it," Curt said. "Eric's gonna use the Barracuda, and they've got surprise on their side."

"How about Fort Stockton?" Dirk asked.

"Ran out of time. I'll check after we've nailed these creeps. Let's take the RPGs in front of the house."

The men gathered up the launchers, a crate of rockets, and the AR-15s. They rushed around to the front of the house.

"There's bushes up there on either side of the road," Curt said. "Let's set up behind them."

"Yeah," Dirk said. They rushed into position.

"You guys know how to fire the RPGs, right?" Curt asked.

Dirk gave a thumbs up. "I'll help Chance," he said in a loud whisper.

They loaded rockets, then got prone behind the cover and watched.

"They just hit the last dirt road," Curt said. "Get ready."

They watched in silence for a few minutes. Then the rumble was coming towards them. Pickup trucks with their lights turned off.

"That's a hit squad," Curt said in a loud whisper. "We'll take them easy. Let them get closer. One rocket per truck if we can. I see three."

"Okay," Dirk said.

Curt took aim at the first truck, firing the RPG when it was forty yards out. The rocket flew out of the launcher, hitting the front of the truck, blowing it sky high, the busted hulk coming down fully engulfed in flames.

"The second one is trying to turn around," Chance said.

"Got him," Dirk shouted. He fired, the rocket hitting the second truck broadside. It exploded and rolled.

"The last truck got turned around!" Curt said.

Chance stood up and took aim, firing, hitting the truck in the back of the cab.

"Bullseye!" Dirk shouted. "Any more, Curt?"

Curt was already looking at his phone. "I don't see any. We'd better get out of here in a hurry, though. Those fires are gonna draw the authorities, and they'll try to take our hardware."

"Yeah," Chance said. They rushed to the burning hulks. "Nobody alive that I can see."

"Hope nobody bailed out of the truck beds while the last two were trying to turn around."

"There weren't men in the beds," Curt said. "I got a good look before I fired at the first one."

"We can drive past this mess," Dirk said. "See, right through there."

"Yeah," Curt said. "Let's finish loading the truck and get the hell out of here."

The men sprinted to the garage and finished loading. Curt unlocked the door into the house and went inside, coming out with a crate.

"What's that?" Chance asked.

"Some moonshine I cooked up last time I stayed here," Curt said. "Rather not have it found."

"Well, we could always make use of that," Dirk said. Chance snickered.

"Maybe when things die down," Curt said. "This stuff will peel paint." He locked the door from the garage to the house, and then pulled the garage door shut and locked it. "Let's go."

The three men jumped into the cab and drove off, Curt watching his phone again.

"Still nobody?" Chance asked.

"Nobody with a cell phone," Curt said. "Maybe it's time to shut yours down."

Dirk fished his out of his pants pocket and gave it to Chance. "Yank the battery, okay?"

Chance nodded and did that, then did the same with his phone. "What about yours, Curt?"

"They can't hack mine," he said. "And I need it to watch for them."

"How about the homestead?" Dirk asked.

"Checking now," Curt said. "The enemy turned around. They're fleeing the scene. I'll bet the folks who tried to attack us warned them that they were visible."

"You're probably right," Chance said. "How about Fort Stockton?"

"Checking that area now," he said.

Dirk made the turn off of the first dirt road and sped up, heading for the highway.

"Nobody showing up around Fort Stockton," he said. "They might be getting wise, though. They might be disabling their phones. Knew it would happen eventually."

"Yeah, that thought crossed my mind," Dirk said. "You see any of them anywhere?"

"Yeah, San Antonio and Houston," Curt said, "but we already knew about that."

"Good, there's the highway," Dirk said. He turned onto it and floored the truck, getting up to about eighty.

"I wouldn't go too fast," Chance said. "Bad time to get pulled over."

"Oh, yeah," Dirk said, slowing down. "Sorry, I'm still buzzing from the battle."

"Dammit," Curt said, looking out the passenger side window. "See that truck behind the bushes on the right side."

"Yeah," Dirk said. "It just pulled out onto the highway."

Chance pulled the AR-15 off the floor and handed it to Curt. "The rear window opens."

"Good," Curt said. "Watch for more. I'll take this cretin out before he gets too close."

"You sure it ain't just some hunters?" Dirk asked. Chance was looking through the back window.

"I'm sure," Chance said. "Texans don't dress like that."

"Yeah, those are frigging Islamists all right," Curt said, turning sideways while Chance slid one side of the rear window open. Curt shoved the other side over and aimed the rifle, firing several times, hitting all three men in the cab. The truck careened into a ditch.

"Got them," Chance said.

"Good," Dirk said. "Keep your eyes open."

They blasted down the highway for several more miles before they started to relax.

13

Conference Room

Maria walked into Kip Hendrix's office.

"Where's the meeting?" she asked.

Hendrix looked up from the papers on his desk. "In the big meeting room upstairs."

"Surprised they aren't holding it at the Governor's Mansion."

"Must be too many people coming," Hendrix said. "This one is going to be interesting. I chatted with Governor Nelson a couple hours ago. He sounded nervous."

"Maybe it's about San Antonio," she said.

"Doubt it," Hendrix said. "The police and citizens already turned the tide of that battle."

"Really? Still sounded pretty bad the last time I checked the internet."

Hendrix smiled. "We don't want to say anything that can be used against us by the enemy."

"Well, it's good news, at least," Maria said.

"Yeah, but something has got Nelson really worried. He tried to hide it, but I know him too well." He looked at the clock on the wall. "I'd better get my coat on and go down there."

"Okay," she said. "I'll be here waiting."

Hendrix put his coat on and walked to her, bending down to kiss her. "See you in a little while."

She smiled, straightening his tie for him before he left.

The big meeting room was packed. Rows of chairs sat around the edges of the room. Hendrix saw Holly and Chief Ramsey sitting at the huge conference table in the middle. They motioned him over.

"Hey, guys," Hendrix said as he sat down between them. "How's it going?"

"I'm nervous," Ramsey said. "The Governor looked worried when I was with him a little while ago."

"I picked up the same thing when I talked to him earlier," Hendrix said. "Anybody find Jerry Sutton yet?"

"Nope," Ramsey said. "Sorry. I don't have a good feeling."

"Me neither," Hendrix said. "Thanks for looking."

"Of course," Ramsey said. "Look, Generals. I think that's Walker and Hogan."

"Wow," Holly said. "Gallagher and Landry too. Something's up."

"Well, it's not San Antonio," Ramsey said. "We're just mopping up now."

"How'd we win so easily?" Hendrix asked.

"There were a number of factors in our favor," Ramsey said. "First of all, the tanks were about out of gas by the time they got there. Those folks that hit their supply depot did a lot more damage to them than anybody thought. All of their mobile refueling equipment was there, along with all of their fuel."

"A couple of your officers were involved, weren't they?" Holly asked.

"Yeah," Ramsey said. "The two who were at that Superstore attack when this mess started."

"I'm sorry about how we acted after that," Hendrix said.

"Ancient history," Ramsey said. "You've got my respect now. You too, Holly."

"The feeling is mutual," Hendrix said.

"Same here," Holly said. "You going to bring your two men back in?"

"Walker and Hogan wanted to use them as the core for a citizen force," Ramsey said. "Along with the other folks who were involved."

"Who else was there?"

Ramsey chuckled. "Remember those rednecks who helped put down the initial attack in Austin?"

"You're joking," Hendrix said. "Good for them."

Ramsey chuckled. "Some of those guys have rap sheets a mile long, but I'm glad to have them on our side now."

"There's the boss," Holly said, nodding towards the door. Governor Nelson walked in with his secretary Brian and a few members of the Texas Legislature. A hush fell over the room.

"Thank you all for coming," Nelson said. He sat at the head of the table and glanced at the thin black microphones hanging down from the ceiling. "Those on?"

"Yep," Brian said. "Just speak normally. They should pick up fine."

"Thanks," he said. "Okay, I think everybody knows everybody except for General Hogan and General Walker."

There were murmurs in the room, but they settled quickly.

Nelson nodded to Brian, who sat at a console and turned on the projector.

"Take a look at the gentleman on the screen there," Nelson said. A man in Islamist garb was standing with several other men, all of them holding AK-47s.

"Who's that?" Hendrix asked.

"General Walker?" Nelson asked.

General Walker nodded to Nelson, and then looked at the others sitting around the table. "He goes by Saladin. His real name is too hard to pronounce. He was seen in the United States last week, with some very interesting company."

The picture changed, to a grainy long shot of three men, standing on the tarmac of an airport next to Air Force One. Several people gasped, and the murmuring was back.

"Holy shit," Ramsey said. "I knew it."

"I'm sure you folks recognize the two men talking with Saladin," General Walker said.

"Governor Sable of California and the President of the United States," Holly said. "Dammit. What does this mean?"

"It means collusion," General Walker said. "We believe that Saladin has command of all the Islamist Forces in the western half of the country."

"Where is he now?" Hendrix asked.

"We aren't sure," General Walker said. "Probably California, but it could be Arizona, New Mexico, or Utah. Maybe even Colorado. He's hard to track."

Ramsey chuckled. "In other words, you don't have a clue from minute to minute."

General Walker smiled. "Yeah, afraid so. We *do* know that he has an uncanny ability to direct his forces from wherever he is. We don't know how he's doing it."

"What about the RFID idea?" General Hogan asked.

"RFID?" Holly asked.

"Just a theory," General Walker said. "He might have implanted RFID chips into all of his men, which would give him a very good view of where his fighters are at any given time."

"I think it's more than a theory," General Hogan said. "One of his fighters had a device implanted. The coroner found it."

"That could have been from a stint in a prison someplace," General Walker said, "but don't worry, we're looking into it. If we find more like that, we'll know."

"Don't you have more than one body?" Hendrix asked.

"That's another thing that points to the RFID theory," General Hogan said. "These folks are very careful about removing bodies from the battlefield, unless they're burned to a crisp or blow into mush. They seem to know exactly where the bodies are."

"What does this creep have to do with Texas?" Hendrix asked. "Is he operating here?"

"No, we don't think he's been in Texas since you guys became a Republic," General Walker said.

"Okay, I'll take it from here," Nelson said. "Here's the bottom line. We're going to lose the support of what's left of the US Armed Forces in Texas, including the counsel of Generals Walker and Hogan. They have to put a full court press on finding Saladin and stopping his command and control structure."

"So what does that leave us with?" Ramsey asked. "The last estimate on Islamic fighters inside Texas that I saw showed nearly half a million men."

"We'll retain the Texas National Guard, but we'll have to recruit citizens. General Walker was working on that. He's handing that job off to Gallagher and Landry."

Ramsey chuckled. "So now I get the importance of the Austin cops and the rednecks," he whispered to Holly and Hendrix.

"No side meetings," Nelson said. "What, Ramsey?"

"Sorry, sir," Ramsey said. "We were talking before the meeting started about how we'll have to rely on citizen teams like the ones who took out that supply dump a few days ago."

"You hit the nail right on the head," General Walker said. "It's exactly what we need. That attack on the supply depot was brilliant. Know where those folks are right now?"

"Some of them are in Fort Stockton," Ramsey said. "I've been in contact with them almost daily."

"Did you know they were going to blow the supply depot?" General Hogan asked.

Ramsey snickered. "No sir, they cooked that up all on their own."

"Good," Nelson said. "We need to get a meeting set up with the leadership of that group and Major General Gallagher."

"Love it," Gallagher said. "I studied what those folks have been doing. Wow. Especially that guy named Curt. He's obviously a genius."

Ramsey laughed. "He used to work for me. You know he had to leave his last police job for punching out a superior, right?"

"I looked into that," Gallagher said. "I don't blame him. He was right."

"Do we know what this Saladin character is planning on doing?" Hendrix asked.

General Walker shot him a worried glance. "We think the Administration and the leadership of California are using him to justify martial law in that state, which they have no plans of rescinding. Ever."

"It's their pilot area," General Hogan said. "If they can pull it off, they'll do the same thing on the rest of the west coast, then work the east coast. Eventually they'll push towards the center of the country from both sides."

"You really think this war is about taking the country totalitarian?" Hendrix asked. "Sounds improbable to me."

"I believe that's part of it," General Walker said. He paused for a moment, looking around the room. "Anybody quotes me on this, I'll deny it."

"Everything stays in this room," Nelson said, his eyes sweeping around. "Understand?"

There was nodding of heads and murmurs of yes.

"Okay," General Walker said. "I believe that the President and others, including the Governor of California, think they can use this guy to make a tipping point in our society. I think they've made some kind of deal on this, where Saladin and his forces disappear after the desired result is obtained."

"There's a *but* coming," Ramsey said.

"Yeah, a big one," General Walker said. "Saladin's forces are huge, and he has more in the pipeline, coming from several directions. The President won't be able to contain these folks. They'll attempt to take over. If we didn't have an armed citizenry, they'd probably succeed, and North America would turn into a giant Afghanistan."

"You really think a bunch of un-trained civilians are gonna be able to make the difference here?" Hendrix asked.

"In a word, yes," General Hogan said. "You remember that old saying about a gun behind every blade of grass? Well, with over 350 million guns in private hands, that's essentially what we have. We need to augment them with more modern equipment and training. In Texas, that's going to be Gallagher's job after I leave."

"And you will pursue this outside of Texas now, I take it?" Ramsey asked.

"Exactly," General Walker said. "We can't do anything about California right now, but we can shore up Arizona, Colorado, and Utah. That's where we'll concentrate. There's several good groups to work with in those areas. I've already started talking to them."

"What's to prevent somebody else from using the citizens to take over the country?" Holly asked. "What's to prevent them from leaping over what remains of the government, and taking charge?"

"Hell, the citizens are already in charge here, remember?" Nelson said. "We all serve at their pleasure, not the other way around."

"But that might lead to a tyranny of the majority," Hendrix said. "All kinds of bad stuff might happen. Revival of Jim Crow, for instance."

"I think we need to give the US population a little more credit than that," Ramsey said.

"I agree," General Walker said, "but we're in uncharted territory here, to be sure."

"Let's assume for a moment that Texas is successful in taking down the invaders inside our borders," Hendrix said. "What then? If the rest of the country falls, won't the enemy come after us?"

"Texas only needs to worry about its own state and New Mexico," General Walker said.

"New Mexico?" Holly asked.

"Yeah," General Hogan said. "The state government of New Mexico is rotten to the core, and they're letting enemy fighters flood in across their southern border. Some of them are coming here. Some of them are going into Arizona, Utah, and Colorado."

"We plan to chase them back into New Mexico and kill them off," Gallagher said.

"That's why the Feds are asking me about our plans for New Mexico," Hendrix said.

"Let's not talk about that in this meeting," Nelson said.

"Okay, sorry," Hendrix said.

"No problem," Nelson said as he stood up. "That's about it for now. I'll be meeting with groups of you over the next couple of days to make assignments. The entire Texas Government will be on this. Think World War II – everybody will be mobilized in one way or another to support the war effort. That's what it's gonna take if we are to survive."

"Sounds like we have our work cut out for us," Ramsey said.

People started getting out of their seats and heading for the door.

"Ramsey and Hendrix, stick around, okay?" Nelson said.

"Sure, boss," Ramsey said. Hendrix nodded.

"I'll see you guys later," Holly said. He left the room. Ramsey and Hendrix watched as the room emptied out.

Nelson looked at his secretary. "Brian, go outside the door and keep people out for a few minutes, please."

"Yes sir," he said. He left the room.

Nelson walked over and sat down next to Ramsey and Hendrix.

"Think that went over okay?" Nelson asked.

"I think you scared the crap out of everybody," Hendrix said, "but in a good way."

"It's bad that we're losing Walker and Hogan," Ramsey said.

"They'll still be working with us on the New Mexico effort," Nelson said, "but you're right, and it worries me. Those guys were valuable in ways I haven't been able to tell you."

"The folks on my side of the fence in the legislature aren't going to buy the alliance of Governor Sable, the President, and Saladin," Hendrix said. "Those grainy photos probably won't do the trick."

"I know," Nelson said. "We'll just have to do the best we can. I still want an opposition party, as long as they stay within the law."

"Agreed," Ramsey said.

"Yeah," Hendrix said. "That isn't why you asked us to stick around, though, is it?"

"No," Nelson said. "Are the Feds still quizzing you on New Mexico, Kip?"

"Every time I talk to them," he said, "but they haven't wanted to talk for a couple days."

"They will again," Nelson said. "I want you to let them *force* some info out of you."

"*Force?*"

"Yeah, Kip, make it sound like you really don't want to admit it," Nelson said. "You know how."

"What do you want me to tell them?"

Nelson chuckled. "Tell them that I plan to annex New Mexico as part of the Texas Republic. Hint that there are other states I'm interested in, and that I'm becoming power-hungry."

Ramsey laughed. "I think I know where this is going."

Hendrix grinned. "You want to double check the story that Walker and Hogan are telling us."

"That's part of it," Nelson said, "but I don't really doubt those two. I think they're both patriots who are being straight with us."

"So what's the other reason?" Ramsey asked.

"I want Saladin to flood the Texas/New Mexico border with enemy troops," Nelson said. "It's going to be a kill zone. I figure it will take us several weeks to put down the invasion here in Texas. Then we can bring our forces to bear and wipe them out."

"What happens after that?" Hendrix asked.

"We rebuild our state, and start planning our re-entry into the union. Then we join the other states and finish this nonsense once and for all. Right now the enemy thinks we'll leave them alone outside of Texas. We're going to make that a fatal error."

"We'll have to weed out a lot of traitors from the Federal Government," Ramsey said.

"Yes," Nelson said. "That's going to be the hardest part. It's not easy to tell friend from foe."

"Okay, Governor, I'll plant the seeds for you," Hendrix said. "Glad to do it."

"Thanks, Kip," Nelson said, reaching to shake his hand. "Ramsey, walk back to the Governor's mansion with me. I want to talk to you about the team that blew up the supply depot, ahead of the meeting with Gallagher tomorrow morning."

"Sure thing, boss," Ramsey said. "See you later, Kip."

"See you guys," Hendrix said. He left the room, feeling like a great weight had been lifted off his shoulders.

14

Park Models

Richardson was getting tired, after another long day on the road.

"There's 771," Lita said, pointing ahead.

"Good, won't be long now," Richardson said.

"The kids are asleep back there," Lita said. "Think we'll be okay?"

Richardson turned onto 771, slowing down from highway speed. "This is a dangerous business, but I've got a good crew. Don't worry."

"How can I not worry?" she whispered. "This is war. People get killed all the time."

"I know," Richardson said. "If you dwell on that too much, you start running scared. Easiest way to get killed."

She reached out and touched his thigh, looking at him with glassy eyes. "I meant what I said back there. We're need to find a courthouse when we're settled."

"Good, I was hoping you'd stay interested in that idea," he whispered.

"You want me that bad?"

"You're kidding, right? I would've married you a year ago if you'd have let me."

"I know," she said. "Wish I would've been ready."

"You sure you're ready now, or is it just the times?"

"The times helped, but that's not all of it," she said. "My view of what's important in life has changed a lot in the last couple of weeks."

"War has a way of doing that to you," Richardson said. "Pretty place."

"It is," she said. "I've been here before with my parents."

"We almost there boss?" Juan Carlos asked as he stretched.

"Yeah, almost," Richardson said. "We're on the main road in right now."

"Good," he said. "I got to pee."

"TMI," Lita said.

Madison punched him in the arm. "Really?"

"I didn't think you were awake," Juan Carlos said.

"I've been dozing," she said. "Hannah's still out. So's Brendan."

"They didn't sleep much last night," Juan Carlos whispered.

"I heard that," Hannah said.

Madison giggled. "Is your man awake yet?"

"Stop it," Hannah said.

"Yeah, he's awake," Brendan said.

"Oh, please," Hannah said.

Madison giggled.

"Looks like 771 turns into 1155 after that bend coming up," Lita said.

"See it," Richardson said.

"DPS vehicles," Brendan said. "See them in the parking lot at the end of the street?"

"Yeah," Richardson said. He pulled up to the gate. A DPS officer stepped forward.

"You Lieutenant Richardson?" he asked.

"Yes sir," Richardson said.

"Good, Captain Jefferson has been waiting for you," he said. "Park over there, by the big building. You'll be directed from there."

"Thanks," Richardson said. He drove forward and parked.

"Can we go in too?" Lita asked.

"Yeah, but they might not let you into the briefing we'll probably get."

"No problem," Lita said. "Let's go."

They all headed to the door of the big building.

"This looks like a fancy restaurant," Madison said.

"It used to be, I suspect," Richardson said. He held open the door for everybody, then followed them inside. There was a desk in the hallway, manned by another DPS Officer.

"You Lieutenant Richardson?" the officer asked.

"Yeah," Richardson said.

"Good," he said. "Go down to the third door on the right."

"Can our women go with us?" Brendan asked, shooting a playful glance at Hannah.

"Yes," the officer said. "You'll get further instructions from Captain Jefferson."

Hannah looked at Brendon as he snickered, shaking her head.

They walked to the door and went inside. It was a large room with two rows of desks. Captain Jefferson was near the back of the room, sitting at a desk in front of the windows. He saw Richardson and motioned him over.

"Good, you made it," Jefferson said, smiling as he took Richardson's hand and shook it.

"Good to be here Captain Jefferson," Richardson said. "You remember Juan Carlos and Brendan, I'm sure."

"Yes, of course," he said, "and Lita. Who are these other lovely ladies?"

"Madison and Hannah," Richardson said.

"Nice to meet you two," Jefferson said. "I won't keep you long today. There's a major briefing tomorrow afternoon, with Gallagher and Landry."

"What happened to Commissioner Wallis?" Richardson asked.

"He's been concentrating on the problem in Dallas," Jefferson said.

"Oh," Brendan said. "They're still worried about what happened on Falcon Lake, then?"

"Afraid so," Jefferson said.

"Are those anti-aircraft batteries out there?" Juan Carlos asked, looking out the window.

"Yeah, and we've got twelve Apaches stationed nearby, too," Jefferson said. "They won't take out this base."

"Where are we gonna bunk?" Richardson asked.

"There's a big trailer park off 771," Jefferson said. "We've brought in some FEMA Park Model trailers. Not the most luxurious in the world, but better than military barracks."

"How about our women?" Richardson asked.

"They can stay there with you if that's what you want," Jefferson said. "It's far enough away from the coast that it should be safe, and you'll be hidden among current residents there."

"Where's the new boats?" Juan Carlos asked.

"They're in a covered dock complex, on the northeast side of this complex," he said. "It's hardened against everything but a large bomb."

"You hope," Richardson said.

Jefferson chuckled. "Yeah, we hope. If we had incoming, I'd rather be there than in this old building here."

"Are the boats ready?" Brendan asked.

"Almost," he said. "They're a new design. There's still some testing going on."

"New design?" Juan Carlos asked. "They still have the M-19s mounted, right?"

"Yeah," he said, "with a night-vision capable sighting system."

"Awesome, dude," Juan Carlos said.

Richardson shot him a glance. "Dude?"

Jefferson chuckled. "It's okay. I love his enthusiasm."

"So does Madison," Hannah whispered. Madison kicked her in the shin. Lita snickered.

"Well, I've rambled on enough," Jefferson said. "I'm sure you want to get settled. Officer Mahoney will take you to your new quarters. The meeting will be at 1400 hours tomorrow. We'll have the briefing, check you out on the new equipment, and send you out on an initial patrol."

"Sounds good, Captain," Richardson said. "Thanks."

The group left the room, heading down the hallway towards the door.

"Just a sec," Juan Carlos said. He ducked into the men's room on the right side of the hallway.

Madison giggled. "I wondered if he was having trouble holding it."

"I could use that too," Brendan said.

"Yeah," Richardson said, following Brendan through the door.

Lita, Madison, and Hannah stood looking at each other.

"You really buying this *our women* stuff?" Hannah asked.

Lita giggled. "As soon as we're settled, I'm gonna find out where the courthouse is. Any of you girls want to join me?"

Hannah and Madison looked at each other and laughed.

"Well, we know where you stand, anyway," Hannah said. "It'll probably take a few days for Madison here. But *only* a few days."

"Go ahead and rub it in," Madison said. "I don't care. I know what I want. At least I've admitted it to myself."

Hannah got a shocked look on her face. "I was joking, you know."

Madison shot her a grin as the men came back out.

"You guys don't have to go?" Richardson asked.

"I'm okay," Lita said. "It was only an hour and a half drive, after all."

"Yeah, you boys just can't hold it," Madison said. She elbowed Juan Carlos.

They went out the door. Officer Mahoney was waiting next to their vehicle, leaning against his DPS Cruiser. He was a large man with dark brownish-red hair and green eyes, clean shaven.

"Officer Mahoney?" Richardson asked.

"One in the same," he said, smiling. "Follow me."

Richardson followed the cruiser, driving back to 771.

"I'll bet they're putting us in that trailer park we passed on the way in," Lita said. "It was huge."

"Probably," Richardson said. "You okay with all this?"

"Living with you?" Lita asked.

"Yeah, and the military operations," he said.

"I'm scared to death of what you'll be doing out there," she said. "As for living together, we already do that whenever we're together. If you weren't in the job you are, we would've moved in together by now."

"I know, but it's kinda being forced on you now," Richardson said.

"I don't look at it that way," she said.

They drove along for about ten minutes.

"He's slowing down," Richardson said.

"I was right. He's turning into that big trailer park."

Richardson followed Mahoney through the gate, and back into the middle of the park. There were new park model trailers here and there, between older units which had been lived in for years.

"There's a lot of new ones in here," Madison said, looking out the window. "I've counted twelve so far."

"They don't look half bad," Juan Carlos said.

"Mahoney just pulled over," Lita said. Richardson parked behind him, and they got out of the car.

"Let's go into this one," Officer Mahoney said. He had a bundle of information packets in his hand. They entered, walking through the furnished living room, stopping at the kitchen counter/nook. "How many units will you be needing? Three?"

The group looked at each other.

"Well?" Richardson asked.

"Don't you think it's three?" Lita asked.

"I think it is," Madison said, turning to look at Hannah.

"All right, all right," Hannah said. "Three." Brendan put his arm around her. She looked at him, not able to keep the smile from washing over her face.

"Fine," Mahoney said, handing a packet to each couple. They were stacks of paper in clear plastic folders with maps on the top. "The map shows the available units. You can tell them by the numbers written on them. They're all basically the same. Colors of the furnishings differ. Feel free to check out several if you want. They each have two parking spaces and a small garden area at the rear."

"Cool," Juan Carlos said.

"You have the keys?" Richardson asked.

"They're all unlocked. Keys are in the drawers on the left side of the sink. Two sets. There's bottled water and a few canned goods and frozen meals already there, but you'll want to get to the grocery store and stock up pretty quickly."

"None of them are next to each other," Brendan said.

"Good, then Hannah won't have to be quiet," Madison whispered. Hannah elbowed her.

"That's all I've got," Officer Mahoney said. "The rest of the info in the packets are owner's manuals for the appliances, and association rules."

"What about stuff like sheets and blankets, kitchen utensils, and all of that?" Lita asked.

"They're all fully stocked with those items," Officer Mahoney said. "You're welcome to change it out for your own stuff, but don't throw it away. It belongs to Texas."

"Got it," Richardson said. "Shall we?"

"Might as well," Hannah said.

"You two will be in bed in about three seconds," Madison whispered. Hannah elbowed her again, but then giggled. "Look who's talking."

Officer Mahoney got an embarrassed look on his face, then nodded and left.

"That was bad, you two," Lita said, eyes dancing.

"Yeah, you girls are worse than us guys," Richardson said.

"Whatever," Hannah said. She took Brendan's arm. "C'mon."

"Yes dear," Brendan said. All of them laughed as they walked out with their packets.

"Hey, we don't have phones," Juan Carlos said. "We threw them in the stream, remember? How we going to get together for the meeting tomorrow?"

"There was a land line in the one we were just in," Lita said. "Saw it in the living room. Let me check to see if it's got the number on it." She rushed back inside, coming back in a few seconds.

"Well?" Richardson asked.

"Yeah, the numbers are on the phone, and I got a dial tone," she said.

"Okay, then let's meet up in a little while and exchange numbers," Richardson said.

"Where?" Brendan asked.

"How about right here," Lita said. "I like the colors in this one. Let's check it out, maybe we'll want it."

"Fine by me," Richardson said. "Meet back in an hour?"

"Better make it at least two," Madison said, shooting a sidelong glance at Hannah.

"Shut up," Hannah said.

"Let's make it three to be on the safe side," Brendan said.

"Okay, but no later than that," Lita said. "We've got some business to take care of."

Madison and Hannah shot each other a glance, then looked back at Lita.

"Why not wait a couple days and make a double?" Hannah asked.

"Yeah, right," Madison said. "Knowing you, it'll be a triple."

"You chicks crack me up," Juan Carlos said. "C'mon, I don't want to waste too much of our three hours."

Lita and Richardson watched the two young couples walk off on different sides of the road, and then went inside the unit.

"You're really serious about the courthouse?" Richardson asked.

"I have a biological reason for being in a hurry," she said. "C'mon, let's check this place out."

They looked at the living room, sitting on the furniture, checking the TV, and getting the general feel of the place. Then they checked the bedroom.

"I like the bedspread," Lita said. "You?"

"I'm not good at interior decoration," Richardson said. "That's your department. If you're happy, I'm happy, as long as we're together."

"Good, glad we got that out of the way," she said, looking at him with a smirk. "Maybe we should look at a couple before we decide. We should check the garden area too, and make note of where the sun is in the afternoon."

"I'm at your disposal," Richardson said, walking up behind her. He threw his arms around her waist and pulled her close. "I love you so."

"Later," she said. "Let's get this part over with."

15

Quail Hunting

Eric put his phone back in his pocket and set down his rifle in the darkness. "That was Curt. The bad guys changed their minds. They're leaving."

"Why would they do that?" Don asked.

"They know we can see them," Eric said. "Curt thinks the Islamists they killed tipped these guys off when they came under attack."

"What if they just gave their phones to somebody else, and are still on the way?" Francis asked.

"That is possible, you know," Don said.

"Yeah, I agree, that is possible," Eric said. "I'm fine with staying here until Curt gets back."

"They know where we are," Francis said. "They might show up again at any time, without warning."

"You want to leave?" Don asked.

Francis thought about it for a moment. "No, not yet. This place is defendable. It would help to put up some electronic surveillance."

"We should chat with Curt about that," Eric said.

"I know a fair amount about surveillance systems," Francis said. "We could definitely cook something up, but no electronic warning system is completely air-tight. You guys know that, right?"

"Yeah," Eric said.

"How long until Curt and the others get back?"

"Another hour and a half," Eric said.

"We can sit here that long," Francis said.

"Agreed," Eric said.

The men sat silently, watching the road, fighting back sleep. Don started to drift off after a few minutes. Francis kicked his leg and he woke up, startled.

"Don't worry, we can sleep later," Francis said.

"I'm beat," Eric said, "but Curt and his team are gonna be worse off. I won't be hitting the sack for a while."

"The sun's coming up," Don said. "Maybe that'll make it easier."

They watched as the wildlife stirred, birds flittering around in the early morning light.

"This place is beautiful," Francis said. "I can see why your family settled here."

"Yeah, it's good to be back here, even in these circumstances," Eric said. "It's home."

"Listen," Don whispered. "Somebody's coming."

"I hear them," Eric said, feeling the hair on the back of his neck rise.

"They're not coming from the road," Francis whispered. "They're coming across that meadow over there." He pointed to the left.

Eric scanned the area, and then smiled. "It's the Merchant girls."

"Wow, who's that raven-haired beauty?" Don asked.

"That's my old girlfriend," Eric said. "Sydney. She's gorgeous, but she was always a handful."

"When was she your girlfriend?" Don asked.

"Oh, when she was about Allyssa's age," Eric said.

"Hell, all girls are a handful at *that* age," Don said.

"The other one is real pretty too," Francis said. "Look at her hair shine in the light."

"That's Amanda," Eric said. "She's the oldest. I think she's prettier than Sydney, but if you tell Sydney that, I'll deny it."

Don laughed. "She looks a little older than me."

"She is," Eric said. "She's wild. Your daughters would scare her away. You'd probably have a better chance with Sydney."

"How old is Sydney?"

"About thirty-five," Eric said. "How old are you?"

"Thirty-nine," Don said.

"That works," Francis said. "Go for it, man. It gets old being the only couple in the family."

Don laughed. "Maybe I've got enough females in my life right now. Two teenagers are enough of a challenge."

"Only one is yours," Eric said.

Don was quiet for a moment. "Chloe doesn't have any family left. I'm kinda her dad now."

"You're a good man, brother," Francis said.

"I have my moments," Don said. "They're close enough now. We'd better make our presence known."

"Yeah," Eric said. "Both of them were crack shots when I knew them. We don't want them shooting us by accident."

Francis chuckled.

"Hey, Sydney! Amanda!" Eric called out. The two women froze, looking around.

"I'm gonna stand up. Don't shoot me!" Eric stood up and looked at them.

"Eric!" Sydney shouted, breaking into a run towards them. Amanda grinned and followed her. She was striking, with bleach-blonde hair and black eyebrows, her rounded figure making her look thick compared to Sydney.

Sydney hugged Eric, then moved back to look at him. "You haven't changed much."

"Hey, Eric," Amada said, her peaceful, calm smile washing over him. She had the same striking blue eyes as Sydney, but with the platinum hair hanging down around her face and shoulders, she had the look of a Viking Princess. There were barb-wire tattoos on both upper arms, and small flowery tattoos on both lower arms, on the insides. She gave him a hug, and he could feel the strength in her arms.

"So nice to see you two," Eric said. "This is Don and Francis. We met up in Deadwood. Guys, this is Sydney and her sister Amanda."

"Oh, yeah, Jason told me that you were in Deadwood," Sydney said. "I'm so sorry for what happened there. You lose people?"

"Yes," Francis said. "We were lucky to get out ourselves."

"You guys going to stick around for a while?" Amanda asked.

"Don't know yet," Eric said. "We've got enemy fighters after us. They know where we are, but at least we can defend this place."

"Hope we didn't bring any problems down on you two," Don said.

"Our place is in a good spot, and it's well fortified," Amanda said. "They might be able to take us, but it'll be real expensive."

"Still tough as nails," Eric said, smiling at her.

"I'm a little more worried than she is," Sydney said. "I like to have a man or two around."

"Well, we've got quite a few men back at the homestead," Eric said. "And some other women, and a couple teenaged girls."

"I heard you have a girlfriend," Sydney said. "Serious?"

"Extremely," he said. "We're as good as married."

"Pity," she said with a small pout.

"Oh, you know *we* ran our course," Eric said. "I have good memories, though."

"So do I." She smiled. "How come you guys are out here?"

"We got tipped off that the enemy was on their way in," Eric said.

"By who?" Amanda asked.

"Our away team," Don said. "They were off picking up some weapons from a stash near San Antonio. They ought to be back any time now."

"How did they know?" Amanda asked.

"Curt. One of our guys. He can track the Islamists by their cell phones," Eric said. "They ambushed three truckloads of Islamists at their weapons cache. Curt thinks they got word back to the fighters on the way here. Told them they were visible."

"Really? Is that why Jason called that blowhard a genius?" Sydney asked.

Eric laughed. "Yeah."

"I think they're wise now, unfortunately," Don said. "Nice while it lasted."

"Curt will probably figure out some new way to track them," Eric said.

"Hopefully," Francis said.

"You guys should come to the house later and meet the rest of the folks," Don said.

"Yeah, we'll do that," Amanda said.

"What were you two doing out here?" Francis asked.

"Looking for game," Sydney said. "I had a hankering for quail. Lots of Bobwhites around here."

"Do tell," Don said. "Love me some Bobwhites. Maybe we can go out together sometime."

Sydney looked him up and down, then smiled. "Yeah, I'd like that."

"Glad we saw you guys," Francis said. "Hearing gunshots back here would've gotten us worried."

Amanda chuckled. "We'll have to get used to other folks living around here, I guess."

"Sorry," Eric said.

"Oh, I like it," Amanda said. "Don't get me wrong on that."

"Listen," Don said. "Vehicles."

"Hope it's our folks," Francis said, straining to see down the road. Dirk's truck came into view.

"Yes!" Eric said. "It's Dirk, Chance, and Curt."

"Good." Sydney giggled. "Watch this guy flirt with me again."

"You love the attention," Amanda said.

"I have a feeling Curt will focus on you, Amanda," Eric said.

Amanda snickered. "What are you talking about?"

"I know you, and I know Curt," Eric said. "You two will get along. Trust me."

Sydney laughed. "Maybe we ought to go. Hunting apparel isn't the best way to trap a man."

Amanda looked at her and shook her head. "Keep it up, little sister. When you going *bird hunting* with this one?" She nodded towards Don, watching his face turn red.

"Curt will like you just fine dressed like that," Eric said. "C'mon, let's go meet them."

"Yeah, let's," Amanda said.

Dirk stopped when he saw them walking towards the road, and got out of the truck with a big smile on his face.

"Hey, guys!" he said. "Everything all right here?"

"No sign of the Islamists," Don said.

Curt and Chance caught up to Dirk as he rushed to the group.

"That's not all good news," Curt said. "They're onto us now. We'll have to figure out another way to watch for them." He smiled at Sydney, and then saw Amanda, freezing his eyes on her, mouth open. She returned the look, then broke into a smile.

"You're Curt, eh? I'm Amanda. Nice to meet you."

"You can pick your jaw up off the ground any time, man," Eric said to Curt, snapping him out of it.

"Shut up, pencil neck," he said. Then he turned back to Amanda. "Nice to meet you too."

"What'd you bring back?" Don asked.

"You won't believe it," Dirk said. "C'mon."

They walked to the truck and looked in the bed.

"What the hell are those big things?" Amanda asked.

"M-19 Automatic Grenade Launchers," Curt said.

"RPGs?" Eric said. "Mortars? Where the hell did you get all this stuff?"

"I could tell you, but then I'd have to kill you," he said.

"Oh, please," Sydney said. Don looked to his side and saw that she'd moved right next to him while he was looking in the truck bed. His heart beat quickened.

"We should get going," Amanda said. "While we still have a chance at some quail. Maybe we could come by your place for a visit this afternoon."

"Yes, please do," Curt said.

"We need to go get some shut-eye," Dirk said. "Been up for over twenty-four hours now."

"Yeah, you guys do that," Francis said. "We'll keep an eye on things for a while."

"Let's go," Chance said. He walked back to the truck with Curt and Dirk. Amanda and Sydney nodded to them and walked back into the meadow.

"Wow," Don said. "You see Curt and Amanda lock eyes?"

"Yeah," Francis said, "and I saw how you and Sydney looked at each other, too."

"Don't know what you're talking about," Don said.

"Yeah, right," Francis said.

"She likes you," Eric said. "I can tell. She got right next to you by the truck too."

"That didn't mean anything," Don said.

"Yeah, right," Francis said again.

The men settled back into their watch, fighting sleep again.

Robert Boren

16

Flatbeds

Moe and Clancy were already at it for a couple of hours by the time Kelly and Junior got to the road.

"Hell, you guys are almost done," Junior said, looking at the flatbed. A tank sat next to it, cannon pointed east on I-10. DPS officers were still cleaning up the wreckage from the mangled trucks another four hundred yards down.

"What's to stop those DPS officers from driving these flatbeds away with our tanks the minute we get them done?" Junior asked.

"Chief Ramsey," Kelly said. "Had a long chat with Jason this morning, before you got up."

"They're trying to recruit us, ain't they?" Junior asked.

"Yeah," Kelly said, "and I'm ripe to be recruited."

Junior sighed. "We've gone respectable. Who knew?"

Kelly laughed.

"Hey, guys, give us a hand with this tire, okay?" Moe asked. They rushed over to help Clancy lift it, and Moe used his rechargeable impact gun to put on the lug nuts. "Gotta charge this up again."

"We're about done anyway," Clancy said. "I just got to hook up the new brake lines on this one, and it'll be ready to go." He got underneath the flatbed with two hand wrenches and got to work, still listening to the conversation.

Jason and Kyle rode over in Jason's Jeep.

"Damn, you guys know how to get things done," Jason said, looking at the flatbeds. "How close are they?"

"Half an hour," Moe said. "We need to decide what we're gonna do. We can park these on the vacant lot across the road from the park entrance until then."

"That's a perfect place to load them," Clancy said from under the flatbed.

"Could we get these flatbeds past that narrow part of the road at the homestead?" Kyle asked.

"I suspect we'll have to park the flatbeds and take the tanks through on their own," Jason said.

"Can the road handle the weight?" Junior asked.

Jason thought about it for a while. "Maybe not," he said. "We could take them in the back way. There's no road, but these tanks should be able to get through."

"How many miles would that be?" Moe asked. "These things get thirsty really fast."

"That's a good question," Jason said. "I'll check it out. I'd say it's under ten miles."

"If we can take these tanks in the back way, doesn't that mean the enemy could do the same thing?" Kelly asked.

"Possibly," Jason said. "Usually when we get attacked the enemy comes via troop transport trucks, or sometimes civilian pick-ups. No way would they make it in the back way with those. Track vehicles are another matter. They don't need roads, as long as the terrain isn't too hairy."

"We're getting a little ahead of ourselves," Kyle said. "We don't know what's gonna happen in the meeting with Ramsey and the Texas National Guard. They might want us someplace else."

"They might even want us to stay here," Clancy said. "I'm seeing a lot of traffic on the message boards about the New Mexico border, and this is a lot closer to that area than Fredericksburg is."

"He's right," Junior said. "They might move us to the panhandle, even."

"Hope not," Kelly said. "Too dry and too damn hot."

"Hell, it's hot right here," Moe said, wiping the sweat from his brow. "It's gonna get worse, too."

"Hey, Moe, I think we can fire this one up now," Clancy said.

"Go for it," Moe said.

Clancy climbed up into the cab. "Still too much blood and guts in here," he shouted out the window as he fired up the big diesel. "Purrs like a kitten."

"Drive it over to the spot we talked about," Moe said.

Clancy shook his head yes and put the bit flatbed into gear, grinding a little. The huge truck slowly moved towards the road.

"There it goes," Jason said. "The others ready?"

"Yeah," Moe said. "How many folks we got who can drive big-rigs?"

"Two of Gray's guys can do it," Kelly said. "So can Junior and Nate."

"You can too," Junior said.

Kelly laughed. "I grind the gears way too much. Wouldn't want to try with the kind of load these suckers are gonna be carrying."

They watched the DPS officers for a few minutes.

"Looks like they're almost done," Kyle said.

"About frigging time," Moe said.

"Maybe they were keeping an eye on us," Jason said.

"In order to take the tanks?" Moe asked.

"No, in order to protect us," Jason said. "The last thing the Texas government wants to do is disarm folks like us."

"Here comes Clancy," Moe said, pointing. "In Nate's truck."

Nate parked and they both trotted over.

"How'd it go?" Moe asked.

"No problem," Clancy said. "Thanks for bringing me back over, Nate."

"No problem. Maybe we ought to take the next two. Somebody could drive my truck back over."

"I'm good with that," Clancy said. "C'mon." They both got into trucks and fired them up, then drove onto I-10, heading back to the park.

"Damn, Nate handles those even better than Clancy does," Moe said.

"He drove truck for a lot of years," Kelly said. "Part of it was smuggling, and he got caught. Kinda ended his trucking career."

"What was he moving?" Moe asked.

"Weed, mostly," Kelly said. "That was when he was a lot younger. He's a little more prudent now."

Junior laughed. "Yeah, but only a little. Want me to take the last one?"

"Help yourself," Moe said.

Junior got into the last of the flatbeds and started it, grinding the gears for a second before the truck lurched forward. "Don't worry, I'll get the hang of it in a hurry," he shouted out the window as he drove onto I-10.

"He's doing all right," Moe said, watching him make the turn off of I-10 towards the park.

"Who's driving the tank back?" Kelly asked.

"Clancy can do that, or one of Gray's guys," Moe said.

"I'll go get somebody," Kelly said, walking to his truck.

"Anybody left here who can fire that tank?" Jason said, looking around nervously.

"Yeah, I can," Moe said. "I'd need a hand up. Why, you see something?"

"No, but I feel like we're flapping in the breeze here," Jason said.

"Battle fatigue," Kyle said. "Kelly will be here with somebody in a few minutes. Want to go back?"

"Let's wait for him," Jason said.

"All right," Kyle said. "Hear anything else from Eric?"

"Not since Curt, Dirk, and Chance got back from their supply run," Jason said.

"I'm glad they got back all right," Kyle said. "Had me worried."

"Me too," Jason said. "One way or another, Curt needs to be reunited with his toy hauler. He's got gimbals to make."

"Yeah," Kyle said.

"Kelly's coming back," Moe said, pointing at the road.

"That was fast," Jason said. He watched as Kelly pulled up next to them.

Clancy jumped out of the truck. "Thanks, man," he said to Kelly. "Want to ride back over in the tank, Moe?"

"Naw, I think I'll take your spot with Kelly, if you don't mind," Moe said. "The tank is too hard on my knees."

"Roger that," Clancy said. He ambled over to the tank and climbed up to the driver's hatch. "See you guys over there."

"Yeah," Moe said, climbing into Kelly's truck.

"You guys did a good job," Kelly said.

"So did you," Moe said. "I heard that depot attack had an impact on the battle for San Antonio."

"Yeah, that's what Ramsey told Jason earlier. Got to give Curt most of the credit for that."

"He's a valuable guy, that's for sure," Moe said.

Kelly watched as Jason and Kyle drove onto I-10, and then followed them.

"You think we're gonna stay here a while?" Kelly asked.

Moe sighed. "I don't know," he said. "Jason said Ramsey wasn't sure yet. Deferred to this meeting they want to have with us."

Robert Boren

"How we gonna hold the meeting when part of us are in Fredericksburg and part of us are here?" Kelly asked.

"I heard Jason say something about a web meeting," Moe said. "What do you think about moving? You've been at both places."

"The homestead is more secluded and easier to defend against an enemy force," Kelly said. "It's also an easy place to get trapped with RVs. That narrow part of the road is bad, and it's got switchbacks. It'd be easy to go off the cliff."

"Big cliff?" Moe asked.

"No, it's not huge, but I wouldn't want to roll down it."

"Any other ways in?" Moe asked.

"Apparently you can get in through the rear of the property, but there's no road. You need serious four-wheel drive. Not those soccer-mom all-wheel drive SUVs. Real four-wheel drive, like a Jeep Wrangler or a modified four-wheel drive truck."

"Or a tank," Moe said. "If it's really ten miles in with no road, fuel might be an issue. These things go through gas like shit through a goose."

"What do they burn?" Kelly asked. "Not gasoline, right?"

"They *can* burn gasoline," Moe said, "but they can burn other fuels too. I used to wonder if that's why the Army decided on the turbine engines, but after reading a little more, I think it was more about engine size and power-to-weight ratio."

"The fuel we blew up at the depot smelled like kerosene," Kelly said.

"Yeah, kerosene, jet fuel, and even diesel fuel will work," Moe said. "Hell, whiskey would probably work. You need some kind of a starter for those, though, to get the engine going. Something more volatile like propane."

Kelly pulled through the gate and stopped at the office. "You want to get out here?"

"Sure," Moe said. "Thanks for the lift."

"Thank you for *everything,* man," Kelly said.

Moe nodded and left the cab, shutting the door and waving as he walked onto the office veranda. Kelly drove back to his space. Junior walked up as he was parking.

"Hey, Junior," he said. "How do those flatbeds drive?"

"Slow and heavy," Junior said. "I suspect they'll feel even worse with tanks on them."

"Probably," Kelly said. "What are you gonna do now?"

"Check on Rachel," he said.

"How'd it go last night?"

Junior's face flushed. "Like a dream, man."

"Good for you," Kelly said. "Think I'll go check with Brenda. See you later."

Junior nodded and walked towards his Brave. Kelly smiled as he watched him.

"Kelly?" Brenda called from the trailer.

"Yeah, coming," he said, closing the door of his truck. He went into the trailer, pausing just inside the doorway to take Brenda into his arms. They kissed passionately.

"Wow," she said. "What was that about?"

"Nothing," he said. "Just feeling the love, I guess."

"How's Junior?" she asked.

"Walking on cloud nine," Kelly said. "You think Rachel is for real?"

"*Oh, yeah,*" Brenda said. "No doubt in my mind at all."

"What happened? I didn't see that coming. Not really."

"Neither did she," Brenda said. "I'm a little jealous."

"Why?" Kelly asked. "You have me."

"That's not what I meant," she said, taking him back into her arms. "I'm jealous because I'm too old."

"You're not too old," Kelly said.

"To have babies, dummy," she said.

"You think that's what Rachel has planned for Junior? She's no spring chicken herself."

"She's still fertile," Brenda said. "She *is* older than she looks. The age difference with Junior isn't nearly as much as I thought it was."

"Yeah, if Junior shaved off that beard of his he'd look younger than me," Kelly said.

"Think he'd ever do that?" Brenda asked.

"Oh, I don't know," Kelly said. "Maybe."

"You heard about this meeting coming up?"

"Yeah, we were talking about it on the road," Kelly said. "How'd you hear about it?"

"Carrie told us earlier," Brenda said. "Makes me nervous."

"Me too, a little," Kelly said. "No sense worrying about it."

"I know," Brenda said. "I'm still worried about Chris. Wonder where they ended up? I can't raise him."

"Hope Simon Orr didn't do something to them," Kelly said.

"I think I need a nap before the meeting," Brenda said. "You want to join me?"

"Oh yeah." Kelly smiled.

17

Violet and Cami

Maria answered the phone, a grim look on her face as she listened.

"Sir, it's Washington DC. The Attorney General's office," she said. "Want to take it?"

"Sure," Hendrix said, feeling his pulse start to pound.

"Line one," she said.

He picked up the receiver. "Hendrix."

"Hi, Kip."

"Franklin, how are you?" Hendrix asked.

"You obviously survived that attack on Austin."

"I did," Hendrix said. "We might have lost Jerry Sutton, though. He's still missing."

"I could look into that for you," Franklin said.

"How would you know anything about it?"

"We have plants within the enemy ranks," Franklin said. "There, I told you something. Your turn."

"We hit the enemy supply depot outside of Austin," Hendrix said. "It impacted the planned attack on San Antonio. We were able to put it down and take out a lot of Islamist forces."

"Oh, please," Franklin said. "We already know about that, and it wasn't the government that did it. You've made things more difficult for the administration. You know that, right?"

"What are you talking about?" Hendrix asked.

"Your damn vigilantes, working with those Austin cops. That's who did it, and it's all over the internet. We've had challenges to martial law in Virginia, Pennsylvania, and New Jersey thanks to that."

"They're working with us," Hendrix said. "Sorry if that's been a problem for you." He struggled to keep the sarcasm out of his voice.

"Sorry if that's been a problem for you," Franklin mocked. "Any more of that nonsense coming?"

"Well, you said it wasn't us, so how would I know?"

"Don't play with me, Kip," Franklin said. "You've got a lady friend. One with a little sister in trouble. You've been down that road before."

"I don't know what you're talking about," Hendrix said, his mind racing to the past. *Violet and Cami.* Dammit. What would Maria think of that?

"You still there, Kipster?"

"Yeah, I'm still here," he said. "You don't know the whole story on that. It wasn't as it seemed."

"You got Violet drunk and had your way with her. After she passed out, you had your way with Cami. We've got testimony."

"They were both taken care of. They left the state. I paid dearly for that, even though it wasn't what Violet said it was." The words stung his lips coming out. "It was also over ten years ago."

Franklin chuckled. "Texas really should cut ties with the Feds if they want to be independent."

"What are you talking about?" Hendrix asked.

"You guys are still using the Federal system for temporary psychiatric hold. We know all about Maria's sister. We know what she looks like. She's just your type."

"You don't know anything," Hendrix said. "I was helping out Maria. As a friend."

"We know about the suicide attempt. We know you helped Maria get her sister committed. They keep records when somebody is taken into custody against their will."

"So what?" Hendrix asked. "When we left the hospital that night, I drove Maria home and then I left. Nothing happened. I didn't plan anything to happen, either." Sweat broke out on his forehead as he flashed back to Cami, her eyes glazing over as he took her the first time.

"Have it your way," Franklin said. "We can make sure that Maria finds out all about that regrettable incident."

Hendrix was silent for a moment, panic subsiding as he remembered what he could say.

"You still there, Kip?"

Hendrix sighed, loud enough for Franklin to hear. *Make it real.* "What do you want?"

"The plans for New Mexico," Franklin said.

"They'll kill me," Hendrix said.

"That's your problem," Franklin said. "Don't worry. They won't find out where the info came from."

"Easy for you to say that," Hendrix said.

"What were the chances that you'd get both of them pregnant, anyway?" Franklin asked. "Makes for a fine story. Texas Legislative leader knocks up his secretary and her sister on the same lust-filled weekend."

"Okay, okay," Hendrix said, lowering his voice. "I'll tell you, but this stuff stops. Understand?"

"You think you're in a position to dictate terms?" Franklin asked.

"You want the info or not?"

Hendrix paused again.

"C'mon, Kip," Franklin said. "I don't have all day."

"We're preparing to pursue the Islamists into New Mexico," Hendrix said, trying to sound scared.

"That's not all, is it?"

Hendrix paused again.

"C'mon, dammit," Franklin said.

"After we've kicked them out, we're going to take over the New Mexico government. They can't handle the situation."

"That's an attack on the United States," Franklin said.

"Nelson said it's only until the war is over," Hendrix said.

"Do you believe him?"

"Yeah, but I don't think the war is gonna be over anytime soon," Hendrix said. "New Mexico might be a possession of the Texas Republic for quite a few years."

"Finally," Franklin said. "That was like pulling teeth. I guess that's enough for today. I'm sending you something as a reminder, so you won't decide to clam up on me."

Hendrix's phone dinged as a text message arrived. He pulled his phone out and opened the message. There was a picture of Cami's naked dead body, laying on a bed, eyes staring into nothingness.

"Recognize that?" Franklin asked.

"No," Hendrix gasped. "She was fine. What happened?"

"She killed herself a year after you *raped* her," Franklin said. "You really ought to watch it with the unstable ones. Hope Maria isn't like that. We know her sister is, so be careful my friend."

Hendrix's anger rose, and he slammed the receiver of the phone down, then put his head on the desk and sobbed.

"My God, what happened?" Maria asked, rushing into his office.

Hendrix lifted his head off the desk and wiped the tears from his eyes. "I can't talk about it here."

"Can you tell me tonight?" she asked.

"Yeah," he said, trying to get hold of himself.

"Why were you crying?"

"Memories of past mistakes they're holding over my head," Hendrix said.

"You're afraid that I'm going to find out about it?"

"No, I'm ashamed of myself. It's been ten years, but I still can't believe what I did."

"Don't worry about it now," Maria said, petting his head.

"I'll be all right," Hendrix said. "Want to go get lunch?"

"I have to go to the hospital," she said. "Celia's case is coming up for review."

"How's she doing?"

"Sounds like she's doing better," Maria said. "She wants out *now*, of course."

"What happens when she gets out?"

"I don't know," Maria said. "She can't live by herself, that's for sure."

"How about your mother?"

"I can't count on her," Maria said. "That's how she ended up at my place."

Hendrix looked down at the desk for a moment, then back up at her. "She'll need to move in with us, won't she?"

"I couldn't ask you to do that," Maria said.

"We're together," Hendrix said. "There's no other place, is there?"

"I don't know," Maria said. "They might not let her out, you know."

"Well, if she's getting out soon, don't worry about it. You know how big our house is. We have room, and I can bring in a caretaker if needed."

Maria kissed him. "How'd I get so lucky?"

"Want me to go with you at lunch?"

"No, that's okay," Maria said. "I know you're backed up. You probably have to talk to Governor Nelson after that last phone call, too."

Hendrix chuckled. "Yeah. Everything went according to plan. That's all I can say now."

"Okay," she said. "I'll get out of your hair. Want me to put in a call to Nelson?"

"No, I think I'll take a stroll over to talk with him. Still don't trust these phones one hundred percent."

"All right," she said, turning to leave. Hendrix watched her in her tight navy blue dress.

"I love what you have on," he said.

She turned around and smiled. "Used to make me nervous wearing this. I know you liked it. Now I enjoy what it does to you."

"I'm gonna make you pay tonight," Hendrix said.

"Hope so," she said softly as she walked back to her desk.

Hendrix left the office for the Governor's mansion. It was warm outside. Too warm for a suit. Passers-by nodded warmly to him as he walked. There were a group of reporters hanging around by the entrance to the mansion.

"Kip Hendrix," one report said. The others rushed at him like ducks fighting over bread on the water.

"Sorry, folks, no time now," Hendrix said. "Maybe when I come back out."

He walked up to the security desk. "Kip Hendrix to see Governor Nelson."

The receptionist smiled at him. "Good Afternoon, President Pro Tempore Hendrix. I'll buzz him for you." She picked up her phone and hit a button as he looked around at the milling people. It was so much busier now than it had been before the war. *Before the Republic.*

"You can go on in," the receptionist said.

"Thank you," Hendrix said. He walked past her desk, into the entry way of the mansion. Nelson's secretary was there to greet him.

"Hi, Brian," Hendrix said warmly.

"Good morning, sir," Brian said. "Can I take your coat? It's devilish hot today, and the air conditioning in this building is barely keeping up."

"Sure, thanks," Hendrix said. He took off his coat and handed it to Brian, then followed him up the stairs to the Governor's private office.

"Have a seat here. Governor Nelson will be with you shortly." He scurried away with the coat as Hendrix sat on one of the chairs against the wall.

"Kip!" Governor Nelson said as he came into the waiting room, hand extended.

"Good afternoon, Governor," Hendrix said, shaking hands. They went into the office together.

"Get a call from the Administration?" Nelson asked, sitting behind his desk. Hendrix sat in a chair facing it.

"Yep," Hendrix said. "It was the usual weasel. Franklin."

"I hate that guy," Nelson said. "You plant the seed?"

"Yep, and I think he swallowed it hook, line, and sinker."

"Excellent," Nelson said. "He get rough with you?"

"Yeah, and it made the job easier, frankly," Hendrix said. "I was actually taken aback when he brought up the incident he used. Didn't think they knew about that one."

"Which one was it?" Nelson asked. Then he shook his head. "Never mind. You don't have to tell me."

"I think I should tell you," Hendrix said. "Might help you plug some holes."

"Okay, go ahead," Nelson said.

"It was about my secretary Violet, from ten years ago, and her sister Cami," Hendrix said.

"I remember Violet, but I don't remember any scandal about her sister," Nelson said.

"Long story," Hendrix said. "I won't tell you details. I'm a little bothered about how they found out. Violet came back to Texas, last I heard. They might have somebody here who's been talking to her."

"They have any recent information?"

"No," Hendrix said. "Not that they told me, anyway. There is one other thing, though."

"What's that?" Nelson asked.

"The Medical Center," Hendrix said. "You know they're still putting info onto the Federal databases?"

Nelson leaned back in his chair, thinking. "I'll have somebody look into that. How do you know?"

"They knew about Maria," Hendrix said. "Not that we're together, but they suspect something, since I was involved in getting her sister committed for observation."

"Interesting," Nelson said. "Deny it and see if they find out more."

"I did. You think there are still moles, don't you?" Hendrix asked.

"Yep," Nelson said. "Hell, that's the main reason I wanted you to float that phony story about New Mexico. I want to see where leakage is coming from. Sooner rather than later, we'll see stories about Texas's plan to annex that state, and then we should be able to follow the stories to the source."

"Sounds like a plan to me," Hendrix said. "That's all I got."

"You think they're going to call you again?"

"Oh, I'm certain they will," Hendrix said.

"How are you certain?"

"They sent me a picture of Cami, Violet's sister, dead on a bed, to prime the pump for next time."

Nelson froze. "You didn't have anything to do that that, did you?"

"No, she took an overdose of sleeping pills about a year after the last time I saw her," Hendrix said. "Believe it or not, I didn't know she'd passed. It was a shock."

"Sad," Nelson said. "Violet's still okay though, right?"

"I really have no idea," Hendrix said. "Maybe we ought to have somebody look into it. She might be seeing somebody about this. Might lead us right to the mole."

"That's a damn good idea," Nelson said. He got out a pad of paper and his pen. "What was her last name again?"

"Sanchez," Hendrix said.

"Okay, I'll put somebody on it."

"Nobody's going to hurt her, right?" Hendrix asked.

"Don't worry," Nelson said. "You know I'm not like that."

"Okay, sorry," Hendrix said.

"You still have feelings for this woman?"

"Not love, no, but I care about what happens to her," Hendrix said.

"Anything else, Kip?"

"Nope," Hendrix said. "I'll let you know when they call again."

"Thanks," Nelson said. "From me and from Texas."

Hendrix chuckled. "You are Texas, old friend."

They shook hands, and Hendrix left.

{ 18 }

Choices

Hannah was walking fast, Brendan barely keeping up.
"What's the hurry?" he asked. She kept up the pace.
"Hannah, stop!"

"What?" she asked sharply, turning back towards him as she slowed.

"Why are you in such a hurry?" he asked. "We've got time."

"I'm just nervous, that's all," she said, "and I want to get one of the units that's further away from the others."

"Why?" Brendan asked.

She stopped and looked into his eyes. "I know myself," she said softly. "It's embarrassing. I've been holding back, too."

He put his arm around her waist and pulled her close. She resisted, looking away from him.

"Hannah," Brendan said.

She turned to look at him, almost afraid to make eye contact. "What? Let go of me."

Brendan let her go and she started walking again. "See that one, with the tree in the backyard?"

"I see it," Brendan answered.

"Let's look at that one, okay?"

"Sure," Brendan said.

Robert Boren

"I'm sorry," she said, slowing until he caught up. "I'll settle down."

"In your own time," Brendan said. "Don't worry about it."

She climbed the steps onto the porch of the trailer. A gentle breeze blew the plants on either side of the unit.

"I like the outside," Brendan said. He opened the door and waited as she walked in.

"Nice colors in the living room," she said, walking around and looking. "What do you think?"

"I like it," Brendan said. "Looks like we get afternoon shade on the porch too. Might be a little sunny in the backyard."

"We won't spend much time back there anyway," Hannah said. She walked into the kitchen and checked cabinets. Brendan noticed her hand trembling as she opened one.

"Hey, you okay?" he asked, coming up behind her. He put his arms around her waist and pulled her close. She froze for a moment.

"I'm sorry," she whispered, looking down at the counter.

"What's wrong?"

"I feel out of control. Dread. Like I'm going to lose you just when we're getting…" She paused.

"Getting?" Brendan asked, turning her to face him. She avoided eye contact.

"Let's finish looking the place over," she said, escaping from his arms. "Bedroom and bathroom."

Brendan watched her walk into the bedroom and look around. He followed her at more of a distance.

"Hannah, I'm sorry," Brendan said. "I shouldn't push you. I'll try not to do that anymore."

She turned towards him, making eye contact and looking away. "It's not you. It's me. You didn't do anything wrong."

"If you don't want to live together, I'm sure they'll give you your own unit, at least until you decide what you want to do. I'll understand."

She looked at him, tears in her eyes. "I don't want that."

"What *do* you want?"

She sighed and sat on the bed facing him. "I don't think I can talk about it right now."

"Okay, I can wait until you're ready," he said, sitting on the bed, keeping a little distance between them. "I won't push you."

They were silent for a few minutes, Brendan uncomfortable with it. He broke it.

"What do you think? Is this the place?"

"I like it," she said. "Do you?"

"Yes," he said. "I think it's perfect."

"Hope it's far enough away," Hannah said.

"Maybe it doesn't matter now," he said.

She looked into his eyes. "What do you mean by that? You think I don't want you anymore?"

"Kinda seems that way," he said. "It's okay. I know we were thrown together. I know everything went too fast. Sorry I took advantage."

A soft smile came over her face. "You're picking up the wrong vibe from me."

"I am?"

"Yes," she whispered.

"Help me out here," Brendan said, feeling himself tremble.

"It's not that I don't want to be with you," she said softly. "I'm afraid you'll be ripped away from me."

Brendan was silent for a few minutes, thinking.

"What do you want?" Hannah asked.

"You," he said, glancing at her face, then looking away.

"Oh, you're crying," she said, moving closer to him. "Sorry I'm being so difficult. This should be a happy time."

"Maybe we should talk this out now," Brendan said. "Can you?"

She looked at him and nodded yes.

"This isn't casual for me," Brendan said. "I've never felt this way about a woman before. I'm sorry we aren't quite in sync."

She looked in his eyes. "I'm *so* much in love with you," she said softly.

"I thought so," Brendan said, "but you're resisting it."

"You have to fight," she said. "You might get killed. I don't think I could take that. I'm scared to death of it."

He petted her cheek, then turned her head to him. "This is war. There's nothing we can do about that. All we can do is get as much of each other as we can, and hope that we both come through it okay."

"Live happily ever after?" she asked, soft smile on her face.

"Do you want that?"

She nodded yes. "Do you?"

He was silent for a moment, looking at her pretty face.

"Maybe you don't love me yet," she said.

"Now *you're* getting the wrong vibe," he said. "I just told you I wanted you."

"I know," she said.

"Okay, I'll cut to the chase. I love you more than anything. More than life itself. I want you to be my wife. I want to have children with you. I want us to grow old together with our family gathered around us."

She looked at his face, touching his cheek, coming in for a slow kiss, light but trembling and passionate. Then she giggled. "Geez, I can't believe this."

"Can't believe what?" Brendan said.

"What I'm thinking right now. God, I'm embarrassed. The girls would have a field day with this."

"What?" Brendan asked, caressing her back as she leaned into him. She shook her head no. "You'll tell them."

"No I won't. Trust me."

She shook her head. "No, it's stupid. Kiss me again."

He took her head in his hands and kissed her passionately, from her neck up past her chin, his mouth slipping onto hers as she moaned. His hands roamed all over her as she trembled in his arms, pushing back against him wantonly, breath and heartbeat racing.

"Oh, geez," she said, breaking the kiss. "Maybe we ought to lock the door. You know where this is gonna lead."

Brendan nodded and stumbled out to the front door, locking it. When he came back she was already naked on the bed. He undressed and climbed over her, caressing her face as he kissed her again, their naked bodies touching, passion building fast.

"Don't wait," she whispered, pulling him into position. "I want you now."

She cried out as he took her, urgently pushing back on him, her eyes rolling back in her head.

"I love you so," Brendan said as he sped up. She was beside her self now, louder than before, egging him on. Then he stopped.

"No!" she cried.

"I *know*," Brendan said softly, watching her twitch beneath him.

"What?" she asked. "C'mon. I need you."

He moved a little and then stopped again.

"Brendan!" she cried, trying to get him going.

"I know what you were thinking. We're gonna do it. Today."

"Brendan," she said. "You don't…"

He moved a few times again and she wailed. Then he stopped again.

"Why are you doing this?" she asked.

"You want to be my wife, don't you?" he whispered to her.

"Don't ask me that now," she said, her breath coming in a rush, her eyes wide as he looked at her.

"Answer the question," he said.

"Yes, dammit," she said. "Yes."

"We'll do it today, when we go to the courthouse with the others," he said.

She froze, staring into his eyes. "No, we couldn't do that."

"We're *going* to do that," he said, starting again. "You'll be mine and everybody will know it."

"Oh God," she said, going out of control.

"You'll do it?" he asked as she came down.

"Yes," she said. "I can't believe I'm saying this."

Their passion burst over them and they were gone, inside each other with total abandon. Nothing else in their world mattered. They lay next to each other afterwards.

"What did we just decide?" Hannah asked, turning toward him. "I'm never gonna live this down. Especially after messing with Madison."

"You'll just have to deal with that," Brendan said. "Remember how those two are. They're liable to be thinking the same thing."

"You really think so?"

"Juan Carlos worships the ground she walks on. Never seen him like that with anybody."

Hannah sighed. "I know, same with Madison. She wants him bad. When those two lock eyes you can feel it across the room."

"We've been putting out the same vibe," Brendan said.

She nodded silently. "Sorry I resisted."

"We just packed a long courtship into a few days," Brendan said. "Both of us resisted as it started to sweep us up."

"When did you know?"

"The morning we left Port Isabel," Brendan said.

She giggled. "Me too. How much time we have left?"

"Until what?"

"Until we have to meet the others," she said.

"Hour and a half," he said.

"Good," she said, rolling onto him. "Let's not tell them until we get there, okay?"

Brendan chuckled. "I like it."

Web Meeting

C urt was nervous. He looked around the Finley property, wondering if they would get attacked there, waiting for the upcoming meeting. *I should be working the gun mounts, not hanging around here.* Eric approached.

"It's happening?" Curt asked.

"Yeah," Eric said. "Be another half hour, though. Want to help me set up the audio-visual?"

"Sure, what the hell," he said. "I'm antsy. I need something to do. All I can think about is getting back to my shop. I've got gimbals to make, and guns to mount."

"I know," Eric said.

They walked to the house and went into the living room. Kim was working on wiring behind the TV set. She smiled when Eric came in.

"Hey, sweetie," she said. "Got most of it done. How we gonna do the call? Do we have to use a phone?"

"Probably," Eric said. "We aren't set up very well for this."

"I might be able to run it through the laptop, if it's got good enough speakers," Curt said. "Gonna have to gather around it pretty close, though, in order for the microphone to pick up."

"I was thinking we put the laptop on a table in front of the TV, down low," Eric said, "and run the video to the TV screen for people who aren't close enough. We'll have to move up to speak, of course. It'll be a pain, but doable."

"How about the folks at Fort Stockton?" Kim asked.

"They'll have an easier time," Curt said. "They've got a pretty good set up in the clubhouse there. They can tie things into the PA system, and they've got real microphones."

Don walked in with Chance, Dirk, and Francis. "Know where the girls are?" Don asked.

"I think they're in the front bedroom," Kim said. "Everything okay?"

"Yeah, just nervous, that's all. I don't want them running around the countryside."

"Need any help?" Francis asked.

"We got it," Eric said. "It'll be a little crude."

"I got some powered speakers in my trailer," Dirk said. "You want them? They'll plug into the headphone jack of the laptop."

"Yeah, that'd be good," Eric said.

"I'll go get them," Dirk said. He left the room, Chance following him out the door.

"You invite the Merchant girls?" Don asked.

Eric turned to him and smiled. "Yeah. I think Sydney likes you."

"Don't say that too loud," Don said quietly. "Don't want to worry my daughter. And besides, probably nothing will happen."

"Yeah, that's what I thought," Eric said. "Then *this* happened." He nodded at Kim. She noticed.

"Hey, I'm a *this* now?" she said. "Brother."

Eric pulled her into his arms and kissed her. "I guess you're a little more than that."

She melted into him. "Don't get me started."

"Knock it off, you two," Curt said.

Eric laughed. "Yeah, I'll remember you said that when Amanda hog-ties you."

"Never happen, pencil neck," Curt said.

Kim looked at Eric and snickered. "He has no idea, does he?"

"No idea about what?" Curt asked.

"No idea about life during wartime," Eric said. "You'll end up with something like *this*." He nodded to Kim, and she punched him in the arm.

"Stop it with that," she said.

"I'm just messing with you," Eric said.

"Winning him over was like pulling teeth," Kim said. "Don't make it that hard on Amanda."

Curt shook his head. "You women think you got it all figured out, don't you?"

"Yeah, as a matter of fact." Kim giggled. "Deny it all you want. It's futile."

"I'm going to check on the girls," Don said. He went to the bedroom and knocked.

"Who is it?" Alyssa asked.

"Dad," he said.

"Come in," Alyssa said. Don slipped through the door.

"Sydney's gonna go after him," Eric whispered to Kim.

"Really?"

"Yeah, you should have seen the sparks fly."

"How do you feel about that?" Kim asked.

"I think it would be great for both of them, but let's not tease him, okay?"

"Agreed," Kim said. "Because of Alyssa, right?"

"And because of Chloe too," Eric said. "They need to feel safe and stable. We don't want to stir the pot."

Dirk and Chance walked in with the speakers and cable.

"Here you go," Dirk said, setting them next to the laptop on the table. "Has a sub-woofer but I took it off. All the bass will just cause a hum."

"Good thinking," Curt said. They finished the setup.

"Francis? You in here?" asked Sherry.

"Yeah, honey, I'm here," Francis said, getting up to walk to her. "What's up?"

"Just wanted to know where you were," she said. "When's this meeting happening?"

"Pretty soon," he said. "We're almost ready."

"We really gonna let Chloe and Alyssa in the room?"

"You don't think we should?" Francis asked.

"I don't want them to be scared," she said. "It's up to Don, though."

"He's in the bedroom with them now," Francis said. "Go talk with them if you want."

She thought about it for a moment. "No, I'll let them have time with their dad. I don't need to be butting in. He'll know what to do."

"Good. I agree," Francis said.

Eric's phone rang. He looked at the number. "This should be it." He answered the phone, walking out into the kitchen for some quiet. After a moment he stuck his head out. "Who has paper and pencil? I need to jot down some codes."

"I've got some in our trailer," Sherry said. "Know right where it is. Be back in a sec."

She rushed out, Francis following her. They were back in less than a minute.

"Thanks," Eric said as he took them to the kitchen counter. "Go ahead." He listened and jotted down numbers. "Okay, we'll be on in a few minutes. Thanks."

"Got the codes?" Kim asked as Eric walked over.

"Yep," he said. "I'll read them off to you. The site is already up on the browser. Just maximize it."

"Okay," she said, sitting in front of the laptop. Eric read the codes off and she typed them in, then hit the submit button. The progress bar showed on the screen as the node logged into the meeting.

"Bingo," Eric said, looking over her shoulder.

"This laptop camera isn't going to show everybody," Kim said.

"That's okay, it's not important," Dirk said.

"Turn the sound up," Chance said. Kim nodded and dragged the bar on the sound icon. A buzz came through the speakers. Then there was a click.

"Who's there?" a voice asked.

"You got the Fredericksburg location," Eric said close to the microphone. "Who's this?"

"We're in the media room at the Governor's Mansion in Austin," the man said. "I'm Brian, the Governor's secretary. The Governor, Chief Ramsey, Major General Gallagher, and Major General Landry will be on in a moment, along with some members of the Texas Legislature."

"Great, thanks," Eric said. "This is Eric Finley speaking."

There was a click, and more noise came over the speaker.

"Who just joined?" Brian asked.

"Fort Stockton," Jason's voice said.

"Hey, brother," Eric said.

"Oh, good, you guys are on," Jason said. "Everything going all right there?"

"So far so good," Eric said. "Never had an attack."

"Hey, pencil neck," Curt said.

A few people from Fort Stockton laughed.

"You need to come up with something new, Curt," Kyle said.

"Seriously," Kelly said.

Junior snickered. "Call me anything but late to dinner."

"Oh brother," Brenda said.

"How many people are there?" Kim asked.

"We got about forty people in the clubhouse," Jason said.

"Here comes the video feed," Curt said. The screen broke into three sections. The laptop video feed from the Homestead was in the upper right-hand corner, and Fort Stockton's much clearer picture in the upper left-hand corner. The media room in Austin was sharp across the bottom half of the screen. Only Brian was visible, making adjustments to the video camera and checking settings on his PC.

"How secure is this meeting?" Curt asked.

"Extremely," Brian said. "Don't worry."

Don came out of the bedroom with Chloe and Alyssa. "Mind if they sit in?"

"It might be a little scary," Sherry said. "Can you two handle it?"

"Yeah," Alyssa said. "Dad told us about it. We have to be grown-ups."

Chloe nodded in agreement, and the three of them sat on some of the extra chairs that were brought in.

"Hello?" said a woman's voice from the kitchen door.

"Probably the Merchant girls," Eric said.

"Come on in," Sherry said, getting up to greet them. Amanda and Sydney came in. "I'm Sherry. Francis is my husband."

"Oh, yeah, we met him earlier. I'm Sydney. This is Amanda."

"Good to meet you," Amanda said.

"I'll do a quick intro," Sherry said. "The conference call is just starting up."

They went into the living room.

"Everybody, this is Amanda and Sydney," Sherry said. She went through the names of everybody, and they found seats, Amanda plopping herself right next to Curt.

"Hi there," she said. "Mind if I sit here?"

Curt smiled at her. "Not at all."

"Look, there's the Governor," Francis said, pointing to the screen.

"Yeah, and that's Gallagher," Curt said. "Met him once, back in the old days."

"Chief Ramsey," Eric said. "Notice how tired all these guys look?"

"Seriously," Kelly said from Fort Stockton.

"Who's that other general?" Junior asked.

"Major General Landry," Brian said. "Head of the Texas Air National Guard."

"Commissioner Holly and Kip Hendrix?" Curt whispered. "The opposition."

"They've changed their views lately," Eric whispered. "They're on our side, don't you worry."

Curt rolled his eyes.

"You know all these folks?" Amanda asked, slipping a little closer to Curt.

"Yeah," he said. "Army days, and police departments."

"You're a cop?" she asked.

"Used to be," Curt said. "Punched out my CO before this war started, so I'm a free agent now."

"Good," Amanda whispered, getting closer. "Wouldn't want you to bust me."

"Bust you for what?" Curt whispered. She moved closer and whispered in his ear.

"Shine. We got a nice operation going."

Curt laughed out loud.

"What?" she asked.

"I'll have to let you try some of *my* stuff. Brought what was left of it here along with the weapons and ammo."

"I'm starting to like you," Amanda said, moving even closer.

"You're going to end up on my lap at this rate," he whispered to her.

She giggled. "Later."

Eric glanced at Kim. "You seeing this?"

"Yeah," Kim said. "Amanda is all over him. Wow."

"Curt doesn't mind, either," Eric said.

"Everybody here?" Governor Nelson asked.

"We're all on in Fort Stockton," Jason said.

"Same here at Fredericksburg," Eric said.

"Good, let's get started," Nelson said. "First of all, let me thank you for your patriotic and extremely effective actions up to now. Kudos. Texas will remember you."

There was silence for a moment, as Nelson gathered his thoughts.

"There's been a new development, and it's going to put more pressure on the people of Texas. A major incursion is going on in Arizona, Colorado, and Utah. The US Army assets we had are being moved there. We have to develop and deploy a citizen force to take up the slack."

"They taking the hardware with them?" Curt asked.

"No, this is mainly personnel, which is even worse," Major General Gallagher said. "We're losing General Walker, General Hogan, and their entire staff."

"I don't like the sound of that," Jason said.

"None of us are happy about it," Major General Landry said. "We *are* blessed with a strong and well-armed population, though, which puts us ahead of the game compared to most states."

"What's happening in the rest of the state now?" Curt asked.

"San Antonio has been re-taken," Gallagher said, "but you already knew that. There's terror attacks going on daily in the Dallas/Fort Worth and Houston areas, mostly in the suburbs. The Houston invasion has stalled. That's probably the best news I've got."

"How about Austin?" Eric asked.

"Thanks to you guys, we've put them down here," Gallagher said. "I don't know who came up with the idea for that supply depot attack, but it was a total game changer in central Texas."

"It also put a huge target on your backs," Chief Ramsey said.

"Yeah, we figured," Kelly said. "So what now?"

"We want your group to be the core of the citizen forces in central Texas," Nelson said. "We want you to work with Gallagher and Landry to build yourselves up. We'll help you with equipment and air support."

"And intel," Gallagher said. "Before we get too far, we need to chat about the Fredericksburg location."

"Uh oh," Eric said.

"Yeah, *uh oh,*" Gallagher said. "The enemy is collecting near Cain. We've hit them with choppers twice now. They keep sending more people into your general area. The only target worth anything to them is you guys. We need you to get out of that area. Fast. Right after this call, if you can."

"Dammit," Eric said. "I was afraid of that."

"Can they come here to Fort Stockton?" Jason asked.

"That's what I suggest," Gallagher said.

"This place is kinda exposed," Kelly said. "We were actually thinking of relocating to the homestead."

"That location seems very exposed because it's so close to I-10," Landry said. "There aren't good places for the enemy to hide in that area; no places where the enemy can gather in numbers large enough to take you on, especially with those tanks you have. We think you're safer there."

"What if they send a column of tanks down I-10?" Junior asked. "That's what I worry about the most."

"We're patrolling that corridor with aircraft now," Landry said. "We'll take them out."

"How do we know your resources won't be pulled away to help in Dallas or Houston?" Jason asked.

"Don't worry about that," Nelson said. "You guys are extremely important, and we want to increase the size of your force. There's other groups like you all over Texas. We need to get you linked up."

Amanda glanced at Sydney, both of them worried.

"You okay?" Curt asked.

"Hey, Ramsey, you gonna have a problem if I move certain manufacturing assets when we leave?" Amanda asked.

Ramsey chuckled.

"What's she talking about?" Nelson asked.

"She's running the largest bootleg outfit in central Texas," Ramsey said.

"Bootleg?" Nelson asked.

"White lighting," Ramsey said.

"Wait a minute," Gallagher said. "What kind of output can you provide?"

"A lot, if I can take all my stuff," Amanda said. "You guys aren't going to burn me when this is over, right?"

"No," Nelson said. "What do you have in mind, Gallagher?"

"The biggest weakness with the M-1 Tank is the fuel requirement," Gallagher said. "Those turbine engines will run on what she manufactures."

Curt laughed out loud. "Now we're talking."

Amanda looked at him, then back at the screen. "I have a bobtail delivery truck. Pretty sure I can fit all the equipment in it, if I have some help dismantling everything and loading it up."

"I'm there," Curt said.

"Count me in too," Dirk said.

"Yeah," Chance said.

"That sounds good," Gallagher said. "I wouldn't hold the whole population out there on that task, though. A few of you work on moving the distilling equipment. The rest of you need to get out fast. Within the next couple of hours."

"We're really in that much danger?" Eric asked.

"Yeah," Gallagher said. "Unlike Fort Stockton, there's a lot of places for the enemy to hide around Fredericksburg, and we can't use air power there without causing a lot of collateral damage."

"Your truck have a trailer hitch?" Curt whispered to Amanda.

"Yeah, why?"

"I'll need to drag my Barracuda home," he said.

"What's a Barracuda?" she asked.

"One heavily armed off-roader," Curt said. "It's got one of the automatic grenade launchers mounted on it."

"Cool," she whispered back.

"We going into any tactical discussions in this meeting, or should we start getting ready to leave now?" Kim asked.

"Does Fort Stockton have enough room for everybody in Fredericksburg?" Ramsey asked.

"How many coaches we talking about?" Moe asked.

"Only a couple," Eric said. "We'll need space for tents."

"Yeah, some of you already have RVs at Fort Stockton," Jason said.

"True," Curt said. "I need to get back to my workshop."

"Workshop?" Amanda asked.

"I got a 3-D printer and some machine tools in the back of my toy hauler," he said.

"I'd rather not get hung up talking about next steps in this meeting," Nelson said. "You guys got the lay of the land. I say we end the call and get moving."

"I agree," Gallagher said.

"Anybody else have anything?" Ramsey asked.

There was silence in both locations.

"Okay, then we'll talk later," Nelson said. "Thanks, and God Speed."

The video feed stopped. Kim closed the connection on the laptop.

"Well damn," Dirk said. "Let's get busy."

"Yeah," Eric said.

Sydney rushed over to Amanda. "You okay with this?"

"Yeah," she said. "I think I can hang out with this character for a while." She nodded at Curt. He glanced back at her, eyes lingering.

"I'm surprised you didn't climb onto his lap," Sydney said.

"I saw you and Don making eyes at each other," Amanda said. "So don't give me any crap."

Curt stood, shaking his head. "Let's get busy." He held a hand down to Amanda she took it and stood next to him.

Don came over to Sydney. "You're going, aren't you?"

"Do you want me to?" she whispered.

"Yes," he said.

"Good," she said.

"I need to help my daughter and her friend get packed," Don said. "You need a way there?"

"I may be here longer, getting our equipment loaded. Don't wait around for me. Protect your girls."

"Okay," Don said.

Amanda followed Curt out to the barn. "There it is," Curt said, as he pointed to the Barracuda.

"Lord have mercy," she said, looking at the grenade launcher. "That thing works?"

"Like a dream," he said. "Want a ride to your place? It seats two."

"Let me check with Sydney first, okay?"

"Okay," he said. He looked her up and down, taking in her curvy figure as she walked away. She turned around and snickered.

"Caught you."

He just smiled at her as she kept walking.

{ 20 }

Doctor's Call

Hendrix drove through his gate and around to his garage, hitting the opener. It was almost seven in the evening. The conference call and meetings afterwards took longer than anybody expected. *Maria's not home yet.* He sat in his car, mind racing to all the bad things that might have happened. Then he pulled out his phone and called her.

"Hey," she said.

"Hey," Hendrix said. "Where are you? I just got home."

"I'm still at the hospital, waiting for the panel to decide if Celia has to stay or not. They're taking a long time."

"Want me to come down there and wait with you?"

"No, sweetie, that's okay. I'll see you in a little while. She won't be getting out tonight. It'll be tomorrow if they allow it."

"So why do you have to wait?" he asked.

"They might have questions," she said. "The doctor asked me to stick around. They should be done pretty soon. Want me to pick up something on the way home?"

"To eat?" he asked.

"Yeah," she said.

"Sure, go ahead," Hendrix said. "Or if you want to go out, we can meet somewhere."

"I want to come home and be alone with you," Maria said. "If you don't mind."

"I'm counting the minutes," he said. "Love you."

"Love you too. What do you want to eat?"

"Surprise me," he said. "I'm good with anything. They fed us between meetings, so I'm not desperate."

"Okay," she said. "See you soon. Don't worry, all right?"

"I won't," Hendrix said.

"Bye."

Hendrix went inside his house and headed for the kitchen. Then he paused and made a detour to the bar in the living room. He poured himself a shot of Jameson and threw it back, then sat on the couch and turned on the TV. He was asleep in minutes.

Maria made it home just after nine, setting a bag of Chinese food on the counter. "Kip?" she called out. She heard nothing but the TV, then walked into the living room and found him asleep on the couch.

"Kip?" she said above him. "Kip."

He startled awake, fear in his eyes until he saw her pretty face smiling at him.

"Oh, sorry," she said.

"Man, I was really out," Hendrix said. "Busy dreams, too."

"Bad dreams?" she asked, sitting next to him.

"Yeah, kinda," he said.

"About us?"

He chuckled. "No, about ancient history. What happened with your sister?"

"They decided to wait a week and talk again," Maria said. "Hungry yet?"

"Yeah," he said, getting up.

"I got Chinese. Hope that's okay."

"Perfect," Hendrix said. "That's better than the comfort food I ate all day today."

"That's what I figured," she said. He moaned as she stretched up to grab plates from the cupboard, showing her figure.

"That blue dress really gets to me," he said, coming up behind her, his arms going around her waist.

She turned and kissed him gently. "Let's eat first. Then you can have your dessert."

He grinned and let her go, watching her put the plates on the kitchen table.

"Grab the food bags, okay?" she asked.

Hendrix nodded, picking them up off the counter and putting then on the table. Maria got the white cardboard boxes out one by one and opened them.

"Smells good," Hendrix said.

"Hope it's okay. The place I used to go to is by my apartment. It's probably gone, judging by what we saw yesterday."

"Which place did you get this from?" Hendrix asked.

"Louis's Garden," she said.

"Oh, I know that place. It's one of the best ones around here."

"Good," she said as she dished the food out. Hendrix sat next to her.

"So what was the deal with Celia? They tell you?"

"It's embarrassing," Maria said.

"Sorry, you don't have to tell me."

"No, you need to know," she said. "Celia tried to come on to one of the attendants. Had his pants all the way off before the other attendants saw it on the monitors."

"Oh," Hendrix said. "I'm surprised they're going to reconvene in a week, then."

"The doctor told me it would have been more like six months if she was a male."

"Well, being a danger to others is considered more of a risk than being a danger to yourself, I guess," Hendrix said.

"What makes you think she's not a danger to others?" Maria asked. "She could ruin somebody's life. It's not always just about physical danger."

"Good point." He took a bite of food. "Excellent."

"Yeah," Maria said. "I was hungry. All I got was snacks from the machines at the hospital."

"You look worried," Hendrix said.

"I think it's risky to bring Celia here, but I don't know what else to do."

"Risky?"

"Of course," Maria said. "She'll go after you."

Hendrix leaned back in his chair as he finished a mouthful of food, then looked at her. "They'll keep her there if she's still showing that behavior. I wouldn't worry too much."

Maria sighed. "I wasn't going to go into this, but I'd better now."

"Uh oh," Hendrix said.

"My mom didn't just kick Celia out because of the substance abuse or the depression-related issues," Maria said.

"Oh," Hendrix said. "You don't have to tell me if you don't want to. I see the worry written all over your face."

"No, I need to tell you this, especially if there's a chance she ends up here for a while."

"All right, go ahead," Hendrix said.

"Mom caught her screwing her boyfriend," Maria said.

"No, really?" Hendrix asked. His mind flashed to Cami but he pushed it back.

"That's why I'm worried. She was doing those behaviors before she had her breakdown."

"Did you tell the doctor about that?"

"Of course," Maria said. "I think we should arrange for her to go to a halfway house instead of coming to live with us."

"Well, sweetie, it's your family, so I'll go along with whatever you decide," he said.

"What if she comes onto you?" Maria asked.

"You think I'll go for it?"

"Not on purpose," she said.

Hendrix chuckled. "I do have *some* self-control, you know."

"You don't know her. She can be every man's wet dream."

Hendrix stopped eating and leaned towards her. "How about this. If we can't get her into a halfway house, let's just make sure that you're always here when I am. Then she can't do anything."

Maria thought about it for a moment. "That would probably work, but my first choice is to have her someplace else. Things could go wrong."

"We've got at least a week to think it through," Hendrix said. "Don't be too worried about it. We'll handle it if we need to, okay?"

"Okay," she said. "I'm done. You want any more?"

"No thanks, sweetie," he said.

"What happened in the meeting today? Can you tell me?"

"Sure," he said. "Let's clean this up first, and sit on the couch."

"Okay," she said.

"Ready?" Hendrix asked, settling next to her on the couch.

"Uh huh," she said, leaning into him, her hand on his chest.

"We're losing the two generals from the US Army. And their staffs too."

"That doesn't sound good," Maria said.

"It's not," Hendrix said. "The Texas National Guard forces are too thin. I've never seen Nelson so worried."

"So what are we gonna do?"

"Recruit citizens to join in the fight," Hendrix said.

"Like a draft?"

"No, more like a group of local militias," Hendrix said. "I don't think we have any choice now, but I don't like it."

"Why? You don't think they can handle it?" Maria asked.

"Oh, I think they can beat the enemy, although it will be a very bloody affair."

"So what are you worried about?" she asked.

"I'm afraid of what happens after the war," Hendrix said. "By the time we get there, we'll have thousands of people who served this way. Anything could happen. What if some bad actors take control of these forces?"

"Oh," she said. "I get it."

"At least Austin is fairly safe now, and we're moving the last of the vigilante group to Fort Stockton, which will reduce enemy presence here even more."

"Where are the enemy fighters now?"

"Some are still around San Antonio, although they're just about defeated there. There's still a big problem in Houston, Dallas, and Waco. The biggest problem is New Mexico."

"New Mexico?"

"Yeah," Hendrix said. "The state government there has lost control of the southern border completely, and the Feds won't help them." He sat silently for a moment, grinding his teeth.

"What's wrong?"

"You can't mention this to anybody. We're playing a game with the Feds on this right now. I made them think that Nelson is planning on annexing New Mexico."

"Oh, that's what the conversation was about with the Attorney General's office today?"

"Yep," Hendrix said. "No turning back now. If Nelson and the other Texas leadership gets prosecuted by the Feds after this mess is over, I'll probably go down with them."

"Is it likely?"

Hendrix sat silently for a moment, then sighed. "Probably not. I think the Administration is going to be exposed, and Nelson will turn out looking like a hero."

"Is that bad?"

"Well, depends on how you look at it," Hendrix said. "I'm in *Texas Patriot* mode for now, and I'm glad to be in that camp. Later we'll have a mess."

"What kind of mess?" Maria asked.

"The Progressive Movement will have a setback that will last for years," Hendrix said. "Regardless of what side you fall on, it's not good to have no opposition."

"Oh," she said. "Can you do anything about it?"

"No, not really," he said. "Protecting Texas is the priority now."

"I think I'm ready to go to bed," Maria said.

"Tired already?" he asked.

"No," she said, getting up and extending her hand. "Dessert, remember?"

He smiled and got up.

Exodus

Curt stood next to Amanda and Sydney, looking at the still. "Wow," he said.

"This all gonna fit in one truck?" Dirk asked. "We've got the pickup, but it's full of weapons right now."

"I think we can get all the important stuff to fit," Amanda said.

"Hear that?" Sydney asked. The sound of engines drifted down the road.

"I hear it," Dirk said. "Probably our folks leaving."

"Let's go check," Chance said.

Curt pulled out his phone and looked for enemy hits. "Don't see any enemy phones, but still a good idea to check," Curt said. "We gotta remember that they're wise to us. I'll help the ladies in here until you get back."

"Why did you look at your phone?" Amanda asked.

"He figured out how to track them by their phones," Dirk said. "We got the drop on the enemy more than once that way." He left with Chance.

"I'll back the truck up to the door," Sydney said. She rushed outside.

"Alone at last," Amanda said, smiling at Curt. "C'mon, we got to take these evaporators apart." She led him to the work bench. They grabbed two cordless drills off the chargers sitting there. Amanda opened a metal cabinet next to the workbench and picked up a caddy full of bits. "Let's go."

"Nice setup," Curt said, looking around. "Too bad we have to leave here."

"We'll be back," Amanda said. "Help me with this first one."

They got to work. Sydney backed the truck up to the door, then got out, unlatched the roll-up door, and pushed it up. Curt turned and looked.

"Damn, that's a big truck. We'll get all this stuff in there."

"I think so," Amanda said.

Dirk and Chance came back in. "That was our folks leaving," Dirk said.

"All of them?" Curt asked.

"Don't know," Chance said. "Both trailers went by. I doubt if all the bikers are gone yet, but they were in tents, so they had to break camp."

"Where we going again?" Sydney asked as she walked in.

"Fort Stockton," Curt said. "Not a bad place, actually."

"It ain't home, but it'll have to do for a while." Amanda said.

"Should take about three and a half hours to get there," Curt said

They continued working, as quickly as they could. It took just under two hours to get everything dismantled and moved.

"Ready to go?" Dirk asked.

"I think so," Amanda said.

"You riding with us, Curt?" Chance asked.

"Naw, I'm going to ride in the Barracuda," he said.

"While I'm towing it?" Amanda asked. "Ain't that illegal?"

"Yeah," Curt said. "Don't care. Anybody who comes up behind us is gonna have a real bad day."

Amanda grinned. "Okay, I'm sold. Let's get her hooked up and blow this joint."

"I'm gonna go lock things down at the house. You want anything from there?"

"Yeah, grab the duffel bag on my bed," she said.

Sydney rushed out of the barn. Dirk and Chance left, climbing into the truck. "We'll get past the switchbacks and wait for you guys," Dirk said.

"Roger that," Curt said.

Amanda watched them leave, then walked up to Curt, stopping to look up at his face. She got on her tiptoes and put her arms around his neck, pulling herself up and locking her legs around his waist.

"What are you doing?" Curt asked, heart fluttering.

She kissed him, hard and long, then pulled back and looked at his face with a shy grin, legs still locked around him.

"What was that for?" Curt asked.

"I wanted to know if it would curl my toes," she said.

"Amanda!" Sydney said as she came out. "Get off him. We need to go."

She slipped back onto the ground. "All right, all right. We're about ready anyway."

"Well?" Curt asked. "Did it work?"

She turned to look at him. "I'll let you know later." Then she looked at Sydney and they both giggled. Curt shook his head.

Sydney pulled the truck forward. Curt hooked the Barracuda up and got into the seat, turned on the engine, and used the sight to swing the gimbal around, pointing the M-19 towards the rear. Then he shut off the engine and strapped in.

"Ready?" Amanda asked.

"I'm good," Curt said.

"I'll lock up the barn," Sydney said. Curt watched as she did that and scurried towards the cab of the truck. Amanda started the truck and drove out of the driveway.

Curt's mind was spinning as he watched the scenery of the woods going by. *Is she for real?*

The truck slowed as they made it to the switchbacks, taking them carefully. Curt felt his palms sweat on the steering wheel as they went close to the edge. It took about five minutes to get back onto the flat part of the road. The truck stopped.

"Hey, Curt, come here a sec," Amanda called out the cab window.

He unbuckled and rushed up to the cab. Dirk and Chance were standing next to the pickup. "What's up?"

"You want us in front of the bobtail or behind?" Chance asked. "To guard the rear."

"Front," Curt said. "I'll cover the back door with the M-19."

"Okay, just making sure," Chance said. "We'll keep within eyesight of you guys."

"Good idea," Curt said. Amanda nodded in agreement and they took off.

Up in the cab, Amanda and Sydney watched the road ahead of them in silence. Both of them relaxed when they got onto Route 290.

"We should be fine now, if the Air National Guard is really out there," Sydney said.

"Hope so," Amanda said. "You got the handguns in the cab, right?"

"Yeah, in the glove box," she said. "Loaded, so be careful if you have to grab one. I hope we're doing the right thing."

"I don't see any choice," Amanda said. "Besides, I saw you and Don looking at each other. You've got him interested. Real interested."

"He's got those two girls," Sydney said. "Might make romance a little difficult."

"But you like him, don't you?"

Sydney looked at her, shaking her head as she let out a sigh. "I don't even know him yet."

"You like what you see," Amanda said. "I can tell."

"Okay, I'll admit that," Sydney said. "You believe Ramsey and Nelson? About our business?"

"Yeah," Amanda said. "At least as long as they need us."

"What was that between you and Curt when I walked in? Did he start it or did you?"

Amanda chuckled. "I did. Wanted to see what he kissed like."

"Well?"

Amanda laughed. "Why should I tell you about that?"

"I didn't hold back about Don," she said. "Just want to know what to expect, that's all."

"Fair enough, sister," Amanda said. "If that kiss would've lasted much longer, I would have been pulling his clothes off."

"You're so bad," Sydney said. "He likes your body, that's for sure. Saw him checking you out a few times. Especially your butt."

"Good," she said. "I saw Don checking you out too."

"No you didn't," she said.

"Oh yes I did," Amanda said, "but then you always were the pretty one. Most guys check you out."

"Like they don't check you out," Sydney said. "Please."

They rode silently for a while, each in their own heads.

"Why isn't there any traffic on 290?" Amanda asked. "This is light even with all the crap going on." Sydney was ignoring her, looking out her side window.

"Hey, I'm talking to you," Amanda said. Sydney opened the glove box and pulled out her .45 auto. "Oh shit, you see something?"

"Yeah," Sydney said. "Two trucks, sitting there watching the road from 441."

"Dammit," Amanda said. "What're they doing?"

"Looks like they're getting on behind us," Sydney said. "Look, Chance saw them too. He just pulled a rifle out from behind the seat in the truck."

Robert Boren

"What should I do?" Amanda asked.

"Keep driving," Sydney said. "Don't stop for anything."

"Hand me the other piece," Amanda said.

"I'll put it on the seat next to you," Sydney said as she pulled it out of the glove box.

Suddenly there was an explosion behind them, then other.

"Whoa!" Amanda said. "Truck on fire behind us, heading for the ditch."

"Where's the other truck?" Sydney asked, eyes wide.

"Still coming."

"Dirk's turning around," Sydney said.

There was another explosion in back.

"Holy crap, that second truck just lifted off the ground about five feet!" Amanda said, looking at Sydney with glee.

"Should we stop for a sec? Make sure Curt's okay?" Sydney asked.

"Yeah," she said, slowing the truck. She pulled over to the side and they got out. Dirk rolled up alongside them.

"Don't see any others back there," he said.

Amanda ran to the back of the truck. "You okay?" she asked.

Curt grinned at her. "I'm a lot better than those Islamist slugs are."

Amanda chuckled. "You're just full of surprises, aren't you?"

"Amanda, let's go before somebody else shows up," Sydney yelled. "You can make time with him later."

Amanda looked Curt in the eye. "Yeah, I suppose I can." She winked at him and went back to the cab. They were rolling down the road again in a few seconds.

{ 22 }

Almost

They were still breathing hard, in the afterglow of their passion.

"You ready to get dressed now?" Madison asked, laying on her side, propped up by her elbow as Juan Carlos looked at her.

"Yeah, I guess we got most of it out of our system," he said. "For at least a little while."

"You're going to wear me out," Madison said, face still flushed. "I think I was almost as loud as Hannah during that last one."

"Yeah, I loved it," he said. "I'd better not think about that, or we'll never get out of here."

Madison giggled and got out of bed. "You like our place?"

"As long as you're in it, yes," he said, getting up.

Madison put on her bra and panties. "You think they're really going to go through with it?"

"What?"

"Richardson and Lita, silly," she said. "You think they're really getting married this afternoon?"

Juan Carlos sat on the bench against the wall and tied his shoes, then looked up at her. "I know he's really into Lita. Can't say that I blame him. She's really nice."

"She is," Madison said. "We might need to go with them and be witnesses."

"Sure that's a good idea?" Juan Carlos asked.

"What are you talking about?" she asked.

"We *will* be in front of a preacher. You might get ideas and twist my arm."

Madison looked at him and laughed, face turning red. "Oh, please."

"Well, you do love me," Juan Carlos. "You admitted it."

"So did you," Madison said. "Two can play this game. How do you know I'd be the one twisting an arm? You men are so sentimental. Gets sickening sometimes."

He looked at her as she checked out her outfit in the mirror with her back towards him. When she turned, she froze.

"What's the matter?" he asked.

"You're looking at me like *that* again."

"Like what?" he asked.

"Shit," she said. "You would, wouldn't you?"

"I don't know what you're talking about."

"Forget it," she said. "We need to get to know each other at least a little bit. All we've done so far is try to stay alive, and pleasure each other."

"Don't worry," he said. "Ready to go?"

"Okay," she said. "Can I have a hug first?"

He pulled her to himself silently and held her tight, feeling her tremble against him. Then he pulled back from her and studied her face.

"Quit looking at me like that," she said softly.

"No. We already know we're in love. Just go with it." He kissed her hard.

"Oh, God," she said when they broke it. "I feel out of control."

"But happy," he said. "I can see it on your face."

"Yes," she said softly, then smiled at him. "Don't get any ideas over there. I mean it. I might not be strong enough to resist."

"We'll see," Juan Carlos said. He chuckled as she punched him in the arm.

They went out the door, walking towards the unit they all started at. Lita and Richardson were leaning against the SUV waiting for them.

"Are we late?" Madison asked.

"No, we're just anxious," Lita said. "Seen Hannah and Brendan?"

"We're coming," Hannah called out. They all turned to see them walking over hand in hand.

"Well, would you look at that," Madison said. "Have a good time? You two have that look."

"What look?" Hannah asked.

"Stop!" Lita said. "Don't say it."

"Let's go," Richardson said. "You guys can be witnesses."

They all climbed into the SUV, and Richardson drove towards the gate.

"Well," Lita said, "did you find yourselves nice units?"

"Yeah," Hannah said.

"Same here," Madison said. "You ended up in the one we started at, didn't you?"

"Yeah," Lita said. "I liked the colors."

"Good," Madison said. "We're two rows over. Space 166."

"We're all the way in the back," Hannah said. "Space 395."

"We know why," Madison said.

"Shut up," Hannah said.

Madison laughed.

"Now, now, let's be nice, ladies," Richardson said.

Lita looked at him and snickered. "Take a right at the next light."

"Got it," Richardson said.

"Nervous?"

"No, happy," Richardson said. "You?"

"Can't believe it's finally happening," she said. "Took me a long time to trap you."

Richardson laughed. "Yeah, like *that's* what happened." His phone rang. He pulled it out. "Dammit, it's Captain Jefferson."

"No," Lita said.

"I'm gonna pull over and take it." He answered the call as he parked on the side of the road.

"What's up, Captain?"

"We need you at the base right away," Jefferson said. "Sorry. Large group of boats were spotted going past the opening to Baffin Bay. Looks like they're on the way to Corpus Christi. We need to nail them before they get there. How quickly can you report in?"

"Ten minutes or so," he said. "I'll have to drop the girls off at the trailer park on the way."

"See you soon," Jefferson said.

Richardson ended the call.

"He needs you at the base?" Lita asked.

"Sorry, sweetheart. Corpus Christi is about to come under attack. We need to go help."

"Oh no," Hannah said.

"Don't worry, we'll be okay," Brendan said.

"Easy for you guys to say," Madison said, her eyes glistening with tears.

Richardson turned the SUV around and drove back to the Trailer Park.

"Just drop us off at the gate," Lita said. "You girls got the keys to your trailers?"

"Yeah," Hannah said. Madison nodded.

"We'll be back in no time," Juan Carlos said, touching Madison's face.

"You'd better be," she said, moving closer to him. "I love you so."

"I know, I love you too," Juan Carlos said.

Richardson pulled to the side of the front gate, and everybody got out.

"You'd better come back," Hannah said.

"I love you," Brendan told her.

She glanced at Madison, then shrugged. "I love you too. Please be careful."

The men got back into the SUV and Richardson took off, tires squealing.

"This is what I was afraid of," Hannah said.

"I know," Madison said. "You guys finally broke through, didn't you? I heard what you said."

She flashed an embarrassed smile, then caught Lita out of the corner of her eye. She was crying.

"Oh, honey, I'm so sorry," Hannah said, rushing to her side.

Madison joined her. "He'll be back, and then you'll get married."

"I know," she said. "I'm just scared."

"How can we not be?" Hannah asked.

"Want to come to my place for a while?" Lita asked. "I noticed some coffee in the cupboard."

"Yeah, we shouldn't be alone right now," Hannah said.

"I agree," Madison said. They walked to the trailer and entered. Lita plugged in the coffee maker and got down a box of Keurig pods. "Regular or decaf?"

"Hit me with the real stuff," Hannah said.

"Me too," Madison said.

They watched quietly as Lita made the coffees.

"Somebody say something," Lita said. "It's too quiet in here."

"Did you really fall for Brendan, or were you just saying that to him?" Madison asked Hannah.

Lita snickered.

"What's so funny?" Hannah asked.

"That boy had you from the first night," Lita said.

Hannah looked back at her, tears filling her eyes.

"I'm sorry," Lita said, rushing to her.

"No, it's okay," she said. "You're right, he did. I tried to slow it down, because of this."

"I know, me too," Madison said. "This is really hard. We're going to be scared to death every time they leave."

"They're pretty good at taking care of themselves," Lita said. "We have to focus on that, and how important their jobs are."

"You already sound like a military wife," Madison said.

"You have a funny look on your face," Hannah said. Madison turned red.

"Out with it," Lita said.

"Oh, nothing," she said. "I think Juan Carlos might try to get me to marry him."

"Wouldn't surprise me at all to see you two married someday," Lita said.

"No, I mean when we're there for your wedding," she said in a hushed tone.

"Oh," Lita said. "How do you feel about that?"

"I told him he'd better not," she said. "If he does, I might not be able to resist."

"Might not?" Hannah asked.

"What's with the silly grin?" Lita said, looking at Hannah's face.

"Nothing," she said. "Look at us. These men have us all messed up."

"True that," Madison said.

23

Bloody Sedan

J ason, Kyle, Kelly, and Junior ran towards the front gate as Eric's Class C motor home rolled in, pulling his Bronco. Frances was behind him, pulling Dirk's trailer. Then came Don's SUV and the rest of the vehicles in a steady stream, bikers bringing up the rear. They all collected in the big parking area next to the front office. Moe and Clancy came out to greet them as they got out of their vehicles.

"Welcome to Fort Stockton RV Park," Moe said.

"Where's Curt?" Jason asked.

Nate and Fritz trotted up. "What's going on?" Nate asked.

"First group of folks from Fredericksburg," Kyle said. "But no Curt."

"He'll be along in an hour or two," Eric said. "He helped the Merchant sisters with their distilling equipment. They're towing his Barracuda. Dirk and Chance are with them."

Carrie, Kate, Rachel, and Brenda ran up. Carrie had Chelsea in her arms.

"You must be Kim," Carrie said. "Welcome to the family."

Kim left Eric's side and greeted her. "So nice to meet you. What a beautiful daughter." Chelsea looked at her with a coy smile.

"Any problems on the way out?" Junior asked.

"Nope," Eric said. "Smooth sailing. It was hard to leave the homestead behind."

"We'll get back there eventually," Jason said.

"Now, if Chris, Jasper, and Earl would show up," Brenda said, worried look on her face.

"You have people who haven't shown up yet?" Eric asked.

"Brenda's ex, co-owner of Texas Mary's," Kelly said, "and a few of our folks. They had a bad apple with them. Hope nothing happened."

"Bad apple?" Francis asked.

"Simon Orr," Junior said. "That's why we came back early, remember? I've got a really bad feeling about this."

"Me too," Brenda said.

"All, meet the people from Deadwood," Eric said as he saw Don and his girls walk up with Francis and Sherry. He introduced them.

"Nice to meet you," Francis said.

"Yeah, very good to be with you," Don said. His girls looked bewildered.

"You're right about one thing," Eric said. "This is right on top of I-10. I can see it from here."

"Yeah," Junior said. "I hope Landry was right about the Air National Guard."

"I'll feel better when Curt gets that Barracuda back here," Kyle said.

"You've got some pretty good weaponry on your truck," Kelly said.

"I know, but a .50 cal just doesn't have the impact of an M-19," he said.

"Boys and their toys," Brenda said, shaking her head.

Jason's phone rang. He looked at it. "It's Curt," he said, worried look on his face.

"Well answer it," Kyle said.

"Hey, pencil neck," Curt said.

"Curt, where are you guys?"

"Almost to Sheffield, making good time," Curt said. "Should be another hour or so."

"Sounds kinda windy," Jason said.

"I'm in the Barracuda, being towed behind Amanda's bobtail truck."

"Oh," Jason said. "Figures. How do you like her?"

Curt chuckled. "She's like a female version of *me.* The rest of the crew get there?"

"Yeah," Jason said. "We're gathered around them up by the office."

"Good," Curt said. "Keep your eyes open. The enemy knows we left."

"Crap, what happened?"

"Had to waste two truckloads of cretins on the road," Curt said. "Not a problem. They didn't even get a shot off."

"But they might have checked in with their leadership," Jason said. "Dammit."

"I'll let you go. Warn everybody."

"Will do," Jason said. "Be careful." He ended the call.

"Everything okay?" Kelly asked.

"They got attacked on the road," Jason said.

"Shit," Kyle muttered.

"Don't worry, Curt wasted them with the M-19. Amanda's pulling the Barracuda behind her bobtail truck. He's riding in it, like he did when I towed him that time."

"Son of a bitch," Kyle said. "They know we've left, then."

"Yeah, that's why he called," Jason said. "We'd better stay sharp."

"Hell yeah we'd better," Junior said.

"I'll get up on the roof with the binos," Clancy said. "All the tanks manned?"

"Yeah," Gray said. "We're ready."

"Let's get everybody settled," Moe said. "Anybody who needs space, come on into the office and we'll get you taken care of."

"Let's go back," Rachel said, putting her arm around Junior's waist.

"I'm ready," Junior said.

"Hey, Jason, where are you guys?" Eric asked.

He pointed towards the southwest side of the park. "Over there. All the spaces around us are taken, though. You'll be further to the east, I suspect."

"Okay, see you in a while." He took Kim by the hand and followed Moe into the office.

"Hey, who's that?" Clancy yelled, pointing to a smoking, bullet ridden sedan creeping to the gate.

Kelly whirled around and looked. "What the hell? Is that who I think it is?"

Brenda looked. "Oh no, that's Chris!"

Kelly and Brenda rushed over as the dieseling engine stopped with a shudder. Junior noticed and whispered something to Rachel, then trotted over to the car.

"Chris, what happened?" Brenda cried as she got to the car. He looked at her through foggy eyes and then passed out. His sister was in the passenger seat, half of her head blown away.

"Get back, honey," Kelly said, looking at the sister's body. "You don't want to see her."

"Oh my God!" Brenda cried. "No!"

"I'll call the doctor," Clancy shouted from the roof, pulling out his cellphone.

Nate and Fritz rushed over. "Oh shit," Fritz said.

"Where's Jasper and Earl?" Nate asked.

"We don't know," Kelly said. "Hope Chris makes it. He doesn't look good."

"Look, his eyes opened," Junior said.

"Chris," Brenda said, getting closer to him. "What happened?"

"Simon Orr," he said quietly, barely conscious. "Turned Jasper and Earl. Said we could leave, but then followed us." He passed out, his breath shallow and raspy.

"Shit, he ain't gonna make it," Nate said under his breath.

"The doctor will be here in about ten minutes," Clancy called from the roof. "He said not to move him until he gets here."

"Got it, thanks," Kelly shouted up to him.

Eric rushed out when he heard the commotion, Kim by his side.

"Is this who you were waiting for?" he asked.

"Some of them," Junior said. "Two still missing, and the bad guy."

"We'll have to hunt this creep down," Nate said, angry rising in him.

"Maybe we should leave it alone," Fritz said. "If Jasper and Earl are turned, we might have to kill them. Don't think I could."

"Here comes the doctor," Clancy shouted, pointing to the driveway. The car stopped, and a thin middle aged man with balding hair rushed over.

"Out of my way," he cried. Brenda and Kelly moved away from the car.

"Dr. Knudsen," Clancy said. "Thanks for getting here so quickly."

He nodded and got his face inside the window, checking vitals. "This man's been shot in the back and shoulder. Who's the woman?"

"His sister," Kelly said as Brenda watched, tears streaming down her face.

"That was a large caliber weapon," he said, looking at the woman's head wound. "At least she didn't know what hit her. Somebody help me when I open the door. I don't want him falling out."

Kelly, Nate, and Fritz stood by the door as the doctor opened it, hands out to catch Chris. He rolled into their arms.

"Let's carry him into the clubhouse," Doctor Knudsen said.

"Shouldn't we put him on a stretcher?" Brenda asked.

"Won't matter," he said. The men lifted Chris and rushed him in as carefully as they could, laying him on a table.

The doctor ripped Chris's shirt off of him and looked at the wounds. "He's bleeding internally."

"Oh no," Brenda said.

Dr. Knudsen looked at her. "You a relative?"

"Ex-wife and business partner," Brenda said quietly.

"He was our friend," Fritz said. "A very dear friend."

"I'm sorry," Dr. Knudsen said, his hawkish eyes glancing around the room. "You know who did this?"

"He said it was Simon Orr," Kelly said.

"Well, you'd better keep your eyes open, because this didn't happen very far away. He was probably shot less than ten minutes ago."

"We would've heard it, wouldn't we?" Nate asked.

"Don't count on that," Moe said. "The wind around these flatlands will play tricks on you sometimes."

"Another car coming," Clancy shouted from the roof. "Pickup truck."

Kelly and Nate glanced at each other, pulled their pistols, and ran out the door. Junior and Fritz followed them. Brenda collapsed onto a bench, eyes wide with fear and grief.

24

Battle of Baffin Bay

Richardson stopped the car in front of the headquarters building and rushed to the door, Juan Carlos and Brendan on his tail. "What's happening?" he asked.

Captain Jefferson turned and saw them. "Thanks for getting here so fast."

"No problem," Richardson said. "Which boat is ours? Anything we need to know about it before we take off?"

"Yeah," Jefferson said. "There's a tech down there waiting for you. The others haven't arrived yet."

"Okay, let's go, guys," Richardson said. They rushed out the door and ran down the path to the boat house.

"You Richardson?" asked a man standing on the dock just under the roof of the boathouse.

"Yeah," Richardson shouted. "Which one is ours?"

"Number 49 there," he said, pointing.

"Damn, it's bigger," Juan Carlos said. "Inboard. Good idea. We got our powerhead shot up on the outboards."

"This is much better protected," the tech said. "I'm Jim Shelton. Nice to meet you guys."

"I'm Juan Carlos, pilot, and this is Brendan, our weapons expert."

"What's going to be different about this boat?" Richardson asked as they climbed aboard.

"First of all, it's faster. A lot faster," Shelton said. "Gets better mileage too, since it's not two-cycle, but it draws more water. You can't get into the shallows as easily. Start her up."

Juan Carlos got into the pilot's chair and hit the ignition. The engine fired up, settling into a raspy purr.

"Nice," Juan Carlos said, grinning ear to ear. "This the navigation system?"

"Yeah, turn it on. Button on the bottom left side of the screen."

Juan Carlos switched it on. The GPS found them within a few seconds, and a map showed up. Then it re-oriented itself, zooming out, showing an X up near the mouth of Baffin Bay. "Hey, is this the enemy?"

"Yeah," Shelton said. "Won't work by itself. We have to focus on the enemy with our radar planes. When we're working together, we can send the info to you, but if there's no radar planes nearby, you'll only get GPS navigation."

"These guns have grenade launchers on them," Brendan said.

"Whoa, I thought these were still experimental," Richardson said.

"I won't tell anybody if you won't." Shelton snickered. "See this lever, over the trigger handle?"

"Yeah," Brendan said, getting into position behind the starboard side gun.

"Flip up for grenades. Down for the .50 cal. Mind the belts. Ammo feed can be an issue with these. We're still working on them."

"Anything different about the M-19?" Juan Carlos asked.

"Only the sight," Shelton said. "See this switch? Turns on the FLIR night vision system."

"Sweet," Juan Carlos said. "It fires the same, though, right?"

"Yep," Shelton said. "Larger grenades than the side guns."

"What's with the seat belt?" Richardson asked, looking at the pilot seat.

"When you floorboard this baby, you move around a lot in the chop," Shelton said. "Some of our testers couldn't hold steady enough to aim the main gun. We found that the seatbelt helped."

"What's the range?" Richardson asked.

"About twice what the old boats were," he said.

"Anything else?" Richardson asked.

"It feels different," Shelton said. "Get used to it on the way down there. Make some fast turns. Try out the guns. Use the navigation system. We were gonna train you guys for four or five hours before sending you into combat. Can't do it now."

"Roger that," Richardson said. "Let's go men."

Juan Carlos nodded, watching as Richardson and Shelton pulled off the dock lines. Then Richardson climbed aboard and got onto the port gun. "Let's go."

Juan Carlos idled out of the slip and turned the boat towards the mouth of the small bay. "Hold on guys," he said as he got past the no-wake buoys.

"Go for it, man," Brendan said, bracing himself.

Juan Carlos gunned the engine. The boat jumped up on a plane and took off like a rocket. "Holy shit, dude!"

"Damn, this puppy flies," Richardson said.

"Seriously," Brendan said. He aimed his gun and let off a small blip of machine gun fire, then flipped the switch and fired a grenade, which flew to the sandy bank and blew up. White sand flew high into the air. "Yes!"

"I guess I ought to try it too," Richardson said. He fired a grenade at a dilapidated shack, blowing it sky high.

Juan Carlos laughed. "Dude, you sure nobody was in there?"

"Yeah, I could see inside through the broken door," Richardson said. He fired off a few rounds of .50 cal. "This thing shoots like a dream."

"I'm going to do a few maneuvers," Juan Carlos said, breaking into a zig-zag fashion. "Feels different steering with a rudder instead of an engine."

"The inboard engine is so much quieter," Brendan said.

"Yeah, we'd be yelling at this speed in the old boat, dude."

"How close we getting to the enemy?" Richardson asked.

Juan Carlos looked at the navigation screen. "Half a mile. They don't appear to be very fast."

Suddenly gunfire came at them from the sides, hitting the bullet shields and the armored sides of the hull.

"Shit, see where that came from?" Juan Carlos shouted.

"I did," Brendan said, turning his gun towards the bank. He fired a grenade at some structure on the beach, and it blew up with a loud rumble.

"You hit their ammo, obviously," Richardson said. "Get those men running away."

Brendan nodded and switched to machine gun mode, strafing the beach, hitting all the men he could see.

"Okay, hold your fire," Richardson said. "We need to save most of our ammo for the enemy boats."

Brendan nodded.

"Hey, dude, they're speeding up. They must have heard that."

"You got it to the floor?" Richardson asked.

"Nah, about three-quarters," Juan Carlos said.

"Punch it," Brendan said.

Juan Carlos pushed the throttle all the way forward. The engine roared and they flew forward.

"Damn, how fast are we going?" Richardson asked, holding onto the gun handles.

"Seventy-five," Juan Carlos said. "That's about it, though. It's to the floor."

"We catching up to them?" Brendan asked. "Never mind, I see the first one. Dead ahead. What's the range on the grenades?"

"Forgot to ask, didn't we?" Richardson said. "Let's hit them with the machine guns first. I know we can hit those last two boats with the .50 cals."

Brendan opened up, bullets ripping into the back of the first boat. "They got armor."

Richardson fired, a little higher, hitting the enemy pilot in the back. The boat veered off course as the other men on board struggled to get the dead pilot out of the way. Richardson sent another volley of .50 cal rounds into them, killing all but one.

Brendan shot a grenade at the other boat. It exploded, blowing the stern off. He followed with a second grenade, which flew through the opening and blew up inside, sending debris from the boat high into the air.

"Look out, man," Brendan shouted. "Don't run into any of that debris."

"Got it," Juan Carlos said, speeding around it. "Damn, look at that big cruiser!" He slowed the boat and fired the main grenade launcher, hitting the upper deck, men flying into the air. Brendan and Richardson both opened up with machine gun fire, cutting the men to pieces as they struggled to get away. Then there was more machine gun fire hitting them from the side.

"Watch starboard," Juan Carlos yelled as bullets flew over his head.

"See them," Brendan yelled, wheeling the gun around and opening fire on a smaller boat racing towards them. "Heavy armor again. Switching to grenades." He let go with two rounds in rapid succession, the first blowing a hole, the second going through and blowing up inside. The boat started to settle, but it was still moving, the enemy sailors who were left trying to get to the main guns on the top deck.

"Get those guys!" Juan Carlos shouted. Both Brendan and Richardson turned their weapons in that direction and opened fire, killing the men on the deck. Then Juan Carlos turned the main gun towards them and fired, blowing up the bridge. Brendan hit them with one of his grenades and the boat exploded.

"Wow, dude!" Juan Carlos yelled.

"Any more enemy boats showing up?"

"Yeah, a couple of the big boats are getting pretty close to Corpus Christi," Juan Carlos yelled. "They're almost to that big bridge."

"Look behind us," Brendan shouted. Two more Texas patrol boats were flying up behind them, pouring on the speed.

"Yeah, dude, let's go get them!" Juan Carlos yelled, moving the throttle all the way forward again, the boat screaming forward as the other two got alongside.

"Hope we get to them before they destroy anything," Richardson said.

"They're trying to duck into that big harbor on the left," Brendan said. He fired a grenade, but it fell short. Then one of the other patrol boats pulled forward and fired again, hitting the closest of the two boats, stopping its engine.

"Nice shot," Richardson said.

"Seriously," Juan Carlos said. He looked into the sight of the main gun and fired two rounds in rapid succession. The first missed, but the second one hit the other boat, which opened up with machine guns, Brendan and Richardson returning fire along with the other two boats. Then Juan Carlos and the pilot of another boat let grenades fly, both of them hitting the remaining enemy cruiser within a split second of each other, breaking the hull in half. It sank quickly in front of them.

"That's it, man!" Brendan shouted.

"No more showing up?" Richard asked.

"No, dude," Juan Carlos said. "Should we stick around?"

"No, let's go back in," he said. "But keep an eye on the display, and slow it down a little bit."

"Got it," Juan Carlos said.

Richardson grabbed the radio mike and hit the key. "Riviera Beach, come in please. Over."

"Richardson? You get them? Over."

"Yeah, Captain. These boats are a huge improvement. Over."

"The others get there in time to join the party? Over."

"Two of them did," Richardson said. "Looks like we have two more approaching. Over."

"Yeah, we sent out a total of five counting you guys. Come on back. We need to chat. Over."

"On our way. Over." Richardson put the mic back on the holder and got back to his gun.

"We get to go back?" Juan Carlos asked.

"Yep," he said. "The Captain wants to talk to us."

"Wonder what's up?" Brendan asked.

"I have no idea," Richardson said.

The boat cut through the water as they all calmed down, getting back to the boathouse without enemy encounters. Juan Carlos pulled into the slip while Richardson and Brendan jumped onto the dock with ropes. Shelton rushed over.

"Well, what'd you think? I heard from Cappy that you kicked some serious ass."

"This thing is unbelievable," Richardson said.

"Seriously, dude," Juan Carlos said as he undid his seatbelt. "Feels weird wearing this belt, but I'd probably have flown out of the seat without it."

"Yeah, we could use something to stabilize us at the guns," Brendan said.

"They weren't really designed to fire weapons at full speed," Shelton said.

"Don't know why not," Juan Carlos said. "Worked pretty well, all things considered."

"Let's get up to headquarters," Richardson said as he tied off the port line. Brendan finished with the starboard line and they rushed up the path to the building.

"Good, you guys are back," Jefferson said. "Nice work out there."

"Nice work with the boats," Juan Carlos said. "Big improvement."

"Yeah, the enemy wasn't expecting it," Richardson said. "Especially the speed."

"Good," Jefferson said.

"What did you want to chat about?"

"We got intelligence on those enemy vessels," he said. "They were going to hit the harbor facilities next to Nueces Bay. We can't afford to lose a facility like that, especially now."

"Yeah, what we have on the gulf coast has to supply the whole damn state," Brendan said.

"Exactly," Jefferson said.

"What were they going to hit us with? A nuke again?" Richardson said.

"That weapon they used to take out the dam at Falcon Lake," Jefferson said.

"No way," Juan Carlos said. "Where are they getting those? Russians?"

"Not the Russian Government," Jefferson said. "At least that's what they're telling us."

"So why'd you call us in?" Juan Carlos asked. "To tell us that?"

"You guys got a better look at the impact of that weapon at Falcon Lake than anybody else."

"We weren't the only boat that survived that, as you know very well," Richardson said.

"My boat was sheltered in a cove where we couldn't see the wave coming," Jefferson said.

"Well, I remember it, that's for sure," Juan Carlos said. "I can still see it. Remember that cheesy movie about the ocean liner that got knocked upside down by the rogue wave?"

"You mean the Poseidon Adventure?" Jefferson asked.

"Yeah," Juan Carlos said. "It was like that. A huge rolling wall of water. The only reason we survived is because we were close to shore when we saw it. It was coming like a frigging freight train."

Richardson was looking at the map app on his phone. "My God, if they let one of those loose in this channel, it wouldn't just take out stuff in the water. It'd take out all the oil facilities along here. See?" He held up his phone to the others.

"We know we have a problem," Jefferson said. "We're trying to find the base for these boats. We have a pretty good idea where it is. Waiting for confirmation, but it's our third try. They keep finding our operatives and killing them."

"Where you thinking?" Richardson asked.

"Mexico, of course," he said. "Below South Padre Island. That's why that area was so crazy. That's why they wanted us out of there."

"Long way," Juan Carlos said. "A lot of it in the open gulf."

"Yes," Jefferson said. "I was thinking the new boats were over-kill. Maybe not."

"Trust me, they aren't," Juan Carlos said.

"Sounds like we have a suicide mission coming," Brendan said.

"I wouldn't go that far," Jefferson said. "We aren't going to send you to your deaths, believe me."

"Why not just station folks all along the coast?" Juan Carlos asked.

"You don't want to play defense against this weapon," Jefferson said. "Wouldn't work. They could clear out the area with one, then cruise through the devastation ten minutes later and get to their target easily."

"We should be using air power for this," Richardson said.

"There are still a bunch of M-1 Tanks and other mobile hardware in the hands of the enemy, all over Texas," Jefferson said. "Lot more people at risk from them. Most of the air power is being used for that at the moment. If we're lucky it'll change before we have to send any boats to the Mexican coast."

"We don't have enough resources for this fight, do we?" Richardson asked.

"No," Jefferson said. "We've got a really dangerous few months ahead of us."

"Maybe Nelson shouldn't have taken us out of the union," Juan Carlos said.

Jefferson chuckled. "The US Government is in on this mess. Nelson figured that out. The military capability that would've stayed active in and around Texas would've been used against us."

"If that's the case, Nelson had no choice," Richardson said. "No choice at all."

"I can just see Hannah's reaction to this," Brendan said.

"*Do not* tell your women about this," Jefferson said. "Or anybody else, for that matter. This is classified. Get it?"

Juan Carlos laughed. "Hell, dude, we don't even have clearances."

"You do now," Jefferson said. "So get serious about it. We're already landlocked by hostile territory. If we lose the harbor facilities along the gulf coast, we're done. The US Government will starve us out."

"We understand, don't we, men?" Richardson asked.

Both of them nodded quietly.

"All right," Jefferson said. "You guys can go back home. You're going to be on call, though, so keep that in mind. I'd lay off the intoxicants."

"Just like the Battle of Britain, eh," Brendan asked.

"Yeah, pretty much," Jefferson said. "Now get out of here."

"See you soon," Richardson said. He headed for the door, the other two following.

"Dammit," Juan Carlos said. "This sucks, dude."

"I know, guys, but suck it up," Richardson said, "and remember what the Captain said. Mum's the word with the girls. Understand?"

"Yeah," Juan Carlos said.

"I understand, boss," Brendan said.

"Good, then let's go home." They got into the SUV and drove away.

{ 25 }

Celebrity Witness

Maria woke up in a cold sweat next to Hendrix.

"Kip?" she asked softly.

He grunted and turned towards her.

"Kip!" she said, a little louder.

"What, sweetie?" he asked.

"Hold me. I'm scared."

He moved towards her, feeling her tremble. "What's wrong?"

"I had a nightmare," she said.

"I'm sorry, sweetie. Want to talk about it?"

She was silent for a moment.

"You don't have to," Hendrix said, holding her in the embrace.

"No, it's okay," she said. "It was about Celia. She broke us up."

"Oh, honey, that's not gonna happen," Hendrix said, pulling her closer.

"I know, but it was so scary," she said. "Go back to sleep. I'll be okay."

Hendrix reached for his bedside table lamp and switched it on, then looked her in the eye. "You'll never lose me. I love you so much."

She reached for him, tears in her eyes. "I know. I love you too."

"Let's get married," Hendrix said. "We'll go in the morning."

"You don't have to do that now if you…"

"I want you to be my wife," he said, looking intensely at her. "Will you marry me?"

A smile broke through her tears. "You know I will."

"Good," Hendrix said. "You don't mind a simple wedding?"

"Not at all," Maria said. "Tomorrow? Really?"

"Really," he said, smiling at her. "Now go to sleep."

She smiled back at him. "You think I can sleep now?"

"Try," he said, "We've got a big day tomorrow."

"All right," she said as he turned off the lamp. They settled against each other. Hendrix drifted off in minutes. She lingered for half an hour, listening to him breathe. *I love this man so.*

Maria woke with a start the next morning, reaching for Hendrix. He was gone. She felt panic for a moment, but then heard him working in the kitchen. She threw on her robe and walked down the wide steps.

"Hey, sweetie," Hendrix said, standing in his pajama bottoms with no shirt. "You finally got to sleep."

"Yeah," she said, hugging him from behind. "Mmmmm, French Toast, huh?"

"Seemed like a good meal for our wedding day," he said.

"You don't have to go through with it just because I had a nightmare."

He turned and pulled her into his arms. "Are you serious? I already told you that was what I wanted, remember?"

"I know, but we don't need to rush into it," she said.

"Are you saying you don't want to get married today?"

She thought for a moment.

Hendrix flipped the French toast in the pan, then looked at her again.

"I want to," she said. "More than anything."

"Good," he said. "Now go sit at the table and I'll bring your breakfast."

They ate leisurely and talked, then went into the bedroom and got dressed.

"Courthouse?" she asked.

"That's what I was thinking," Hendrix said, as he watched himself put on his tie in the mirror. "I've got to make a call before we go."

"No problem," Maria said. "I've got a little more work to do on my makeup anyway. I want to look my best."

"Do you want your mother to attend?" Hendrix asked.

She thought about it for a moment. "No. We're on the outs because of what happened with Celia. I don't want to deal with her."

He nodded, kissed her forehead and went into the living room, taking his phone out of his pocket. He made a call, speaking in hushed tones, then sat on the couch and waited.

"Ready?" Maria asked, coming out in a smart navy blue dress with white collar.

"You look beautiful," Hendrix said as he got up. "I'm so proud to be with you."

She smiled as he walked over and took her into his arms, kissing her.

"Don't muss my makeup," she said. "You can do that later."

He escorted her to the car, and they drove away.

"Don't we need a witness to do this?" Maria asked.

"I got that covered," Hendrix said. "Don't worry."

She smiled. "Everything well in hand."

"Always," he said.

The courthouse was busy. Hendrix parked in a VIP spot, and they walked through the sunny morning into the main entrance, heading through the metal detectors.

"How romantic," Maria said as they grabbed their metal objects out of the basket. They both chuckled and went to the elevator.

"You know which floor?" she asked.

"Top floor," Hendrix said. The doors opened into a foyer with white lattice photo areas and flowers.

"Wow, never been up here before," Maria said.

"I've attended weddings here," Hendrix said.

Suddenly there were Capitol Guards rushing into the room, looking at everybody, checking the corners. Maria looked around nervously. "What's going on?"

Hendrix chuckled. "Our witness has arrived."

Governor Nelson walked in with his wife, beaming. "There's the happy couple!"

"Governor, thanks so much for coming," Hendrix said, shaking his hand warmly.

"Wouldn't miss it, old friend," Nelson said. "You remember Sandy."

"Of course," Hendrix said. "Good to see you again, Sandy."

"Great to see you, Kip."

"This is Maria," Hendrix said.

"Nice to meet you both," Maria said. "It's such an honor."

"The honor is ours," Nelson said. "Shall we?"

"Ready, honey?" Hendrix asked.

Maria took a deep breath. "I'm ready." The two couples walked through the double doors to the chapel.

They were done in less than ten minutes.

"That was much nicer than I expected," Maria said, arm in arm with Hendrix as they came out the chapel door.

"They do a nice job," Nelson said. "You two *are* going to take a few days off, I hope."

"I'd like to," Hendrix said. "I'm fine with being on call, of course. We both understand the state of things."

"Yes, we do," Maria said. "If you need us, call."

"I'll try not to do that," Nelson said. "Things around here are going pretty well at this point. We have the right people doing the right things all around the state. Texas can do without you two for a little while."

"Thanks so much for being here," Hendrix said, shaking hands.

Nelson bent down to kiss Maria, and then took his wife's hand and left, the security detail following.

"Well that was certainly a surprise," Maria said.

Hendrix smiled at her. "I thought you'd like that."

"It was exciting," she said.

"What do you want to do now?" Hendrix asked as they stepped into the elevator.

"Is that a trick question?" Maria asked, turning towards him. He took her into his arms and they kissed passionately as the elevator traveled down.

"Well?" he asked.

"I want to stay in bed for most of the day," she whispered.

"Oh, *really now*?" Hendrix asked.

She got next to him and whispered in his ear. "It's a good time. You've got work to do."

"You mean?"

She nodded yes.

He moaned. "Let's hurry."

They rushed out to the car and drove home.

Maria rushed towards the garage door.

"Hold it," Hendrix said.

"What?" she asked. "Aren't you in a hurry?"

He chuckled and caught up to her, unlocking the door. He pushed it open and picked her up.

"Oh!" She giggled. "I like this."

He stood just inside the threshold and kissed her, then put her down.

"I'm so much in love with you," Hendrix said, feeling himself tremble.

"You are," she said. "I feel it whenever I'm with you. I can't believe we found each other. This is the best thing that's ever happened to me." She pulled him in for another kiss, moaning as he took hold of her and hugged her tight. They broke the kiss and rushed upstairs to the bedroom, clothes coming off as they went. Hendrix was beside himself with love as he watched her naked form climbing on the bed.

"Your face is so flushed," she said when she turned towards him. "You okay?"

"I'm more excited than I've ever been in my life," he said.

"You are? Even more than the first time?"

"This time's for real," he said as he joined her on the bed.

"Because we're married?" she asked has he came over her.

"And because we're working on our family," he said, settling on top of her.

"Oh, God," she swooned. "I love you so much, Kip."

They flew into ecstasy, focused on only each other, lost in their passion, then laying back, passion still strong but too tired to keep going.

"You've made a mess of me," Maria said.

"Yes I have," he said. "You mind?"

She giggled. "We're not done yet."

"We're done for a while," Hendrix said. "I'm not seventeen anymore."

"Nor am I," she said.

"Want a snack? Or maybe some champagne?"

"We have some cold?"

"I put a bottle in the fridge before we left."

"Tricky," she said. "Sure."

"Be right back," he said, throwing on a robe and rushing down the stairs. He got the bottle out of the fridge and grabbed two glasses, then noticed Maria's phone on the counter with a call memo on the screen. He picked it up and put it in the pocket of his robe.

Maria came out of the bathroom, using a washcloth to take her makeup off. "Geez, you should have told me my makeup was so screwed up."

"I like you that way," Hendrix said. "Especially after what we just did."

She flashed him a shy smile as he opened the champagne and poured them each a glass.

"Thanks," she said as she took a sip from her glass. "It's good."

"Ought to be," Hendrix said. "It wasn't cheap. Oh, you had a call flashing on your phone." He pulled it out of his robe pocket and set it on the dresser.

"Uh oh," she said, picking it up. "Don't recognize the number. They left a message."

"Go ahead and listen to it if you want to."

She nodded, hit the playback button, and put the phone to her ear, eyes wide.

"Oh no, what happened?" Hendrix asked.

She put the phone down. "Celia. She escaped."

{ 26 }

Interrogation

The dirty, primer gray pickup truck raced for the entrance to the Fort Stockton RV Park.

"Shit, Kelly, that's Jasper and Earl," Nate said.

"I know," Kelly said. He turned to the crowd. "Women and children, run towards the back of the park. Armed men get ready."

"Is this an attack?" Clancy asked.

"Don't know yet," Kelly shouted.

Kyle and Jason ran back over with Junior. Eric and Kim came out of the office with Francis and a few other people.

"What's going on?" Eric yelled.

"Two guys who Chris said were turned by Simon Orr just showed up," Kelly said. "We don't know what the situation is yet."

The truck rolled to a stop. Jasper and Earl came out with their hands up.

"Don't shoot!" Jasper said, looking at his friends with guns drawn.

"Clancy, keep an eye out for anybody else coming," Moe shouted.

Kelly, Junior, Nate, and Fritz approached slowly.

"Chris said Simon Orr turned you guys," Kelly said.

"They had us convinced to join their militia, until we overheard them talking," Earl said. "They're planning to come here and take your weapons."

"Yeah, we ain't gonna stand with that. Not for one second," Jasper said. "Honest. Our guns are behind the seat in the truck. We aren't carrying. You can frisk us."

"We will," Fritz said. "Cover me, boys." He walked over and frisked both men. "They're clean."

"Okay, c'mon, let's go talk," Kelly said. "In the clubhouse."

"I'll keep watch," Clancy said.

"Make sure we have the tanks on alert," Jason said.

Kelly rushed over to Jason. "Call Curt and tell him what's up."

"You read my mind," Jason said, phone already in his hand. "Find out how many men this Simon Orr character has."

"Yeah, that's job one," Kelly said.

"You think we can trust those guys?" Kyle asked.

"Don't know," Kelly said. "Maybe after things have settled a little you guys ought to join us. Show us some of your police interrogation skills."

Kyle laughed. "Yeah, maybe those detective classes I took will come in handy after all."

Jason shook his head as he walked away with his phone to his ear.

Kelly joined the others in the Clubhouse. Jasper and Earl were sitting in chairs against the far wall, the other men standing in front of them. Kelly grabbed a chair and brought it over. He sat down in front of them.

"How many men does Simon Orr have?"

Jasper and Earl looked at each other. "We saw about thirty," Jasper said. "They're at a dilapidated factory north of Penwell, off I-20. Orr said there were more on the way."

"They coming here?" Nate asked.

"I think so, but they won't just bust right in during broad daylight," Earl said. "They know they're not strong enough."

"You guys should hit them," Jasper said. "Before they get much stronger."

Kelly and Junior looked at each other, then back at Jasper.

"You wouldn't be leading us right into a trap, would you?" Junior asked.

"We've fought together," Jasper said. "Drank together. Hell, we saved your ass at Texas Mary's, remember?"

"I remember," Kelly said. "What does Simon Orr's militia want to do?"

Jasper and Earl looked at each other again, nervously.

"C'mon, dammit," Nate said.

"They want to gather up as much equipment as they can and take it into Utah," Jasper said. "To some base they're putting together near Capitol Reef National Park."

"Why?" Fritz asked.

"This is gonna sound crazy," Earl said. "You got to believe us."

"Go on," Kelly said.

Suddenly the Dr. Knudsen started CPR on Chris, on the table in the other side of the room.

"Dammit, we're about to lose Chris," Junior said, looking over.

"No," Jasper said, tears forming around his eyes. Earl shuddered as he looked over, choking up.

"Answer the question," Kelly said, his focus intense.

"They told us it was to defeat the Islamists in that state," Earl said, "but then we overheard them saying they were gonna give it to the Islamists for a whole lot of money."

"It's the God's honest truth, Kelly," Jasper said. "I heard it too."

"Chris just died," Dr. Knudsen said, pulling the blanket over his face. "I'm sorry, guys."

"Brenda's going to take this hard," Kelly said, fighting back tears.

"What happened with Chris?" Nate asked.

"We got to this abandoned factory," Jasper said. "Simon wanted to wait for his other people to show up, so he could bring them here. Chris wanted to keep going, to join you guys as quickly as possible."

"What about you two?" Junior asked.

"Simon Orr told us he wanted to link up with you guys and join the fight here, then enlist you to go to Capitol Reef for some big battle," Jasper said. "We believed him. We were okay with waiting there for a couple more days."

"When Simon's people showed up, Chris got real standoffish," Earl said. "He didn't like them."

"Did you?" Nate asked.

Earl got an ashamed look on his face, then looked down. "I thought they were okay, until this afternoon."

"Chris decided to leave because of the new folks?" Kelly asked.

"He was already leaning that way," Jasper said. "He didn't trust Simon Orr. You know Chris. He's not exactly a joiner, and he has a solid gold bullshit detector. We should've picked up on it."

"Go on," Fritz said.

"So Chris took off with his sister," Earl said. "We got suspicious when Simon Orr and a few of his men disappeared all of a sudden. We snuck up and listened in on a few of them talking after Simon left."

"They caught us," Earl said.

"What happened then?" Nate asked.

"They ain't alive anymore," Jasper said. "Their buddies might be coming this way now."

"No way," Earl said, glancing at him. "They know they're not strong enough to take this group on."

"How do you know *we'll* let you stay?" Fritz asked, "or let you live, for that matter?"

Earl and Jasper looked at each other with terror in their eyes.

"No, we're not with them," Jasper said. "I swear."

"What do they know about us?" Kelly asked.

"They know you have tanks, and they heard about Curt's stuff," Earl said.

"You tell them?" Junior asked, moving towards them in a menacing fashion.

"Cool your jets, Junior," Kelly said. He looked back at Earl. "How'd they find out?"

"They must know somebody who saw," Earl said.

"Yeah," Jasper said. "If they're really selling hardware to the Islamists, they might have heard it from them."

"I'm not buying this," Junior said. "Maybe we ought to gut these two and hang them from the gate post out there."

"Dammit, Junior, I told you to cool your frigging jets," Kelly said.

"Our friend is laying there dead," Junior shouted. "He said these guys are turned."

"He didn't know what we found out," Earl said. "I swear. He'd already left with his sister by the time we found out."

"You believing this crap, man?" Junior asked. "Really?" He looked from one to the other, spoiling for a beat down.

Nate and Fritz looked at each other, then at Kelly.

"What?" Kelly asked.

"I think the good-cop, bad-cop routine worked," Nate said. "They're telling the truth."

Kelly and Junior looked at each other.

"What do you think, Junior?" Kelly asked.

Junior exhaled and laughed. "Yeah," he said. "Sorry, guys. We had to. You know."

Jasper and Earl looked relieved and got out of their chairs.

"Wait a minute, we ain't done," Kelly said. "I want to know everything you do about their base and the people there."

"Sure, no problem," Jasper said, sitting back down.

"Hey, Nate, go get us some paper and pencils, okay? We're gonna need these guys to draw some stuff."

"Got it," Nate said. He rushed out the door.

Brenda came in, breaking down when he saw Chris's covered body. "Oh no!" She ran over to Kelly and they embraced, both of them crying.

"We're so sorry," Jasper said, breaking down himself. Earl looked at them, numb look on his face.

"Did they do it?" Brenda asked, nodding at Jasper and Earl.

"No," Kelly said. "We don't think so."

"Simon Orr's going to come after us, isn't he?" Brenda asked.

"He might," Kelly said. "Don't worry, we'll take him."

Nate came back with the paper and pencils.

"Okay," Kelly said. "First, let's see what the facility looks like. Jasper, you go over there and draw. Earl, you go over on that side of the room and do the same."

"I thought you believed us," Jasper said.

"We're gonna be cautious," Kelly said. "Sorry. I'd hope you'd do the same with us if the situation was reversed."

"He's right, Jasper," Earl said. "C'mon."

They went to opposite ends of the room and got to work.

Jason walked to the door with Kyle and motioned to Kelly and Junior. They rushed over, Brenda by Kelly's side.

"You get Curt?" Kelly asked.

"Yeah," Jason said. "He's only about ten minutes away now."

"Good," Junior said.

"You get the lay of the land from Jasper and Earl?" Kyle asked.

"Yeah, we think so, but we're still being cautious," Kelly said.

"What'd they say?" Jason asked.

"They overheard some of Simon Orr's people saying they want to sell our weapons to the Islamists in Utah for big bucks," Junior said.

"Jerk weeds," Kyle said. "When Curt comes back we ought to go kick their asses."

"We don't want to go waltzing into a trap, guys," Junior said. "We got Jasper and Earl drawing their base for us."

"Separately, so they can't collaborate," Kelly said.

"Sure you've never been a cop?" Kyle asked with a twinkle in his eye.

Kelly laughed. "No, but we've been on the receiving end of those tactics."

"Yeah," Junior said.

Jason laughed, shaking his head. "Well, I'm impressed, man."

"The new folks settled yet?" Kelly asked.

"Getting there," Kyle said. "We've got a pretty powerful force brewing here, even before we get additional help from Nelson and Ramsey."

"Damn straight," Junior said.

"We need to screen anybody new they send us," Kelly said.

"Yeah, I agree," Jason said. "Too many moles in too many places."

"Truck coming!" Clancy shouted from the roof. "No, two trucks. One of them's a bobtail."

The four men ran out to the gate and checked.

"Hey, guys, it's Curt," Clancy shouted. "That off-roader of his is hitched to the bobtail. He's riding on it."

"Yes!" Junior said, wide smile on his face.

The two trucks pulled to a stop just inside the gate. Curt climbed out of the Barracuda and unhitched it from the bobtail, then backed it away and drove it next to the office, aiming the M-19 down the road. Then he rushed over to meet Amanda and Sydney as they got out of the cab.

Dirk and Chance trotted over to them.

"Curt," Kyle said. "How you doing?"

"Just fine, pencil neck," he said. "You remember Sydney and Amanda, right?"

"Only met Sydney," Kyle said. "Good to see you again. Nice to meet you, Amanda."

"Glad you're here," Jason said. He glanced at Curt, catching him with his eyes on Amanda. Curt noticed, face turning red.

"They finally met, huh?" Jason asked Sydney. "I figured there'd be sparks flying."

"You trying to marry this boy off?" Amanda asked. "Same old Jason."

"Yeah, shut up pencil neck," Curt said.

"Pencil neck again," Junior said. "Welcome to the group."

"Yeah, welcome," Kelly said. "This is my woman, Brenda."

Brenda looked at him, misty. "Still gives me a tingle when you call me that. *It's disgusting.*" She turned to Amanda and Sydney, smiling. "So nice to meet you. Welcome. I'll introduce you around after you get settled."

"That'd be great," Amanda said. "You know where Don is? Sydney's going crazy."

"Shut up," Sydney said. Amanda laughed.

"You're sweet on Don, huh?" Dirk asked. "I figured that was coming."

"Here he comes," Chance said. "Let's get back to camp. I need to rest a little."

"Yeah," Dirk said. "For sure."

The two walked to their truck, nodding to Don as they passed him.

"Go get her, man," Dirk whispered. Chance cracked up.

"Everybody's teasing us," Sydney said as Don got to her. "It's embarrassing. We haven't even done anything."

"Don't let them bother you," Don said. "Their hearts are in the right place. Heard you saw action on the way over."

"Yeah, we got attacked, but Curt saved the day with that crazy off-roader of his," Sydney said.

"Well thank God for that," Don said. "I worried the whole time you were gone."

"Don't say that so loud," she whispered, glancing around. "Bad enough as it is."

"Sorry," Don said. "Look." He nodded at Curt, walking with Amanda by his side.

"Those two were made for each other," Sydney said, shaking her head. "She's a handful. Hope Curt's ready for that."

"I barely know Curt," Don said. "I came into this with Eric. Didn't meet Curt until he came to hit that supply depot."

"I know," she said. "How's your daughter and her friend?"

"Shook up, but good. I think they feel better now that we're part of a larger group."

"This feels so exposed," Sydney said. "I hope we really have the air support they said we did in the meeting."

"Yeah, me too," Don said. "Where you gonna stay?"

"I don't know," Sydney said. "Amanda will probably end up with Curt."

Don chuckled. "Yeah, probably. I'll need to find someplace. We have Dirk's trailer, but it won't sleep everybody in our group. Dirk, Chance, Francis, and Sherry pretty much fill it up. The girls were sleeping in the back of the SUV, and then in the house back in Fredericksburg."

"What about you?"

"Tent," Don said. "Not the best. I'll have a chat with Moe. I think there's a few park models here. He also has some consignment RVs for sale. Noticed them when I was walking around the far side of the park, past the office on the road."

Sydney laughed. "Think the society is together enough for those types of transactions?"

"That's a good question," Don said. "Do you like me, or am I getting the wrong impression?"

"I like a man who's not afraid to ask a direct question," Sydney said.

They walked along silently for a few minutes. Then Don pointed. "There's those RVs for sale. See them? In his storage area."

"Yeah," she said. They walked towards them. "None of them are in perfect shape."

"Yeah, I know. Look at that little trailer. I'll bet my SUV will tow it."

"Only five grand," Sydney said. "Must have some issues."

"It's old," Don said, looking at it. "You never answered my question."

She stopped and looked him in the eye. "I'm not ready to answer yet. You going to be okay with that?"

"Yeah," Don said.

"Good," she said. "We'll see what develops."

"You aren't going to ask if I like you?"

She giggled. "No, I don't think I need to. Better go find my sister. We have a still to set up."

"I'll walk you over to the office," Don said.

They got back there in a few minutes. Don saw Moe sitting on the steps of the office, talking to Nate. He went towards them as Sydney joined Amanda, Curt, and Kyle, who were standing by the Barracuda chatting.

"You're Moe, right?" Don asked.

He and Nate looked at him. "Yeah," Moe said, standing up. He extended his hand and they shook. "You're Don, aren't you?"

"Yeah," he said. "I saw that little trailer back there for five grand. It still for sale?"

Moe got a grim look on his face. "The owner got killed in the Austin invasion," he said. "Haven't been able to find the next-of-kin."

"So you can't sell it?"

"I got permission to sell it," he said. "I hold the money in case the next-of-kin show up."

"You don't look too hopeful," Nate said.

"I'm not," Moe said. "He was killed at his house. Tank round blew the place up, from what Austin PD told me. Sad. He had two small kids. Wife had left him. That's why he was selling the trailer."

"So maybe she's the next-of-kin," Don said.

"Their divorce was final, and he got the trailer," Moe said. "You want to look at it? I'll take you over there."

"Well, since I don't have a place to sleep tonight, that would be good," he said. "Know how many it sleeps?"

"Six," Moe said as he got up. "It's pretty crowded with that many in it, though. It's about right for a family of four. Fridge is a little small, and the shower ain't much, but we've got showers in the park."

They walked toward the storage area, Don glancing back. Sydney was watching him, but she turned away quickly when they locked eyes. *There's my answer.*

"Caught you again," Amanda said.

"Stop it," Sydney said.

Curt laughed nervously. "You want to see my workshop? I should get back there and set up to make gimbals."

"Yeah, I'm game," Amanda said. Sydney nodded yes.

"Let's go then," he said. "I've got some beer in the fridge."

"I could use one of those," Kyle said.

"Where's Dirk's truck?" Amanda asked.

"He's about forty yards from Curt's rig," Kyle said. "We might have to wait until they wake up to move the truck closer."

"No problem, I got stuff to set up before I need the weapons anyway," Curt said.

"Hey, Jason, you want to go back?" Kyle shouted. Jason was talking in a circle with Kelly, Nate, and Junior.

"Later," Jason said. "We're still busy down here for a while."

"Okay, I'll let Carrie know," he said.

"Thanks, man," Jason said.

"You two are close, aren't you?" Amanda asked Kyle.

"Jason's my partner on Austin PD," Kyle said. "And we were friends before that."

"You still work for Austin PD?" Sydney asked.

"Yeah," Kyle said. "They put us on paid leave after the incident at the Superstore in Dripping Springs."

"Shit, you're *those* cops?" Amanda asked. "I should have figured that out."

"Oh, you heard about that?" Kyle asked.

"It was all over the news," she said. "Fredericksburg isn't that far from Dripping Springs, you know."

"So Kelly and his guys are the rednecks who were involved in the early battles?" Sydney asked.

"Yeah," Curt said.

"We're going to have a *big* target on our backs," Sydney said, eyes wide.

"Yeah, the enemy would love to destroy this group," Curt said. "We'll handle them and then some."

"Yeah, I'll bet you will," Amanda said.

"There's my baby," Curt said, pointing to the big toy hauler.

"That looks pretty new," Amanda said.

"It's a couple years old," Curt said as he led them to the back. "Help me with the ramp, pencil neck."

Kyle shook his head and helped Curt lower the ramp, exposing the garage.

"So I take it you just drive the Barracuda in here when you travel," Amanda said.

"Yeah," he said. "I could tow it too, but I usually don't."

"What's that sticking up there?" Sydney asked, pointing to the barrel sticking out over the roof.

Curt chuckled. "My last project. I've still got to finish it. That's a remote-control machine gun. I can fire it from the driver's seat if I'm being followed."

Carrie came out of her coach and walked over.

"Hi," she said. "Where's Jason?"

"He's not quite finished up at the clubhouse," Kyle said. "He'll be along."

"Okay," she said. "You ladies hungry? I can whip up something for you."

"No thanks," Sydney said. "We snacked on the way here. You're pregnant, aren't you?"

"Yes," she said, then glanced over as Kate walked up. "So's she."

"Hey, don't tell everybody," Kate said.

"You said we could after Kyle found out," Carrie said.

"Yeah, I'm proud of my handiwork," Kyle said.

"Men." Amanda shook her head. "You two really want to be knocked up in a time like this?"

Carrie and Kate looked at each other and cracked up.

"What's so funny?" Sydney asked.

"You two have no idea," Kate said. "Too bad Rachel isn't here to join in the fun."

"Who's Rachel?" Sydney asked.

"Junior's woman," Kate said. "Wonder if she's been successful yet?"

"Wait, you have somebody trying to get pregnant *right now?*" Amanda asked.

Kate laughed. "I just found out I was pregnant two days ago," Kate said, "and yes, we did it on purpose." She put her arm around Kyle's waist and pulled him closer.

Amanda and Sydney looked at each other and chuckled.

"You two better watch out," Carrie said. "It's catching."

"No way," Amanda said.

Kate snickered. "I can see it now. A little Curt running around."

"God help us," Carrie said.

"Oh, please," Amanda said. She looked over at Sydney, who was eyeing her with a big smile on her face. "Shut up, sis."

"I'm right here, you know," Curt said, looking embarrassed as he climbed the ramp into the garage. "Hey Kyle, want to give me a hand?"

"Sure," Kyle said, climbing up after him. They extended a table from the wall and moved the 3-D printer onto it. Curt plugged it in, then brought over his laptop and turned it on.

"Nice setup," Amanda said as she climbed up.

"What are we gonna make first?" Kyle asked.

"Well, let's see. We got Dirk's truck. We could set that up the same way we did your truck, with the .50 cal. I could make another gimbal from that drawing."

"Dirk gonna be okay with that?" Kyle asked.

"He suggested it," Curt said. "Then there's Jason's Jeep. I'll have to design a new gimbal for that. Probably mount an M-19 on that one."

"You want to put one on my bobtail?" Amanda asked.

"That's not a bad idea," Curt said. "Sure, I could do that. I'll probably have to beef up some structure to put it on. I can use roll bars for the pickups and the Jeep, but there's probably nothing that sturdy on the top of the bobtail."

"Should I bring it over here?"

"Where you planning on setting up the still?" Curt asked.

"How about that space over there, by the back fence?" Kyle asked. "It's fairly flat and there's some cover between it and the road."

"Yeah, that'd probably work," Amanda said. "I can park next to it."

"That way you can bed down with Curt," Sydney said from outside. Carrie and Kate snickered with her.

"Two can play that game, Sydney," Amanda said. "I saw Don going with Moe to check out your love nest."

"Oh please," Sydney said.

"Let's start a pool," Kate said. "Which one of them gets knocked up first."

Curt turned and chuckled. "You women are just gonna keep going, aren't you?"

"You know you want it," Kyle said.

"Shut up, pencil neck."

"Did I hear that somebody else is getting knocked up?" Rachel asked as she walked over.

"Hey, girls, this is Rachel," Carrie said. "Junior's woman." Kate and her giggled.

"You think that bothers me." Rachel chuckled. "I pretty much owned that one before he got back here."

"You girls joke a lot, don't you?" Sydney said, face turning red.

"Yeah, sorry," Kate said. "You'll get used to it. I did."

"Oh, they messed with you too, eh?" Sydney asked.

"Well, Carrie did, the first time I was with Kyle. It was at a barbeque at their house, after the Superstore attack."

Carrie laughed. "Yeah, that was a hoot."

"It was embarrassing," Kate said. "I didn't even know if I liked the guy yet. I was reluctant to go out with him."

"That changed in a hurry," Carrie said.

"It did," Kate said. "I couldn't believe it when you said that Chelsea had my seat."

"Chelsea?" Amanda asked.

"My little girl," Carrie said. "When we walked into the backyard, she was sitting on Kyle's lap."

Kyle snickered. "I forgot about that. Seems like so long ago."

"It does," Kate said. "I thought you were such a blowhard."

"But you spent that night with him," Carrie said.

"Shhhh," she said.

"When did you fall for him?" Sydney asked.

She laughed. "I'm not saying."

"Hey, I'd like to know that," Kyle said.

"Never you mind," she said.

"Shit, it was the first time you saw him, wasn't it?" Carrie asked.

"No," Kate said.

"It was?" Kyle said, coming out of the garage. He took her into his arms. "I knew it." He kissed her hard. The other women giggled. Curt rolled his eyes.

"Okay, okay," Kate said. "You had me from the start. Satisfied?"

"I felt the same way," Kyle said.

"I know," she said. "How much longer do you have to help the genius there?"

"Why, you got something else for me to do?" he asked.

"You see, this is the problem," Curt said, shaking his head. "Too much kanoodling, not enough work."

"Oh, we're gonna do more than kanoodle," Kate said. "C'mon."

"Yes, ma'am," he said, following her back to their trailer.

Curt sighed. "Thanks a lot, girls. I wasn't done with him yet."

"I'll help you," Amanda said.

"With what?" Sydney cracked.

"Stop," she said. "Why don't you go decorate the love nest with Don."

Curt made a few adjustments with the 3D printer and turned it on. "There. It can crank out the gimbal for Dirk's truck while we do other things."

"I've got stuff to do," Carrie said. "Talk to you all later."

"I probably should go find out what Junior's up to," Rachel said. "Oh, excuse me, *my man.*"

Carrie and Sydney chuckled.

"I guess I'll go see what's going on down at the clubhouse," Sydney said. "Call me if you need help with anything, Amanda. I'll be back over before too long, and we can start setting up the still."

"Okay, hon," Amanda said. "Sorry I teased you."

"It's okay," Sydney said. "Same here. Was kinda fun, though. We haven't been able to laugh much lately."

"True that," Amanda said, watching as she walked away. "What now, Curt?"

"Let's bring your bobtail over here," Curt said. "I'll help you set up the still, and then we can take some measurements. I'll have to do a new CAD drawing to feed into the 3D printer."

"Okay," she said. They walked down the ramp and headed for the front gate.

"How long have you known those other gals?" Amanda asked.

"I've known Carrie for years, since before she and Jason were married. I've only known Kate and Rachel for a short while. Met Kate on the way here, and Rachel after I got here."

"Interesting," she said.

"You knew Jason and Eric from way back, I take it."

"Eric used to date Sydney," Amanda said. "I used to flirt with Jason, but I could never get him interested. I was a little too wild for him."

"Yeah, I'll just bet you were," Curt said.

"Not sure how to take that," Amanda said.

"I just know him, that's all," Curt said. "You aren't his type. Didn't mean anything bad by it."

"I know," she said. "I can be hell on wheels, and I gave my parents a real run for the money."

"Got the keys?" Curt asked as he opened the cab door for her.

"Left them in it," she said. "Who's going to steal it from here?"

"Good point," Curt said. He rushed around to the passenger side and got in as she fired up the diesel.

"Where you going?" Clancy asked from the roof.

"Back by my space," Curt shouted. "We want to get the still set up."

"Okay, see you two later," Clancy said.

Amanda put the truck in gear and drove forward, glancing at Curt every so often.

"You didn't tell me how you felt yet," Curt said. "About earlier."

"You're right, I didn't," she said. "Why, you interested?"

"I *was* wondering," he said.

"It showed promise," she said.

"That's all?"

"My, but you get more talkative when we're alone, don't you?"

"Maybe I like some privacy in situations like this," he said. "Can't believe you guys joking around so much."

She giggled. "You know that's how girls get."

"Well?" he said. "You gonna get more talkative?"

"What do you want me to say?" she asked, looking at him.

"Just the truth," Curt said, locking eyes. She started to go off the road, then snapped her head forward and righted the truck.

"See what you almost made me do," she said.

"Sorry," he said.

"Okay," she said. "Sydney will probably tell you anyway."

"Sydney?" he asked.

"She asked me the same thing when we were driving here," Amanda said.

"What'd you tell her?"

"I said that if the kiss would have gone on any longer, I would've been pulling your clothes off," Amanda said, as she parked the truck. "There, satisfied?"

He chuckled.

"Shit, I shouldn't have told you that," she said.

"Why not?" Curt asked. "I was thinking the same thing."

"I know," she said. "C'mon, we've got work to do."

They got out of the cab and headed towards the back. Amanda unlocked the padlock on the door latch, and then stood aside as Curt pushed it up. He climbed onto the back and helped her up, then pushed her against the wall, just out of sight, holding her wrists above her head as he kissed her hard. She moaned, pushing back at him, passion rising fast.

"Oh, geez," she said when they broke the kiss.

"Did that curl your toes?" he asked.

"It did more than that. C'mon. Work before fun. Let's get this stuff unloaded."

"Woman after my own heart," he said. They got to work.

Air Power

L ita, Madison, and Hannah sat together waiting.

"Listen," Lita said. "Somebody just parked outside."

Hannah got up and ran to the window, peeking out. "It's them."

"All of them?" Madison asked.

"Yes," Hannah said. Lita rushed to the door and opened it as the three men walked up.

"Thank God," Lita said, rushing out to Richardson. "I was so worried."

Hannah rushed to Brendan, Madison to Juan Carlos.

"Can we go home?" Madison whispered to Juan Carlos.

"You don't want to go to the courthouse?" he asked.

"It's too late, isn't it?" Madison asked.

Lita broke her kiss with Richardson. "Yeah, we missed it today," she said. "Maybe we can go early tomorrow."

"Best we can do at this point," Richardson said. "I'm so sorry, honey."

"Do you have to go back in tomorrow morning?" she asked.

"We're on call," Richardson said.

"Yeah," Juan Carlos said. "Kinda sucks. No beer. Gotta stay straight."

"I know, that blows," Brendan said. "I could use a couple beers right now."

"Well forget it, guys," Richardson said. "You heard the Captain. Could be a lot worse."

"True, they could make us live on the base," Juan Carlos said.

"Don't give them any ideas," Madison said, coming in for another kiss. "Let's go home. Please?"

"Okay," Juan Carlos said. They walked away hand in hand.

"Can we go home too?" Hannah asked.

"Thought you'd never ask," Brendan said.

"Please do," Lita said, glancing at Richardson.

"I'll call you in the morning," Richardson said.

Brendan nodded, and took Hannah home as Lita and Richardson watched them walk away.

"C'mon," Lita said, pulling him inside.

"You okay?"

"I was scared to death. How bad was it?"

Richardson chuckled. "Believe it or not, it was fun. We got new boats. They're a lot more capable than what we had. A whole lot safer too."

"Good," she said. "Mission accomplished, I assume."

"Yeah, we stopped an attack on the port at Corpus Christi," he said. "Would have been really bad if we hadn't. The oil infrastructure would have been destroyed."

"Wonder if we're still getting oil from other parts of the US?"

"Doesn't sound like it," Richardson said. "That's why they moved us down here – to protect our coast. Without our ports we'll be starved out, and all of our biggest oil refineries are down here."

"They're going to come after you guys, like they did around Falcon Lake and at South Padre Island," Lita said.

"They're probably gonna try," he said, pulling off his shirt and kicking off his shoes. He plopped down on the couch. "I agree with Brendan. A beer would be real nice right about now."

"Don't," Lita said. "I want you sharp."

"So do I," Richardson said. "Believe me."

"What do you want to do?" Lita asked.

"Go to bed," he said.

"We should save some for our wedding day," she said.

"I meant to sleep. I'm exhausted."

She smiled at him. "Good. You don't want something to eat first?"

"What do we have?"

"Not much. There's some Mac and Cheese in the pantry. I could whip that up."

"Sure, I'd go for it."

"Good, then you just relax and I'll make it, okay?"

"I'm liable to doze off."

"Then doze off," Lita said as she walked into the kitchen.

Richardson watched her puttering in the kitchen. It gave him a warm, happy feeling.

"Turn on the TV if you want," Lita said.

"No, I think I'll just watch you," he said.

"Oh, brother."

After about ten minutes, Lita came to the couch with two bowls.

"Smells great," Richardson said, taking one. He dug in.

"Okay?" she asked.

"Perfect," Richardson said.

"You think we should go through with it tomorrow?"

"Having second thoughts?" Richardson asked.

"No, no," she said. "Not at all, but things *are* a little crazy. I could wait a week or two. See if things calm down."

"I think we ought to go for it," Richardson said, "but I'll wait if you think it's better."

"Let me sleep on it," she said. The finished their meals. Lita turned on the TV and put it on a sitcom. "Stupid show, but I don't want to see anything serious."

"Me neither," he said, settling back on the couch. Lita got up and took the bowls to the kitchen, then went into the bedroom. She came out wearing a nightgown.

"Wow," Richardson said. "You're looking good."

"Wedding day, remember," she said, sitting next to him, close enough to touch.

"You're not making it easy," he said.

She giggled. "Yeah, I want you nice and fired up."

"Trouble maker," he said, turning to kiss her.

"Uh uh uh, don't start," she said.

"Fine," he pouted in mock indignation.

They watched TV for another hour and then staggered into bed, both of them falling asleep in minutes.

Richardson's phone rang at just after 2:30 AM. He grunted, then reached for his bedside table, knocking the phone on the floor.

"Dammit," he said, turning on the light and picking it up. He answered it.

"Richardson?" Jefferson asked.

"Yeah," he said. "What's up?"

"Sorry to wake you. We need to get back to Corpus Christi again. Radar sees boats coming from out in the middle of the gulf."

"Dammit," Richardson said. "You sound worried."

"I am," he said. "Get dressed. I'll call your guys."

"You need their numbers?"

"No, we know which trailers they picked," Jefferson said. "Get ready to pick them up."

"Okay, Captain," Richardson said. He set his cellphone down and got up to get dressed.

"So this is what they mean by on call," Lita said, fear in her eyes. "What's wrong?"

"Boats coming from the gulf to the Corpus Christi area," he said. "Sorry, sweetie."

"Nothing to be sorry about," she said, sitting up. "Need any help from me to get ready?"

"No, thanks," he said. "I just got to get dressed and go pick up the guys."

"Okay," she said, getting out of bed.

"You don't have to get up," he said.

"Like I'm going to be able to sleep now. The girls may want to come over. They don't like to be alone when you guys are in harm's way."

"I could see that." He sat on the end of the bed and tied his shoes. "I'm about ready."

"Okay, sweetie," Lita said. "Hold me for a sec, okay?"

He rushed to her arms, holding her tight, then kissing her. "Don't worry. I'll be back."

"I hope so," she said. "This is hard."

"I know," he said, kissing her one last time.

"Be careful," she said, watching him walk towards the door, tears running down her cheeks.

The two other couples were walking over together when he got down the steps of the porch.

"I was going to pick you guys up," Richardson said.

"We wanted to come down here anyway," Madison said. "You think Lita is going to mind?"

"She expected you," Richardson said. "I was gonna bring you here."

Brendan and Juan Carlos said their goodbyes and got into the SUV. Richardson drove towards the front gate as they watched, Lita coming out to join them.

"This is horrible," Hannah said. "How are we gonna live with this?"

"Seriously," Madison said. "I'm so scared."

"Come inside," Lita said. "I'll crank up the coffee maker."

"Might as well," Hannah said. "I'm not falling asleep, that's for sure."

Madison nodded in agreement as they went inside.

"They didn't say much about what was happening," Madison said.

"Richardson said there were boats approaching Corpus Christi from the Gulf."

"They can see them?" Hannah asked.

"Radar," Lita said. "Want something to eat?"

"I don't think I could hold it down," Madison said, on the verge of tears.

"Me neither," Hannah said, "but thanks. Coffee would be good, though."

"Wonder if they'll attack here, like they did at Port Isabel?" Madison asked.

"I hope not," Lita said from the kitchen.

"You don't think they would, do you?" Hannah asked. "We barely got out of Port Isabel alive."

"I know," Lita said, coming out with two cups of coffee. She set them on the coffee table and went back into the kitchen.

"Are you guys going to try the courthouse again tomorrow?" Madison asked.

"I'm not sure yet," Lita said, coming out with her coffee. She sat in the chair opposite the couch. "We talked about it a little last night. We might wait until things die down a little bit."

"What makes you think things are gonna die down?" Hannah asked.

Lita was quiet for a moment. "You're right, we don't know that it will. It could actually get worse. That was Richardson's opinion, I think."

"So he still wants to go through with it as soon as possible?" Hannah asked. "Good."

"Why good, Hannah?" Madison asked. "What are you planning?"

"Nothing," she said. Both Madison and Lita eyed her. "Nothing!"

"Okay, have it your way," Lita said. "You have to follow your heart."

"Juan Carlos would do it," Madison said. "I had to warn him not to. More than once."

"You'd have to agree, you know," Lita said.

"Look at her," Hannah said. "If he pushes it, she won't be able to resist."

"Stop it," Madison said, face turning red. "You're in the same boat that I am."

An air raid siren went off. The women froze, looking at each other.

"Oh no!" Lita cried. "We're under attack!"

"You think so?" Hannah asked. "Maybe it's a drill."

"At this time of night?" Madison asked. She rushed for the door, the others following.

"I don't see anything," Lita said, scanning the dark sky.

"Me neither," Hannah said, voice trembling.

A fireball rose into the air, the sound hitting them a split second later.

"That's the base!" Lita said. "I hope our men left before that happened."

"Oh, God," Hannah said, breaking down.

"Pull yourself together," Madison shouted. Other people in the trailer park were coming out to look.

"Listen," Lita said. "Choppers. They're coming this way!"

"No!" Madison cried. "The guys leave any guns around here?"

"You want to shoot at the choppers?" Hannah asked. "That won't do any good."

"They might land the choppers and put troops on the ground," Madison said.

"Shit, she's right," Lita said. "C'mon."

Lita rushed inside, the others following. She went into the bedroom and pulled open the closet, looking at the floor.

"Not much there," Hannah said.

"Two handguns, a rifle, and this thing," Lita said, holding up the SMAW.

"They left that?" Madison asked.

"Probably don't need it on those new boats," Hannah said. "Brendan said the side guns have grenade launchers on them."

"You know how to fire this thing?" Lita asked.

"I think I do," Hannah said. "I was right next to Brendan when he used it on the way here, remember? I watched. Is the ammo there?"

Lita handed the SMAW to Hannah and looked back in the closet. She pulled out a wooden crate. "Here."

"Good," Hannah said, grabbing several grenades and putting them into her pocket. "Let's go. Grab the other guns."

"They loaded?" Madison asked.

Lita looked at the rifle. "The rifle is."

"Give me a pistol," Madison asked. "I know how to shoot those."

Lita handed her one as they rushed to the door, sticking the other one in her waistband.

"Look, that chopper just hit our trailer," Hannah cried. "Bastards."

"Shit, do you think they knew where our places are?" Madison asked, terror in her eyes.

"Get away from this place!" Lita shouted. They ran towards the clubhouse in the middle of the park as the chopper fired into the trailer Madison and Juan Carlos were using.

"There's your answer," Lita shouted. "Look, here comes another chopper. It's heading to my place."

Before the words sunk in, the trailer exploded in flames. Then the chopper started descending towards lawn in the front of the park.

"They're gonna come get us," Lita cried.

Hannah got down on one knee and loaded the SMAW, then pointed it towards the chopper as it set down. "Good, no moving target." She aimed and pulled the trigger. Nothing happened. "Dammit."

"Safety," Madison said.

"Oh, yeah," Hannah said, looking at the side of the weapon.

"C'mon, they're starting to pile out," Lita said, aiming the rifle at the men in the side door. Then Hannah pulled the trigger again, a grenade flashing out the barrel, hitting the chopper and bursting it into flames.

"Yes!" Madison said.

Lita fired the rifle, hitting one of the men who was running away from the fire. Madison joined in with her handgun, trying to hit the second man but missing. Lita fired the rifle again, killing the man.

"Look, there's another chopper landing," Madison cried, pointing to their left, at a field just outside of the RV Park.

"I hear more choppers coming," Lita said. "Better blow that second one, and then let's find a place to hide."

Hannah tried to pull the spent cartridge out of the SMAW and reload it. "It's stuck, dammit."

"Hurry, there's men getting out of that second chopper already!" Madison yelled.

{ 28 }

White Flags

C urt and Amanda were putting together parts of the still when a buzzer went off in the garage of the toy hauler.

Curt smiled. "The inside gimbal for Dirk's truck is done. I need to take it off and start the outside piece."

He walked up the ramp, Amanda by his side. She gasped when she saw the gimbal part sitting on the build table. Curt lifted the plexiglass cover back on its hinges and carefully picked up the gimbal with oven mitts.

"That's beautiful," she said.

"Yeah, it is, isn't it," Curt said as he sat it down. He closed the plexiglass cover, then loaded more material into the printer and sat in front of his laptop.

"You just pick another drawing and let her rip, eh?" Amanda asked.

"Yeah, if I'm using the same material," he said. "This is metal. It can also use plastic and other materials, but I have to change the heads," He selected the second gimbal part in his list of drawings and clicked the start button. The 3-D printer whirred into motion. "Okay, we got another forty-five minutes or so."

They walked down the ramp and went back to the still.

"Is your still at the house where the weapons were?" Amanda asked.

"Yeah," he said. "It's dismantled right now. If we're here long enough, maybe I'll go get it."

"What's the output?"

"A whole lot less than your system," he said. "Mine's just for personal use. I give a lot away to friends, of course. My last chief loved it."

Amanda cracked up. "You were giving illegal hooch to your police chief?"

"Hell yeah," Curt said.

Amanda shook her head. "We're living in a strange world."

"I'll say," Curt said. "How'd you get started at this?"

"Family business," Amanda said. "We've made our living off of this over the years, when the legit farm activity wouldn't pay enough."

"What did you do at the farm?"

"Raised horses and hogs, mostly," she said. "That's why my dad and sister were gone. They sold off the remainder of our stock. We couldn't get reliable deliveries."

"Where are they again?" Curt asked.

"Montana," she said. "Hopefully they're still alive. Haven't been able to reach them for weeks."

"I think Montana is still safe," Curt said.

"Maybe," she said. "I've seen threads on the internet about Islamists coming down from Canada."

"Me too," Curt said, "but never about Montana. The threads I saw were about Washington and Idaho."

Horns started honking near the east side of the park.

"Oh, crap, what's that for?" Amanda asked, eyes wide.

"I don't know," Curt said. "We better find out."

Kyle and Jason both rushed out of their RVs.

"What's going on, man?" Jason yelled.

"I don't know," Curt said. "Maybe we better grab our weapons and head towards the clubhouse."

"Somebody's really laying on those horns," Amanda said as they stared moving.

"Where's Kelly and the others?" Kyle asked.

"Still at the clubhouse, as far as I know," Curt said.

Clancy was still on the roof, watching I-10 westbound with binoculars.

"What are you seeing?" Jason yelled.

"Tanks," he said. "Looks like five. No, six. They stopped. They're waiting."

"Son of a bitch," Jason said. "Where's our damn air power?"

"Call Ramsey," Kyle said.

"Yeah," Jason said.

Gray ran over. "We got the tank cannons aimed at them. Want us to fire?"

"How visible are our tanks to the interstate?" Curt asked.

"Not very," Gray said. "We got them dug in a little to lessen the visibility. Did that while you guys were gone."

"Good," Jason said, phone to his ear. "Somebody kill the damn car horns."

"Who you calling?" Gray asked.

"Chief Ramsey," Jason said.

"Maybe we shouldn't panic just yet," Clancy yelled from the roof. "Maybe those folks are joining us."

"That's why Jason's making the call," Kyle shouted back. "They should've told us if that was the case, though. Otherwise how do we know if we should fight them or not?"

"You got that right, pencil neck," Curt said.

"You gonna fire up the Barracuda?" Amanda asked.

"No, it's no match for an M-1 Tank. We might need it to escape."

Don and Sydney ran over, Moe trying to keep up behind them.

"What the hell is going on?" Moe asked.

Kelly, Junior, Nate, Fritz, Jasper, and Earl rushed out of the clubhouse.

"What the hell is going on out here?" Kelly shouted.

"Tanks," Clancy yelled. "Sitting on I-10, to the east."

"They're not moving?" Don asked.

"No," Clancy said. "They're just sitting there."

"Hear that?" Sydney asked. "Squeaking. Coming from there." She pointed west. Clancy whirled around, binoculars still at his eyes.

"Oh, shit," Clancy said. "Four more tanks, stopped on I-10 to the west. We're being surrounded."

"Oh no," Amanda said, clutching Curt.

Eric and Kim trotted over. "What's going on?" Eric asked.

"Tanks parked on either side of us, out on I-10," Jason said.

"No," Kim said, looking up at Eric. "What are we gonna do?"

"What about Ramsey?" Curt yelled as Jason walked over.

"No answer," Jason said. "We're going to have to fight them."

"They'll win," Curt said. "They got us outnumbered."

"Yeah, we don't want to get into a tank on tank battle if we can help it," Eric said.

Carrie, Kate, Brenda, and Rachel ran over, Carrie with Chelsea in her arms.

"What's happening?" Kate asked.

"Tanks sitting on the east and west of us, on I-10," Kyle said.

"Dammit," Rachel said. "What about this air power we were promised?"

"We don't know," Kyle said.

"Should we head into the hills?" Carrie asked. "In the four-wheel drive vehicles?"

"Not yet," Curt said.

"Hey," Clancy shouted. "Both groups are holding up white flags. Looks like they want to talk."

"No way," Curt said. He climbed onto the roof. "Let me take a look."

Clancy handed him the binoculars. Curt took a look at both.

"Well, they ain't Islamists," Curt said. "They look like military to me. Our military."

"Texas National Guard?" Clancy asked.

"Yeah," Curt said. "This doesn't smell right. They would've sent an envoy to talk to us before showing up with tanks, if they're legit."

"Yeah," Jason said. "I think Curt's right."

"Try Ramsey again," Curt said. "Anybody else you can call?"

"He's our contact," Jason said. "Bothers me that nobody is at the switchboard."

"You called the Austin Police Station and got no answer?" Curt asked. "That's not good. You got a cell number?"

"It's probably not safe," Jason said.

Curt jumped off the roof and rushed over. "You're kidding, right? What's his cell number. My phone isn't hackable."

"You see any enemy on there?" Kyle asked.

Curt pulled out his phone and checked his scanning program. "No, nothing. Give me the number."

Jason went to his contacts and found Ramsey's number, then read if off. Curt punched it in and made the call.

"Ringing," Curt said. There was a click.

"Ramsey," a voice said.

"Hold it. Gonna put you on speaker." He motioned for the others to gather around.

"Hear us?" Curt asked.

"Yeah," he said. "What's going on? Why'd you call me on this line?"

"No answer at the station," Jason said.

"What?" Ramsey asked. "Son of a bitch."

"What's that noise?" Kyle asked. "You in the car?"

"Yeah," Ramsey said. "Can't stay on long. What's the matter?"

"There's six M-1 Tanks sitting east of us on I-10, and another four sitting west of us on I-10," Jason said. "They got us bottled up."

"Oh, no," Ramsey said. "This is bad."

"So you don't know who they are?" Jason asked.

"No," he said.

"They're waving white flags," Curt said.

"Something happened," Ramsey said. "Something big."

"C'mon, Ramsey, spill," Curt said.

There was a pause on the line.

"Out with it," Jason said.

"It's the Governor," Ramsey said, "and Landry and Gallagher."

"What about them?" Jason asked.

"They're all missing. I'm out with a security detail looking for them now."

To be continued in Bug Out! Texas Book 5!

Cast Of Characters

Texas Hill Country Group

Jason – Austin PD. Young man with family. Brave, trustworthy, great in a fight, loyal. Six foot four and handsome with thick sable hair. Considered to be a high-potential employee by Austin PD. Responsible. Mid 30s.

Carrie – Jason's wife. Strong, brave, witty, smart. Short dark hair and delicate, pretty face. Girl next-door type. Has calming effect on Jason and others. Good in a fight, brave to a fault. Pregnant. Mid 30s.

Chelsea – toddler, daughter of Jason and Carrie. Cute, rambunctious.

Kyle – Austin PD. Partner of Jason. Large man, built like a linebacker, with sandy blonde hair and a sly grin. Cheerful, funny, great in a fight, puts on front of being player, but really a romantic. Worships girlfriend Kate. Mid 30s.

Kate – strong, beautiful, emotional, witty. Former news reporter for a local Texas TV station. Fell hard for Kyle, carrying his baby. Temper. Early 30s.

Kelly – leader of Rednecks. Huge man with long brown hair and a beard. Tough, gruff, smart, great judge of character. Strategic thinker. Man's man. In love with Brenda. Mid 50s

Brenda – half-owner of Texas Mary's Bar and Grill in Dripping Springs. Voluptuous with bleach blonde hair and a slightly wild look. Deeply in love with Kelly. Extremely intelligent. Runs business side of Texas Mary's. Strong but worries about Kelly constantly. Good in a fight. Mid 50s.

Junior – Kelly's best friend. A tall rail of a man with a thick beard, usually wearing a battered cowboy hat. Funny, crazy, smarter than most people realize, good in a fight, strong, loyal to the death. In love with Rachel. Early 50s.

Rachel – picked up on the road. Black hair and brown eyes, short and thin, with a face of delicate beauty. Former drug abuser with difficult past. Lost only child to SIDS, which broke up her first marriage and led to the drug abuse. Leans on Junior, needs strong man in her life. Late 30s.

Curt – former police officer in Austin, and most recently San Antonio. Large man with a military haircut, clean shaven. Punched superior officer in San Antonio. Genius. Renaissance man. Understands many technical disciplines, creative, skilled. Has temper but with heart of gold. Likes to tease his friends. Would die for them. Skilled fighter who can turn the tide of a battle on his own. Sense of humor can be very crude but funny. Mid 40s.

Simon Orr – dangerous leader of militia movement, trying to take over Kelly's group. Large man wearing cowboy garb. Shadowy, cruel. Crossover character from original Bug Out! Series. Wants to become warlord. Playing against every side except his own. Mid 40s.

Sydney – one of the Merchant girls living outside of Fredericksburg, next to Jason's family homestead. Grew up with Jason and his brother Eric. Former teenage girlfriend of Eric. Beautiful, smart, funny, avid hunter and tracker, runs family moonshine business with her sister Amanda. Raven hair and stunning bright blue eyes. Mid 30s.

Amanda – Sydney's older sister. Raunchy, wild, aggressive, knows what she wants and goes for it hard. Beautiful, deep blue eyes like Sydney, hair bleached blond, contrasts with jet-black eyebrows. Tattoos. Smart, good negotiator, runs family moonshine business with Sydney, more technically savvy. Early 40s.

Gray – leader of the bikers, originally from southwest Texas. A large man with black hair and a black beard. Brave and resourceful, suspicious of strangers, but loyal once he's gained respect. Late 40s.

Cindy – Gray's wife. Nervous, small dainty blonde with tattoos and piercings. Pretty face ravaged by a hard life. Early 40s.

Moe – owner of the Fort Stockton RV Park. Overweight and balding with a gray and brown beard, shrewd and strong, strategic thinker, protective, kind. Mid 60s.

Clancy – Moe's nephew. Scraggly thin man with a wicked grin and long stringy brown hair. Works at the Fort Stockton RV Park. Smart as a whip with good intuition. Outdoorsman. Protective of the group, good with technology, good at organizing and getting things done. Mid-30s.

Brushy – owner of an RV Park overrun early in the story. He's been missing for a while. Small man with a huge beard and long hair, about sixty years old. Good in a fight, fearless, crazy, funny.

Pat – Brushy's sister, owner of the Amarillo Oasis RV Park. She's a couple years younger than Brushy, with a similar look. Short, robust, friendly, smart. Brave, angry at the invaders.

Jax – huge man with a blonde beard and a shaved head. Joined the group with a huge group of citizens. Gung ho, brave to a fault, cunning and loyal.

East Texas/Florida Group

Eric – Jason's brother. Over six feet tall with a trim but massive build. Was living in Florida before the war started. Private Investigator working elder fraud cases in retirement areas of central Florida. Brave, very athletic. Fast, good with guns and other weapons. Smart, charismatic. Loved by everybody. Loyal to a fault. Mid 30s.

Kim – Eric's girlfriend. Red-haired, freckled beauty with a slim build. Tough as nails but gentle, head over heels in love with Eric. Mid 30s.

Dirk – leader of Deadwood, Texas group. Medium sized man with a muscular build. Gruff, shrewd, brave, sentimental. Loves family and friends. Large man, muscular build. Late 50s, but a young late 50s.

Chance – best friend of Dirk. Short and chubby but quick, good in a fight. Wise cracks a lot. Good mixture of smarts and bravery, but cautious. Mid 40s.

Don – single dad widower with teenage daughter. Large man, average build with a conservative haircut. Kind and gentle, smart, protective. Lonely, misses wife. Brave but not really a fighter. Took in daughter's best friend when her family passed. Late 30s.

Francis – Don's older brother. Local political figure in Deadwood. Older man, spry for his age. Smart, good strategic thinker, understands the meaning of events better than rest of group, sage. Mid-60s.

Sherry – Francis's wife. Younger than him by ten years. Still pretty, trying hard to live during wartime but having trouble. Depression. Mid 50s.

Alyssa – Don's daughter. Pretty, a little self-centered. Misses mother. Terrified of enemy after attacks on Deadwood. 17 years old.

Chloe – Alyssa's best friend. Orphan taken in by Don after both parents killed. Mousey, kind, smart, helps Alyssa to cope. 17 years old.

Alex – Owner of the MidPoint 66 Café, who met the group during the I-40 battle. Older man, bald and heavy set, robust, funny.

Kitten – Daughter of Alex. Middle aged, chubby with light brown hair and a pretty face. Waitress at her father's Café.

Stanton Hunt – War Chief of the Mescalero Tribe. Brave man, thoughtful, severed in the Army for years, friends with General Hogan.

White Eagle – adviser and spokesperson for the Mescalero Tribe. Doesn't trust the white man. In favor of keeping an alliance with the Islamists. Dangerous man.

DPS Patrol Boaters Group

Juan Carlos – young, handsome Hispanic, full of vigor and enthusiasm. Skilled boat pilot, brave and cunning. Family in Texas since before the Alamo. Loves the state, patriot. Mid 20s.

Brendan – partner of Juan Carlos. Also young and handsome, ginger redhead. Loves to joke and tease, but can be serious. Good with weapons, natural fighter. Mid 20s.

Lieutenant Richardson – Leader of Juan Carlos and Brendan. Handsome man of average size and build with light brown hair. Tough, strong, thoughtful, loyal, brave. Headed for higher rank. Mid 30s.

Lita – girlfriend of Lieutenant Richardson. Beautiful Hispanic woman with model's figure and expressive eyes. Witty, smart, brave. Emotional, worships her man. Protective, mothering. Mid 30s.

Madison – girlfriend of Juan Carlos. Emotional but brave, beautiful with thick blonde hair and curvy figure, college girl forced to quit due to war. Head over heels for Juan Carlos. Mid 20s.

Hannah – best friend of Madison and girlfriend of Brendan. Dark haired beauty. Slim dancer's figure, athletic. Self-conscious, afraid to be hurt, passionate, very deeply in love with Brendan. Can rally in a fight if needed, surprisingly brave when pushed. Terrified of losing Brendan in the war. Mid 20s.

DPS Commissioner Wallace – overall head of DPS Organization. Strong, cunning, thinks several steps ahead of most others. Black man, large and imposing. Loves his men. Feeling is mutual. Early 60s.

Chuck – Gun shop owner in downtown San Antonio, Texas. Big man, brave, expert gunsmith. In love with Carol.

Roberto – owner of a property near Purgatory Creek. Large Mexican man, middle aged, with a good heart, brave but cautious.

Kris – small white woman with gray hair, middle aged, married to Roberto. Brave and strong, used to hardship from childhood. Generous and loving.

Gerald – Roberto's friend. Redneck always ready for a fight. Long gray hair, thin, always wearing a railroad cap. Brave to a fault.

Jay – Roberto's friend, and friends with Gerald. Lanky black-haired man in his early fifties. Sensitive but will fight hard when pushed.

Hector – Another friend of Roberto's. Overweight Mexican man in his mid-forties. A little crazy. Demolition expert. Always ready to bring dynamite to any party.

Harley – DPS Lieutenant, stationed at the new South Padre Island base. Good man with goofy sense of humor and an easygoing manner.

Leadership

Kip Hendrix – President Pro Tempore of the Texas Senate, and the leading liberal in that body. Large man, bald, with a wrinkled face but a dashing look. Has corrupt past, problems with sexual harassment, but down deep has a good heart. Trying to be better. Very complex person. Old friends with Governor, loves him even though they were estranged for many years. Multi-level thinker, good intuition, protective of those he loves, nasty enemy to have. Deeply in love with

Maria, although he viewed her as just another conquest at first. Early 50s.

Maria – secretary to Kip Hendrix. Hispanic beauty with curvy figure and a haunting face, well liked and respected by all around her. Knows how to get things done in Texas government. Fell hard for Kip Hendrix, now loyal to him above all else. Late 30s.

Governor Nelson – Charismatic conservative leader of Texas. Handsome in a rugged way. Patriotic, honest, strong, but opinionated. Old college buddy with Kip Hendrix. Strong bonds between them, even though they are political opposites. Thinks several steps ahead of others, takes risks when he knows he's right. Loved by the people of Texas, for the most part. Has solid-gold BS detector. Early 50s.

Brian – Governor Nelson's secretary and right-hand man. Black man. Cunning and loyal to the Governor. Protects him at all times. Much more important person than most people know. Mid 30s.

Commissioner Holly – ultra left-wing member of the Police Commission. Friends with Kip Hendrix. Tall and skinny with a goatee. Smart but far from open-minded. Constantly knocking heads with the Austin Police Department. Holding his nose to support Governor Nelson while the war is on. Mid 50s.

Jerry Sutton – aid to Kip Hendrix. Political operator. Clean shaven and pudgy. Tries to do a good job. Cares more about power than political philosophy. Early 30s.

Chief Ramsey – Austin Police Chief. Overweight but still burley, with the look of a redneck. Old friends with Governor Nelson. Didn't get along with Kip Hendrix in the past, but friends now, fighting a common enemy. Brave and loyal, strong leader, cares more about his cops than himself. Early 50s.

Major General Gallagher – head of Texas Army National Guard. Old-time soldier, tough and strong, unafraid. Loved by his men. Mid 60s.

Robert Boren

Major General Landry – head of Texas Air National Guard. Cocky but cautious about using his resources, almost to a fault. Late 40s.

General Walker – US Army General, stationed in Texas until the war broke out. Near genius intelligence, charismatic, uncanny ability to turn a defeat into a victory. Feared by the enemy. Crossover character from original Bug Out! Series. Mid 50s.

General Hogan – US Army General, friend of General Walker. Black man, loved by his men, tough, no-nonsense. Strategic thinker, takes risks, understands people. Fine leader. Crossover character from original Bug Out! Series. Mid 50s.

Saladin – evil leader of the Islamist forces in the western states. He is not in Texas, but the Texas leadership is aware of him and his plans. Crossover character from original Bug Out! Series.

President Simpson – current President of the United States.

Major Josh Carlson – Second in command over the Texas Air National Guard. Right Hand Man of Major General Landry.

Celia – beautiful but troubled sister of Maria. Mental issues; depression and addiction.

Private Ken Brown – General Hogan's son. On special assignment to help the Fort Stockton team.

Private Jose Sanchez – on General Hogan's staff. Childhood friend of Private Brown. On special assignment to help the Fort Stockton team.

Captain Smith – near genius Texas Army National Guard officer with rank of Captain. Pilots effort to mass-produce Curt's gimbal system for vehicles. Designs adjustable mounts for mini-guns.

ABOUT THE AUTHOR

Robert G Boren is a writer from the South Bay section of Southern California. He writes Short Stories, Novels, and Serialized Fiction.

Made in the USA
Las Vegas, NV
23 January 2021

16415291R00157